Famous bounty hunter Talisha Artul is not having a good day. A hostile alien planet full of bandits and refugees, an entire group of mercenaries all told to kill her and take her armor, and it's barely even noon. All she wanted was to earn a paycheck and make her mother proud. They've barely shared a kind word since she came out of the closet as trans and took her mother's name.

Now she's travelling with an android cowboy with split-personality issues and an eight-foot-tall warrior woman to beat a group of vengeful pirates and the galactic federation's military forces to uncover an ancient alien temple. Talisha soon learns that despite her legal standing, there is little that separates her from these marginalized cutthroats and outcasts. They're all victims here, all pawns in their shadowy employer's game.

MERCS!

Dorian Dawes

A NineStar Press Publication

Published by NineStar Press
P.O. Box 91792,
Albuquerque, New Mexico, 87199 USA.
www.ninestarpress.com

Mercs!

Printed in the USA
First Edition
June, 2018

Print ISBN: 978-1-948608-88-6

Also available in eBook, ISBN: 978-1-948608-78-7

Warning: This book contains sexual content, which may only be suitable for mature readers.

Chapter One

"WERE THESE SERIOUSLY the best mercs you could hire?" The cigarette moved in the corner of Madame Inspector's mouth as she spoke. She flicked her fingers across the pile of folders strewn across her desk. "Absolute rubbish."

A little man with lily-white skin stood fidgeting with his spectacles in the doorway, clutching a briefcase close to his chest. Madame Inspector scared the living hell out of him. She liked it that way and would have smiled at his discomfort if she thought it'd make him squirm just a little bit more.

He took a tentative step, but she held a palm up and he froze where he stood. *Good dog.*

"Madame Inspector, I assure you they are highly qualified." The overhanging lamp cast a glare over his glasses. "I've assembled before you the most dangerous individuals in the galaxy."

Madame Inspector scowled, spreading out the files and pictures of each motley outcast passing themself off as a mercenary. "These bozos are more danger to themselves than anyone else, Mr. Snidely. Crooks and ruffians."

"That's why they're perfect for the position," Snidely said. He mustered up the courage to give her a wicked smile. "They're completely disposable. Should be easy to turn them on one another when we're done."

Madame Inspector leaned back in her seat. She tapped the ashes of her cigarette into the tray and stared at him until his smile melted into open-mouthed fear. She said nothing, waiting for him to wither before the cold deadlights of her eyes.

"Mr. Snidely," she said, a voice like gravel. "Not once have I witnessed one with as much audacity...or initiative. Good work. You're dismissed."

Snidely bowed his head and ducked hurriedly out of her office. She frowned as he left. The kid had gumption, ambition. They could be useful qualities in the right doses. She'd have to test him.

ARCHIMEDES IV, A war-torn rock populated by refugees and outlaws. It'd been deemed unfit for life by the Council of Thirteen following a resource war that'd decimated the planet and irrevocably altered the landscape. Some forests remained, having evolved to meet the harsh environmental conditions. The trees had become predators themselves, feeding off unwary travelers.

With its constant dangers and inhospitable environment, Archimedes IV had been abandoned by the Intergalactic Peacekeeping Federation, which made it the ideal location for all sorts of criminal scum to stash their ill-gotten gains. So long as they hid away in backwater filth, the law paid them no mind. It was out of their jurisdiction.

Talisha Artul had no jurisdiction. If the job told her to go, she'd go. The IGF had found her as reliable a resource as her mother. Abandoned science station deemed too dangerous to send in a full squad? Talisha was there with her arm cannon and jet pack.

Becoming a space-faring licensed bounty hunter had a few perks. The pay was decent—a huge bonus considering over half her funds were split between expensive hormone treatments and helping support her mother's orphanage. Being able to traverse the galaxy and visit other worlds definitely ranked high on the list. Getting shot at on a daily basis was a minor drawback in comparison.

Reservations about this latest assignment scratched at the back of her mind as she sorted through the information provided to her on her tablet. An anonymous corporate employer had contacted her, leaving the legality of the assignment in question. She'd have to make a call to the appropriate channels to make sure her licensing fees had been taken care of. New information presented itself that she'd be assigned to a task force after previous assurances that she'd be working alone.

She threw the tablet against the ship console. "Shit!"

Talisha preferred working alone for multiple reasons. Silence kept her head clear and victory assured in any firefight. Other people introduced far more variables than she was comfortable with.

Maybe Mom would know what to do.

Talisha grabbed the headset from a compartment just above her and slipped it over her head. She made a sour expression at the tablet as she slumped back into her seat. A few moments later, her mother's voice crackled into her feed.

"Talisha? Thought you'd be on-world by now," Ms. Artul said.

"Mom, when is it okay to back out of an assignment?"

"Uh-oh. What happened?"

Talisha filled her in on the particulars of the assignment, making notes of the new last-minute information.

Her mother thought about that one for a while. "Your reputation is pretty strong right now. You could probably afford to back out."

"What about you?" Talisha asked. "How's the orphanage doing?"

"Expensive. Feels like there's new orphans every day. People keep dying and leaving behind their little ones. This planet's in need."

"Do you have enough to make it through the month?" Talisha propped her elbows against the console and scratched the back of her neck with one hand.

Ms. Artul muttered under her breath in Swahili, then spat out, "Don't you dare. If you don't feel good about this mission, don't take it."

"You can't order me around, Mom. I'm just being stubborn and paranoid...like you."

"I wish you hadn't called then." There was a lengthy pause. "Fucking hell, kid."

Talisha's eyes watered. These were the types of conversations that drove people to drink. She gritted her teeth and pursed her lips, fingers shaking.

"I'm taking the job," Talisha said, then threw the headset against the console.

BLUEBIRD HAD SEEN her fair share of overcrowded dung heaps in her time—claustrophobic messes violating every single fire safety law in the galaxy; easy places to get stabbed and looted before you even had a chance to know what had happened. Folks in a hurry could trample your corpse without even noticing. By contrast, the spaceport on Archimedes IV was practically empty. A dumpster left at the back end of the long passage looked like it'd been overflowing for years. Shit and graffiti marred the walls, and it was nearly impossible to see through the teller's window for all the grime and filth covering it.

Bluebird sniffed. She might come to like it there. Smelled just like home.

The poor terminal worker did a double take at her through the glass. "P-p-passport."

By this point, Bluebird had become well accustomed to most people's reactions to her appearance. She was proud of the severe scarring that marred one side of her face, the mark of a fine battle. Bluebird also knew that most people had never seen a Karstotzkiyan in their lives and were unaccustomed to seeing eight-foot-tall women with striking blue hair and hardened jowls. It's where she'd gotten the nickname Big Ugly Bluebird. She liked it.

"Identification provided!" She slammed a meaty hand against the counter and slid a thick wad of papers through the slot beneath the window.

He stared at the mess of documentation and sighed. There were official licensing documents in the scattered heap to be certain, but there were also receipts to fast food joints, hair salons, old concert tickets dating decades back, etc. Bluebird grimaced, feeling a twinge of guilt. It'd take this poor man hours to sift through it all. She rummaged around in her pockets from some additional cash and deposited it atop the mess of documentation.

He sighed. He gulped, staring at the blue veins bulging beneath her thick muscles and the giant satchel strapped to her back. She did her best to give him a reassuring smile but was certain she only came across as even more imposing. Oh well, it couldn't be helped.

He put a stamp on top the chaotic mess of pages and handed them back to her. "You know what, this is fine. Have a lovely stay on Archimedes IV."

"You are most efficient. Thank you!" She gave him a thumbs-up and snatched the documents beneath her arm. She sauntered out the spaceport with a satisfied smile.

DR. ISAAC NERGAL had been living on Archimedes IV for the past three years. Quarantine. Nobody wanted what Nergal had. Far as the rest of the galaxy was concerned, he could rot there.

The mutation had left Dr. Nergal with discolored green skin, covered in bumps and tumors. He was a gangly creature dressed in a full-body protective suit. It'd once been white but had long since been stained with dirt and blood, and god knows what else.

A man lay on a gurney in the dank pit that served as Nergal's operating room, wounded from a wild animal attack. He was bleeding from a pus-filled stump on his leg. Nergal glided around him, studying the condition beneath a harsh UV lamp.

The man sobbed. "Please, Doc. Ya gotta do something about this. Burns so bad!"

Nergal shook his head, a ghoulish smile forming on his lips. "Oh, I'm afraid it's far worse than that. As sharp as a til-beast's incisors are, their digestive systems can't easily process most foods, so the venom works as a stomach acid, breaking you down into digestible morsels before they open their maws and swallow you whole."

"Christ, Doc. I got a wife to look after," his patient pleaded, tears and blood streaming down his dirty cheeks. "I don't wanna die."

"Luckily for you, I've a fetish for disease and poisons," Nergal chided, slapping him gently on the face with the back of his greasy rubber glove. "But this isn't charity work."

Sweat appeared on the patient's body as his blood-shot eyes widened. "I got money. Okay. Just do what you need."

"I'm a bit above your pay-grade. If I'm going to take something out, I want to put something back in. Understand?"

The man's voice shook. "W-What are you gonna do?"

Nergal laughed. "Calm down, boy, I'd like to imagine having some ethical standards. I've simply some chemicals I've been itching to try."

"They won't kill me, will they?" the patient asked, then screamed. He could see the bit of flesh around the wound already beginning to liquefy, revealing the bone beneath.

Nergal fixed him with a cold stare. "Do I look like the doctor who would kill my patients?"

"Fine!" came the panicked grunts. "Do it."

Nergal's eyes glinted from behind the visor as his mouth widened in a maniacal grin. "Time for your medicine."

He flew to the shattered glass cabinet behind him and quickly retrieved a small syringe and filled it with an irradiated green liquid. Sinister laughter escaped him as he held it in front of his face. He could have kissed it.

"Have you ever witnessed such beauty? Not a serum exists like this in any known galaxy. It is life and death itself collected!" Nergal shouted this last bit, holding the syringe high over his head.

The patient threw his head back and howled. "Doc! Please! I am literally dying right now! Literally!"

"Oh, don't be such a baby!" Nergal rolled his eyes, then jammed the syringe into the man's leg.

Almost immediately the wound closed. Whatever flesh had been torn apart by the bite and venom rapidly reformed before the startled patient's eyes. Even his skin took on a healthy new glow. In a matter of seconds, it was impossible to tell if he had been wounded at all.

"Doc, how? How is this possible? You're a miracle worker!" The patient leapt from the table. "I feel great!"

Nergal watched with keen eyes. "And now for the secondary effects."

"Secondary effects?" The patient's smile faded. His eyes grew wide and he clutched his stomach, hearing a faint gurgle.

"One version of Chemical X indeed heals and rejuvenates the body, closing any wounds, and even gives you a bit of an adrenaline boost for just that added kick in your step. It makes my services invaluable to any cutthroat venture needing a medical expert," Nergal explained, tapping the edge of the syringe with a finger. "But that's not what I gave you."

Veins bulged on either side of the patient's bald head as the gurgling in his stomach grew. He lifted his shirt to see his stomach form into a pot belly with visible veins. Muscle tissue expanded around his torso in discolored lumps.

"What's happening to me?" He trembled, then screamed.

"Looks like you've made a friend. A tumor, to be precise," Nergal commented. "Ah! It's so cute! It's got hair...and teeth! Are those fingernails?"

More lumps appeared beneath the man's clothing and on the sides of his head, expanding outward into hideous little blobs. He became a grotesque amalgamation of displaced flesh and teeth. The patient's screams grew stifled as his tongue pushed against the roof and sides of his mouth. It forced his jaw open to see more of the pus-colored growths swelling rapidly around his tongue.

"Halp Hap!" The man struggled to form coherent sentences as he fell to his knees before the uncaring eyes of the doctor.

Nergal shook his head and his shoulders drooped. "Another failed test subject. Pity. Don't worry. It's for a good cause."

Sighing, Nergal ignored the quivering patient to retrieve a dusty shotgun from the tray of rusting surgical implements. The man stared back at him, scarcely able to see through the pustules blossoming around his head.

"I'll send you a consultation fee," Dr. Nergal said, then pulled the trigger.

The mass exploded into gory fireworks, sending the excess flesh slamming against the walls and equipment. Some of it landed with a loud splat. The smell was unbearable, like rotten eggs and roadkill.

Nergal slung the bloody shotgun over his shoulder and pouted. "Such is the price of progress."

Whistling, he packed his bags and prepared to leave. With any luck, he'd never have to see this dump again.

THE WIDE-BRIMMED hat fell over the LED lights of his eyes as he leaned back in his chair. His snakeskin boots were propped on top of the chipped wooden desk of the sheriff's office. His robotic limbs needed a rest after a long day of scaring varmints and outlaws out of Dover Town.

Weren't too many engineers around who could give him the proper tune-ups he needed. Even then, supplies were scarce. Some days he wondered if he was gonna break down eventually from all the wear and tear on his body. An android contemplating his own mortality. Heckuva thing. He shook his head.

Sheriff Rogers had been commissioned eight years ago by the citizens of Dover Town to protect and defend them from the various scumbags on Archimedes IV. They'd had to scrimp on his programming, so personality matrixes from old western holovids had been dumped into him to make up for it. Result was a six-foot-tall death machine with a charming disposition and a rough Southern drawl for an accent.

A single jail cell sat at the end of the office, so he could keep an eye on any drunk that needed a place to sleep for the night, and that's about all it was used for. Troublemakers in Dover Town were one of three types: someone you could talk down, someone you could quiet overnight, or someone about to find themselves in ownership of several new holes.

The office doors swung open. Rogers sat forward in his chair, noting the wide-eyed dirty youngster stumbling into his office. Brick, was it? He wanted to call him Brick anyway. Kid was built like one, all short and stocky.

"Sheriff Rogers, ya gotta come quick!" The kid was jumping up and down and he looked damn near out of breath.

"Easy scamp." Rogers walked to the front of the desk and knelt to the boy's eye level. "What's got your gears in a twist?"

"Some fellas rolled up into town. They all look pretty scary and armed."

Rogers sighed and straightened. "How armed would ya say?"

"The tall ugly one had a huge cannon!"

The citizens of Dover Town hadn't bothered requesting an android capable of facial expressions. Otherwise, Rogers might have gone slack-jawed and wide-eyed. He'd debated whether or not he wanted the hassle of facial expressions. There'd be advantages, such as the ability to smile when he felt like it or even cry. Right now he was grateful for the simplicity of little blinking lights. No kid should have to see their sheriff spooked by the mention of cannons.

"All right, Brick," he said. "You run along home to your mother. I'll see about greeting these strangers into town. Make sure the rest of your friends know not to be playing in the streets today if ya see 'em."

"Think there's gonna be a fight?" Brick looked more excited about the possibility of violence than Rogers was comfortable with.

"Oh, I'm sure it's nothing." Rogers ruffled the boy's hair.

While the kid did his best to duck away from the android's cold metal touch, Rogers gripped his gun beneath his cloak. His fingers were programmed to detect the ammo count of any weapon they touched. He'd taken the revolver off the first bandit he'd killed in his tenure as sheriff. It was fully loaded.

An antiquated aesthetic disguised the cutting-edge technology within the six-shooter. Its tiny bullets were capable of ripping through any surface. He'd taken out drones, heavily armored thugs and the like with a single shot. He was equipped with other mechanisms of destruction, but he'd come to prefer the revolver. One clean shot meant shorter firefights, and shorter firefights meant reduced civilian casualties.

He shooed Brick out of his office and stepped into the arid desert heat. Rumors of the incoming strangers must have spread quickly. The streets were all but deserted. He made a literal scan of the streets, swapping to thermographic vision to look for the approaching strangers.

Rogers spotted the big one with the cannon first. Subject identified: Karstotzkiyan female. Their species had been near-driven to extinction several decades prior when the IGF colonized the galaxy. The heat signatures from her cannon were strong, and she carried the massive thing on her back like it was weightless. He let out a preprogrammed whistle sound he'd retrieved from a holovid. He hoped she wasn't looking for a fight.

Another figure approached from the east end of town, this one even shadier and more dangerous looking than the last. Subject identified: human male, though drastically mutated. He put out no heat signature whatsoever. Only the readings of his protective suit had been picked up on the scanners.

"What is even going on," Rogers whispered.

A heat spike alerted him to the presence of another human woman entering the local tavern. She wore alien power armor from head to toe. It had all the colors of a sunset. The avian-inspired design suggested it might be Valran in origin, though he'd previously assumed the species to be a myth.

He blinked twice. "Run diagnostics on captured visuals from scanners."

One of his recent upgrades he'd managed to arrange for himself was access to the Galactic Database of Wanted Criminals and Known Threats. He'd found it useful for identifying suspicious cowpokes who rolled into Dover Town looking for trouble.

"Dr. Isaac Nergal—quarantined to Archimedes IV following a laboratory accident involving the experimentation of the worst toxins and viruses known to this sector of the galaxy. Reports indicate the spreading of contagious viruses via skin contact. Subjects experience extreme pain instantly and die within minutes. Avoid contact and alert the IGF if seen."

"Oh dear."

"Agda Valencia aka Big Ugly Bluebird or Big Ugly—former general of the Sapphire Knights deployed by the Ingle Corporation. She slaughtered every single member of her squad and deserted, stealing prototype military-grade equipment. Most notable of the stolen equipment is a prototype plasma cannon. Its exact specifications are considered classified. She has been making a living as an illegal mercenary traveling from planet to planet. Bounty is currently two million credits, dead or alive. The plasma cannon is to be immediately returned to the Ingle Corporation."

"Huh!"

"Talisha Artul—licensed bounty hunter with a growing reputation and notoriety for her high success rate. Consistently deployed by the IGF against space pirates and other wanted criminals. The suit of armor and ship are both Valran in design, and, as of this current report, are the only known remaining artifacts of the lost alien species within the galaxy. No knowledge exists of how Talisha or her mother who wore the armor before her came to acquire such powerful relics."

"You gotta be kidding me," Rogers groaned upon reading the final report. He sighed and gripped the brim of his hat, tightening it around his head. "All right, time to go to work."

The spurs on the edge of his boots rattled as he made his way down the dusty, empty streets. His spurs had been called useless, and he'd been teased for them by the locals. Maybe it was a flaw in his programming, but he liked having them. He found the sounds pleasurable, and it suited his motif. Weren't nothing wrong with a little self-expression so long as he did his job right and proper.

As he neared the saloon, he could hear a slew of voices from behind the wooden doors. That was odd. The saloon was never a rowdy place, mostly occupied by old prospectors sitting together to glumly reminisce. Rogers kept his fingers near the holster of his gun.

The yelling and carousing came to an immediate halt the second he burst through the swinging doors. He surveyed the room cautiously, counting far too many heads than he was comfortable with. All of them had faces mean as a rattlesnake and twice as deadly.

"Evening, folks," Rogers tipped his hat to the saloon patrons. "Welcome to Dover Town. Thought I'd pop in and introduce myself."

He heard a gun click. A scaly-skinned individual with a wide-brimmed hat had a gun with a barrel as big around as his head pointed directly at him. Rogers let out a sigh.

The scaly fiend chuckled. "Would you be the sheriff of this quaint little community?"

"Sheriff Rogers, law-keeping and security android at your service." He raised both hands in the air. "Now would you mind getting that pea-shooter out of my face?"

No such luck. The gunman flicked a switch on the side of the gun, causing it to hum gradually to life, the cylinders on each side spinning and whirring. "There's a bounty on yer head, Mistuh Rogers. Someone thinks you'll be mighty valuable."

Cold metal pressed against the turquoise scales on the back of the gunman's neck. The stocky dark-skinned woman with the weird alien armor was there. She had the long barrel of a thin blaster pressed tightly against his skin. Thick natural hair bounced in ringlets along the sides of her glass-cutting cheekbones. Most striking were her eyes. They held a stern gaze as deadly as any weapon. "Name's Talisha," she said. "Chances are, if you recognize this armor, you know who I am and what I can do. Now, if you're interested in not having your head blasted off, I'd suggest you lower your gun like the nice robot said. He's just trying to do his job and keep the law around these parts. I think we oughta let him, don't you?"

Another gun was raised. A double-barreled sawed-off shotgun aimed in Talisha's direction by the creepy guy in the hazmat suit. He took a bold step forward, his feet thudding against the floorboards with each agonized movement.

"Dr. Nergal, pleased to meet you. I know of you, the law-abiding bounty hunter," he said, grinning widely. "But the problem lies in the fact that there's no law on this backwater planet. You have no power here save for that which you can back up with lots and lots of guns and this robot is worth quite a bounty."

"I'm-I'm technically an android," Rogers added, but doubted anyone was listening.

It was an unpleasant sensation, standing in the middle of a room of armed hooligans all discussing him like a piece of property. He supposed in some way he was, though he'd never thought of himself as such. He'd always hoped he'd be seen as a member of the community, what with all he'd done for these people over the years. Not everyone would see him as a person deserving of all the same rights and decency. This scene was a harsh reminder of that fact.

One of the tables was snatched from beneath a group of leering armed men and held aloft by the large Karstotzkiyan. The men fell cowering before her feet even as she flashed them a wide smile. She hadn't even bothered with the huge blue cannon resting snuggly on her back.

"Shootout would risk damage to the sheriff," she explained, holding the table threateningly. "Our employers paid handsome money to acquire him and his weaponry. This is a retrieval mission."

Nergal slowly swung his shotgun to face her. "A retrieval mission with a competitive element attached. The whole booty goes to the first three mercenaries who bring the android to the designated location."

"I was told nothing of this," Talisha barked. "You're making this up."

"You're a part of it, darling." Nergal retrieved a sheet of paper stuffed into his belt. There were several chemical stains on the corners, and god knows what else, but Talisha's photo next to Roger's was clearly recognizable. "If you happen to die in the scuffle, our employer has a bonus to whoever can bring them your fabulous armor."

Talisha glared. "Motherfuh—"

A warning shot fired into the ceiling interrupted her. All eyes turned to the android in the cowboy hat, brim lowered over his eyes. Sunlight poured through the hole in the ceiling, creating the perfect spotlight in the dim atmosphere.

"Is it true? Did the good folk of this town really decide to auction me off to the highest bidder? Like I was some sort of frigging steer?" His voice was cold as his smooth metal skin, but the anger in his words carried well enough. The sheriff was pissed.

Bluebird looked at him, her eyes softening. "I am sorry, Mr. Cowboy. I have a receipt as proof of purchase. Perhaps it would be better if you come with us. There is nothing left for you here."

"I've spent my entire life cycle for these people," Rogers fumed, finger quivering over the trigger. "I've chased out varmints and scoundrels. I've protected and cared for each and every member of this community, and all without so much as a thank you, but I didn't mind 'cause I thought I was one of them. I thought I was a part of this place. It was my home. And now? Now you're telling me they've sold me off for a paycheck? Who's gonna protect these people when I'm gone? I don't, no, I *won't* believe it."

Nergal sneered. "Face it, cowpoke. You're an outdated model with a problematic quirk in your programming. You're no cowboy, and this isn't a holovid. With the credits and guns offered to this community by our employers, they'll have more than enough to protect themselves and plenty of luxuries for years to come. Seems to me the citizens of Dover Town are getting the better deal."

The lights in Rogers's eyes dimmed, then went red. He made a full sensor sweep on every one of these low-life scumbags. They were well-armed, highly-trained, professional mercenaries and all wanted a piece of him. Well, they could come and get it.

"I don't much like being sold," he said. "I'm still sheriff and you're all unwelcome here. Get out my goddamned town."

Bluebird cursed and threw the table in his direction. "He's going to attack!"

His android reflexes were swift and his movements quicker. Anyone without special lenses would have seen little more than a blur as he dove to the right and fired with pinpoint accuracy. A single bullet flew through the skulls of three men lined together. Others who thought they could hide behind overturned tables found themselves bleeding from bullets and splinters.

Talisha lowered her helmet's visor and blasted the head off the scaled man. A woman tried to grab her from behind only to get shoved off when Talisha jetted into the air. High energy burst fire from her arm cannon shredded through her attacker's armor as if it were paper.

Nergal cackled as he strewed casually through the carnage, stepping over fallen bodies while creating new ones with each shotgun blast. He turned his gun several times on Rogers, who took care to avoid the pellets scattering across the saloon. The wide arc of those shots scared him the most. Massive blasts like that were the hardest to dodge.

Bluebird had fallen into a corner. Rogers assumed she hadn't pulled her cannon out yet because it was likely to bring the whole saloon down around them. Despite her size, he wasn't too worried about having to face off against her. She was a shiny blue target in a ruckus and many hoped to secure her high-tech weaponry. She'd be left holding her own against them for a while.

A man tackled her. He was hurled into an unconscious stupor against the wall. A second went down in a single punch, bloody teeth flying a dozen different directions. By this point, they were coming at her in groups, and she could only kick and punch and throw so many of them.

With a roar, she knocked a man off her wrist to activate a domed barrier shield about herself, pushing them away. Bullets deflected off the barrier and back at their shooters, some of them getting killed instantly. She laughed and charged back into the fray, using the shield to turn herself into a giant wrecking ball, smashing and trampling everything in her path.

The battle lasted only a few minutes, a violent parade of bullets and lasers that utterly destroyed the saloon. Every surface of the building was covered in holes. It was a wonder any walls remained. Bodies littered the floor and stairwell, and blood soaked every floorboard. Nergal, Bluebird, Talisha, and Rogers were all who survived.

Bluebird folded her arms across her chest and snorted, a large smile forming over her unprepossessing features. "That was a good fight," she said, nodding approvingly at the bloodbath.

Rogers gestured at her with his six-shooter. "Doesn't have to be over yet, Bluebird."

Talisha lowered her arm cannon and blaster. "But it doesn't have to continue. I'd hate to use all my resources on unnecessary posturing."

Nergal nodded. "It's a shame I can't claim the additional bounty on your armor, but all the same it's simply not worth the effort to pry it off you."

"And you, tin-man?" Bluebird nodded at Rogers. "These people do not deserve your protection. Fuck them. Come with us. Claim big treasure."

Rogers holstered his weapon. "Treasure?"

"The lost alien treasure of Archimedes IV, buried eons ago before this planet was first colonized." Nergal slung the shotgun beneath his arm and knelt to inspect one of the dead bodies at his feet. "I once thought the treasure a myth, but clearly some are intent on finding it and willing to spend a lot of money to do so."

"But not enough to pay everyone they hired to come looking for it." Talisha stared at the gore with a look of disgust.

Nergal shrugged and stood. "Oh, I wouldn't be too offended, m'dear. It's good business when you're hiring a bunch of desperate individuals to go searching for a treasure that may or may not exist. If they all kill each other, you don't have to pay them. Eliminates fools and weaklings and you get the most out of your money."

"It's unethical," Talisha snapped. "It violates the contract between bounty hunters and their employers. Changing the terms of the bounty like that is despicable and poor business practice. I've a mind to leave this planet and report them to the IGF."

"Ah, but they've no jurisdiction out here," Nergal argued.

Talisha glowered at him. "So you've said."

Bluebird chuckled even as she scowled. "Fuck the IGF. They can't even get their initials right. Intergalactic Peacekeeping Force, hah! It should be IPF. *I Piss Freely*! So, tin-man, you with us?"

The ceiling fan chose that exact moment to fall and crash directly behind her. Both Nergal and Talisha reacted immediately, raising their weapons for another fight. Bluebird took a casual glance behind her and shrugged.

"You big babies!" she bellowed, then laughed. "It is only a fan!"

Rogers sighed. "Fine. Seems like someone went to a heckuva lot of trouble to purchase me. Suppose that makes me their employee."

"You're more their property, technically speaking. As an android, you don't qualify for human rights." Nergal seemed all too eager to point this out.

Rogers stared at him. "Don't make me shoot a walking sack of disease and pestilence now, ya hear."

Nergal giggled. "Oh, you're too kind! This is going to be such fun."

Rogers ignored him and touched his fingers lightly to the bullet-ridden saloon doors. Their hinges groaned and collapsed, sending the doors clattering to the ground. He sighed and stepped out into the streets. A crowd of onlookers had gathered, fixing him with wide, frightened stares.

How had he not seen it? They'd given him these same looks for years. Nergal was right. They'd never view him as anything other than a weapon. Now they'd have newer weapons, weapons they could control, weapons that didn't think. He felt the rejection of their stares and moved passed, head held high.

His shoulders went rigid and his fists clenched. He'd not the capacity for facial expressions, but his body language could communicate emotion just as well as any organic being He was in pain.

"It isn't right," Talisha said.

Bluebird shrugged. "What in the universe is? Fairness and order are lies told to us by the powerful."

Talisha folded her arms over her chest. "Didn't take you for a philosopher."

"Just an observer," Bluebird sniffed dismissively. "Take Sheriff there. Only dangerous because they wanted him to be. All his weapons and powers are a product of his environment. They created him and now they fear him. I've seen it before."

Bluebird's stance parted, as if awaiting fresh combat. Her hands shook and her teeth grated together. She gripped the strap of her cannon like a security blanket.

Talisha raised an eyebrow. "You okay there?"

Bluebird froze. She melted into a smile and let out a hearty laugh, placing her hands on her hips. That breezy self-assured confidence returned. She smacked Talisha on the back, sending the smaller woman stumbling.

"We are going to have fun, you and I," Bluebird said with a wink.

Dr. Nergal had been sticking the various corpses around on the floor with a syringe and extracting blood from the bodies to be stored in vials in a pouch worn about his waist. He moved over each corpse singing a cheery ditty to himself. He stopped, fondling an off-white trench-coat, somehow having remained clean and bulletproof despite the shooting. Only the corners were tattered and torn.

He turned around to Bluebird and Talisha and gestured both arms outward in a showy, dramatic reveal. "Ta-dah! How do I look?"

Talisha folded her arms over her chest. "You're wearing a chemical-delivery apparatus over a tattered coat and a hazmat suit. Absolutely ridiculous."

"I like it!" Bluebird grinned. "Hideous but distinctive."

Nergal took a sweeping bow. "Coming from you, my dear, those are words of high praise. With some tailoring, it'll prove useful for carrying around my...concoctions."

"I've read your file," Talisha said. "There was nothing in it about tailoring."

Nergal moved in terrifyingly close, his visor a mere inch away from her face. She raised her arm cannon to his chin in a warning measure. He smiled lecherously, resting his chin against the barrel of the cannon.

"There is much about me that isn't in my file, bounty hunter."

"I'm well aware. I saw the research station over Pluribon. How many died by your hand?"

"Hundreds, thousands, millions, billions..." Nergal waved his hands about his head, as if plucking the numbers straight out of the air. "What does it matter?"

"Exaggerating the deaths of innocents is in poor taste," Talisha said, her tone icy. "Even for you."

Bluebird swatted them away from each other with a casual swipe of her thick, meaty hand. "Might we dispense with shared body counts on the road? Our quarry is reaching city limits."

Chapter Two

MR. SNIDELY WAITED by the scorpion, a tactical open-roofed vehicle capable of carrying six passengers with a large machine gun mounted to the rear end. Scorpions offered little in the way of protection but could outrun most vehicles on any terrain. Protection didn't interest him anyway. Shields endangered those who hid behind them, luring them into complacency.

Snidely knew the dangers. He'd handpicked the worst mercenaries and bounty hunters in the galaxy for this assignment, and it wasn't 'cause he thought they'd protect him. All great gambles had an element of risk to them. If you're not willing to bet it all, then there's no point in playing.

He'd always been fairly small, borderline petite. His features were narrow and angular. The lenses of his spectacles made him look more like a fly than a man. He spent most of his time in a darkened little room staring at a monitor all day, rendering him sickly and pale. Barely in his twenties and already he stooped like a withered old man.

Snidely could see four figures approaching from Dover Town. He parted his thin pink lips into a wide, unsavory grin. He steepled his fingers and allowed himself a celebratory chuckle.

"Calculations proved correct, only four survived. Shame about the armor. Would have been useful. Might've gotten a raise if I'd managed to secure it. Pity."

As they neared, his smile faded. The android, the mercenary, the doctor, and the bounty hunter all had guns trained on him. This was unexpected, though not out of the realm of plausibility. His only question was why he hadn't elected to wait *inside* the scorpion.

Snidely threw his hands in surrender as they approached. He nodded politely as Talisha approached. "Ah. Yes. I'm Blake Snidely, your representative. Lovely time at the saloon?"

Beads of sweat appeared on the sides of his face. His heart leapt into his throat. No one had ever aimed a gun at him before.

Bluebird stepped forward, the plasma cannon in her arms humming and whirring as it charged. "Do you see this? Her name is Ethel. She does not like you."

"I was told one thing," Talisha added, taking her place beside Bluebird. "These folks were told another. Thought you could get your grubby capitalist hands on some alien technology, did ya?"

Snidely attempted a casual shrug despite his shaking. "I imagine I'm not the first. Though capitalist is a bit hypocritical, don't you think?"

Nergal shook his head. "Tsk, tsk. Don't speak, lovely. We've come to the conclusion that while we might be hired killers looking to make some extra credits, you're an absolute idiot. You arranged for all those people to get killed as a litmus test. Brilliant, up until you double-crossed the likes of us. Ever see what happens when I kiss someone?"

Snidely almost shit himself. His face went somehow even paler. His eyes watered and his knees buckled. It'd gone too far. This was it, he was going to die.

"What do you want?" he whimpered.

"Who are you working for?" Talisha snapped. "What are they after?"

"I can't say," Snidely said, his voice harried. "If I tell you, losing my job will be the least of my worries."

"I'd say Nergal's kiss is more your worry right now," Bluebird sneered.

In response, Nergal moved a gloved hand to his visor gradually lifting it but an inch off his face. Snidely recoiled from the stench. It was the unmistakable smell of death.

"All right," he panted. "It's Plymouth. I work for Plymouth."

Talisha's brow furrowed. "Never heard of them."

"No files on such a company exist on the Datanet," Rogers said, taking a moment to process the statement. "He's a lying dog."

Snidely stammered, backing away from Nergal. "Y-y-ou might have heard of our subsidiaries. The Ingle Corporation, perhaps?"

Bluebird spit. She threw her cannon to the ground and charged. She snatched Snidely off his feet by his collar and raised her fist with a mighty roar. He screamed, shielding his face with his elbows. One punch from a Karstotzkiyan could shatter his entire skull.

"You work for Ingle!" Her screams were deafening.

Rogers cocked his pistol and aimed it at the back of her head. "Drop him, Agda."

"This slimy sunnuva *beetch* bought you from your home!" Bluebird roared, not breaking eye-contact. "Who will miss him if I crack his head open like runny eggs?"

"That's right, and as such I'm his legal property. That puts him under the protections I formerly provided for the good folks of Dover. So, if ya don't mind, put down my boss."

Bluebird growled. "I would be doing you a favor, metal-man."

"That you would, but that also doesn't get us very far, now does it?"

"We're more than Ingle if that helps," Snidely whimpered. "We're a shadow conglomerate that covers everything from the Cobra Media Network, to the Crimson Expeditionary Forces. All work for us at Plymouth, even the ones that look like they're competing."

"Why the secrecy?" Talisha said. "If your claims are true, that makes you the wealthiest and most powerful corporation in the galaxy."

"It's common practice actually," Snidely said, "If you'd put me down, dear Agda, I'd be happy to explain it to you."

"Big Blue, be a dear?" Talisha asked, lowering her arm cannon.

Bluebird squinted at the tiny man squirming in her grip. "Only because the pretty woman said so, do I let you live. Understood?"

"Completely!" Snidely yelped a bit too loudly.

Bluebird released her grip, letting him fall a good three feet to the ground. He collapsed into a crumpled heap in the sand, coughing and sputtering. He rose, knees almost buckling beneath him for a second, and brushed the dirt off his expensive suit.

"Shadow companies," Talisha said. "Explain."

"Right, well it's all very simple. Operating in public leaves one open to scrutiny, the rise and falls of public opinion and how it affects the stock market," Snidely explained. "Add any political turmoil to that mix, in a galaxy where planet-destroying weapons are gradually becoming a thing, and you can imagine why many corporations would want a private backer."

"Someone to fall back on in case they get blown to smithereens or dissolve completely to financial ruin," Nergal said. "It's insidious. I love it."

Snidely nodded. "That's where companies like Plymouth come in, monolithic entities whose primary function is the purchase of other companies looking for a big brother to watch over their shoulder, as it were. We stabilize economies, and most importantly, when was the last corporate war you've heard of? Fifteen years ago, if I'm right?"

"Fourteen," Bluebird muttered darkly. "I rose in ranks quickly in that war. When I was part of the Sapphire Knights. I was a hero in those days."

"And you want to know who brokered the peace between Ingle and Havron? Plymouth. Both companies have been operating alongside each other ever since. Now, each company is for the most part allowed to run the way they see fit, with only the occasional oversight, so of course some things do slip through the cracks."

"Don't insult me," Bluebird spat. "I can see you aren't to blame, though. You're nothing more than a stooge."

"I'm sure your shadow status also lets you engage in a lot of extra-legal loopholes too," Talisha said, her disgust for the man rising by the second.

"Ah!" Snidely raised a finger and smiled. "Not so much as one might think. Yes, we do have teams of legal people to work alongside our assct companies to help protect our interests, but extra-legal activity is something we're loathe to partake in. The IGF isn't necessarily oblivious to our existence, but with no certifiable proof and no reason to go looking for it, they've come to leave well enough alone, and that's honestly just a better way to do business. Don't you think?"

"And the treasure?" Nergal said, his eyes glinting with greed. "I'm far more curious about the treasure than your silly secret paperwork. What does such a corporate powerhouse want with a lost alien treasure?"

"In all honesty?"

Snidely opened the door to the scorpion and dug around inside for a metallic briefcase. He brought it to the hood of the vehicle and flipped it open, retrieving a datapad from its contents. A three-dimensional, emerald holo-projection flickered into view over the pad. It depicted a topographical layout of the planet before splitting off into an adjacent screen revealing what appeared to be a vast trapezoidal structure. Esoteric alien symbols appeared in vertical formations on either side of the image.

"A Valran Temple," Talisha said. "There aren't supposed to be any left in the galaxy."

"So they're real..." Nergal breathed. "I'd always thought them the stuff of superstitious locals."

"Plymouth has been aware of the existence of the Valran ever since your mother started showing up on our radar," Snidely explained.

"Mom doesn't talk about them much." Talisha shook her head.

Snidely sniffed. "I can't imagine she would. Rumor has it she was raised by the Valran before they perished under mysterious circumstances. Many rumors do circulate about that woman and her armor."

"But what about the temple?!" Nergal shrieked, pointing eagerly at the screen.

Snidely's eyes glazed over as tones of longing crept into his voice. "The appearance of the original Talisha Artul led us to believe that more remnants of Valran technology were scattered throughout the galaxy. They were a nomadic people after all.

"We've found some artifacts here and there, but nothing like what was uncovered here." Snidely clasped his hands neatly in front of him. "Plymouth would like to know what the Valran knew. It's possible they recorded everything in a database within the temple."

"But the treasure," Bluebird's shoulders stiffened. "Was that a lie too?"

"Knowledge is better than treasure," Snidely said, shrugging.

She turned her back on him and walked away, throwing her hands in the air in disgust. "Ugh, I wanted loot. Bluebird go bye-bye."

Snidely was unprepared for how fast and far Bluebird could stride. He raced after her on spindly legs, promising a hefty sum in exchange for her services. The datapad lay abandoned on the hood of the scorpion. Talisha folded her arms over her chest and continued staring at the graphic display.

"Rogers?" she said, rubbing her hand over her chin. "Is there any way to verify this?"

Rogers stood still for a moment. "I could hack the datapad, get a good reading on what this city-slicker's up to. Not sure if I've a right to seeing as how this fella owns me and all."

Talisha groaned. "Rogers, ignore Nergal. The man is a sadistic terrorist and mass murderer. He's unlikely to say anything of value."

Nergal sneered in her direction. He went immediately back to staring at the holographic image with rapt fascination. A hungry look had entered in his eyes.

Talisha placed a firm hand on Rogers's shoulder, then removed her helmet. "Listen, after this job. I'm gonna see what strings I can pull with the IGF to have you declared sentient. That renders anyone's ownership of you illegal. You wouldn't be the first, so it's completely doable."

"Why would ya do that for me?"

She looked dead serious. "It's the right thing to do. No better reason than that."

He nodded and snatched the datapad up in his fingers. "I can wirelessly transmit my conscious into any machine connected to the Datanet."

Nergal's mouth fell open, stunned. "We had androids of your make and model back on Pluribon. None of them could do such a thing."

"I tweak now and again, Doctor." Rogers fell silent. The holo display flickered as his brain probed the files contained within.

Nergal shrugged his shoulders and looked to the horizon. Whatever Snidely said to Bluebird must have convinced her. She marched back to them at her own pace with the tiny man riding her shoulders.

Nergal turned to Rogers, licking his lips. "Better hurry, cowboy. The boss is on his way."

"Gonna have to prematurely disconnect," Rogers said hurriedly.

The projection fizzled for a moment and the lights faded from Rogers's eyes. Talisha stared worriedly. She snapped her fingers several times in front of his face.

"Rogers? Sheriff? You okay there?"

"Sentient androids sending their consciousness floating through the Datanet," Nergal muttered, then made a disapproving click of his tongue. "Unprecedented. Who knows what he might have picked up in there? Likely killed him."

"You're so helpful, Doctor," Talisha groaned. She shook Rogers's shoulders. "Dammit! Wake up!"

The lights returned to the android's eyes and the projection flickered back into view just as Bluebird and Snidely arrived. Talisha returned her helmet to her head and hid her panic beneath her visor. Bluebird dropped Snidely unceremoniously to the ground.

Bluebird smiled. "He agreed to double our prices. All of them. Robot also goes free. It is only fair."

"A woman who is not to be underestimated," Talisha said, nodding. "So, how about it, Snidely? Where is this temple?"

"Hold yer horses." It was a gravelly voice, new and unfamiliar, still tinged with Rogers's twangy accent, but far meaner. The android retrieved his pistol and aimed it at Snidely's head. "Rogers was willing to take your bullshit, but now I'm in charge and I'm thinking I want a share of the loot."

"What do you mean, Rogers isn't in charge?" Snidely sputtered.

"Multiple operating systems. Multiple personality subroutines. This one just woke up. Name's Cyrus, ya heard it?"

"I'm hearing it now," Snidely said with a nod. "Very well, you'll get your fair share of the credits. Six million credits, split four ways. Sound reasonable enough?"

Talisha stared, dumbfounded. She could hardly believe it was true. Then again, she'd seen stranger things. She shook her head and tried to ignore her growing sense of unease.

Cyrus lowered the pistol and nodded. "I think we'll get along just dandy. Let's hit the trails, I'm eager to shoot something."

"Won't be that easy," Snidely coughed, turning the datapad off and sliding it back into the briefcase. "The Valran put a great deal of security into this temple, and only the proper key can open it. It's currently being held by a tribe of bandits several miles from here."

"We kill bandits. Take key. Go to temple. Claim treasure." Bluebird shrugged. "Not difficult. Let's go! I will drive."

"Sure. You drive. Why not?" Snidely groaned, pinching the bridge of his nose between his fingers.

Nergal laughed at his expression, an unpleasant wheezing noise full of more menace than mirth. Snidely's heart sank deep into his chest as he understood he'd be spending a significant amount of time with these individuals.

"Tried to manipulate the game and feeling in over your head now, Mr. Snidely?" Nergal asked.

"A biological terrorist, a famous bounty hunter, an eight-foot-tall fugitive with a cannon, and an android with a split-personality," Snidely said, adjusting his tie. "This is nothing compared to the shark-infested waters of the boardroom. I should be fine."

Nergal's eyes narrowed watching Snidely climb into the back of the Scorpion. He rubbed his thumb and finger together, turning to gaze at the barren wasteland. "Of course. Everything is under control."

PLYMOUTH WAS TOO smart to have its primary offices and functions confined to a single location. They spread across several satellites cloaked on the fringes of IGF-protected space. The Mayflower was Plymouth's cutting-edge military-grade satellite, armed with a mean-ass laser capable of wiping all organic life on a planet's surface. It'd only fired once in its original testing phase. They'd had to lay off six million employees just to cover the cost of a single shot.

Some had already suggested using it to clear Archimedes IV before sending out a clean-up team. They were terminated shortly thereafter. The proposition would have been ludicrously expensive, setting back any potential profits gained.

Still, Madame Inspector was not one to leave things to chance. She ordered the Mayflower to Archimedes IV. The Valran Temple had taken priority.

She stood on the edge of a balcony overlooking several stations on the front end of the satellite, her arms folded behind her back. A domed window showed the ruined planet of Archimedes IV and the black void of space beyond. A part of her twinged with jealousy that the little pissant Snidely got to traipse about down there, while she hadn't set foot on a planet's surface in 35 years. It couldn't be helped at this point, she was too important to Plymouth's operations and held too many secrets to risk it all by gallivanting around with mercenaries.

Footsteps echoed behind her. She groaned softly, leaning against the bronze railing of the balcony. A single moment without interruption was impossible. These incompetents simply could not exist without her oversight.

"Madame Inspector." The voice belonged to a man in a long white coat approaching her, his face filled with terror. "Unidentified vessels approaching the western hemisphere of the planet. We thought you should know."

"Got visual?"

He handed her his datapad. She flipped through snapshots of thin black aircraft built specifically for hit-and-run tactics. Her brow furrowed and her lip curled. Not them, dammit. Smoke rose from the sides of the screen, and the datapad burned hot in her fingers. She threw it to the ground and stamped it beneath her high-heeled boot.

"Pirates," she snarled.

"Madame Inspector?" The man in white knelt and immediately stooped to sweep up the bits of shattered datapad.

"Ignore that!" She barked, snapping her fingers in his face. "Only one pirate fleet has the capabilities of transferring a virus through holo-imaging: Captain Ching Shih. Do a full manual restart of all computers on the satellite."

"I assure you our protections are completely fool-proof. No way a virus could-!"

"Yet it got through to your datapad when you transferred the images," Madame Inspector glowered. "I'm not about to hand over the most powerful weapon in the galaxy to a gang of hoodlums who got lucky! Is that understood?"

The man nodded, turning three shades paler. "What do you think the pirates want on Archimedes IV?"

"With any luck, to resupply and lay low," she said, turning her back on him.

"Shall we send an alert to Mr. Snidely and his task force?"

Madame Inspector folded her arms neatly behind her back. "That won't be necessary. The real threat is up here. Ching Shih's viruses have crippled entire fleets. All your efforts now will go to ensure the defenses of our network."

"Yes, Madame Inspector, but why aren't we warning the task force? I thought the Valran mission was a priority."

Her shoulders stiffened. "What is your name?"

"Madame Inspector?"

She turned on him, nostrils flaring. "Your name, peon. What is it?"

"J-Jackie," he stammered, shaking as his mistake became all too clear to him.

"Are you interested in my job, Jackie?" She took a threatening step toward him. "You must think you know better if you're questioning me."

It didn't matter that he was a good foot taller than she was, with broad shoulders and a thick frame. It didn't matter that she was small and old as dust. Every dainty clack of her heels may as well have been a rumbling earthquake for the way he sweat and trembled.

"Curiosity and nothing more, I swear it!"

She placed a hand delicately against the side of his cheek and smiled coolly, her eyes hungry like a shark's. "Curiosity is the mark of ambition. See that it doesn't get you killed, hmm?"

He nodded hurriedly. "Of course, Madame Inspector."

She patted the side of his face dismissively with a fingernail and waved him off. "Get going. You disgust me."

TALISHA'S SPRINGY COILS of hair danced behind her head, propelled by the blast of air from the open roof of the scorpion. She had one arm hanging out the side of the vehicle while her eyes scanned the craggy desert vista for potential threats. Conversation had been thankfully minimal. Turned out that aside from professional interests, the mercs had little in common.

Cyrus sat across from her, hat pulled tightly over his brow to keep it from blowing away. He twirled his pistol about his fingers once in a while, displaying a propensity for idle amusement. At other times he would stare with that expressionless face at one of the other occupants of the vehicle. He caused even Bluebird to turn away with an unsettled grimace.

"How's Rogers?" Talisha called to him.

Cyrus shrugged. "Oh he's around in there. Prolly asleep."

"I'm not familiar enough with your working model," Talisha said. "But I'm not sure multiple operating systems is common."

"That was Rogers tinkering around with his hardware and programming," Cyrus said. He tapped the side of his skull for emphasis. "He felt while his consciousness was scrounging around another system, there should be someone in the driver's seat. That's where I come in."

"Sorry if I sound nosy. Just robotics and tech are a pet hobby of mine."

"Do I fascinate you, ma'am?" Cyrus chuckled.

"Well, you are unique. Never met too many cowboy androids in my line of work."

"With all due respect, ma'am, I'm likely far from the strangest thing in this here galaxy."

"Fair enough. Can't compete with a telepathic jellyfish monster that killed an entire IGF battalion, resurrecting them as mindless slaves."

Cyrus froze. "Ya gotta be pullin' my leg there, right?"

Talisha's brow furrowed. "I still see its hideous, bulbous form in my restless dreams; a writhing nightmare to assault the senses, protected by a hoard of living dead."

All eyes turned on her and conversation fell silent for a solid minute.

Bluebird chose at that specific moment to begin singing in the language of her motherland. It was an anthem of a sort. They must have been grateful for an end to the silence. They allowed her to reach the third chorus before clamoring for its end.

Nergal rubbed the sides of his temples. "I've concocted some terrible tortures in my time, but nothing like that. Big Ugly, you are, indeed, a true sadist. I salute you."

Bluebird frowned. "On my home planet, we had big vocals for big music."

Nergal snorted. "You're Karstotzkiyan. Everything about your people is big. It's why your people made for such good cannon fodder in the corporate wars."

Bluebird's nostrils flared. She took the steering wheel and jerked it hard to the right. The scorpion flew on two wheels for several terrifying seconds, tossing the occupants mercilessly against the sides. She slammed her thick boots against the brakes, bringing the car to a sudden halt, flinging Nergal into her fist. He scrambled to his knees, gasping.

Bluebird smiled at him. "You are a brave and foolish man to speak like that to me."

Nergal's hands ran panicked over his visor. He stumbled to the doors of the vehicle. His fingers slipped against the doorknob.

"It was just a punch, don't be such big baby," Bluebird said.

"You put a crack in my visor, indigo imbecile!" Nergal shrieked, exploding out of the vehicle. "All of you have to get out of here! This vessel may already be contaminated!"

"Contaminated?" Cyrus chortled. "Sucks to be a meatbag right now."

Talisha slammed her visor shut. Her armor could identify and purge toxins. Snidely and Bluebird had no such protections. She blasted out the scorpion with her jet pack, snatching them both beneath her arms and setting them down several yards away from the vehicle.

Bluebird slapped Talisha's back, laughing heartily. "For such a tiny woman, you are strong!"

Snidely adjusted his suit jacket, fingers agitated. "It's the armor. Imbues the wearer with enhanced strength. Nothing else like it in this universe."

Cyrus shrugged his shoulders and stood, sighing audibly. "I'll go ahead and do a scan for any pathogens, I guess."

Nergal crawled a good distance away from the Scorpion where he could remove his visor and headgear. For the first time, all could see the lurid green discoloration of his skin and the bulging blackness of his veins. Some of his stringy black hair fell about his shoulders in matted knots. There were patches of bald spots along the sides of his head. He looked at the group with narrowed jaundiced eyes before turning away. He shrugged off the pack of equipment on his shoulder and rummaged through it, swearing all the while.

"I saw a rat once, sickly and dying," Bluebird mused. "We tried to help it, but it bit and clawed the shit out of anyone who came near. That is what Nergal makes me think of."

"Most of what happened to Dr. Isaac Nergal is classified," Snidely said in a low voice. "As are the two million lives he claimed aboard Space Colony Tychus over the planet Pluribon. Our belief at Plymouth, though, is that it was all a horrible accident."

Talisha folded her arms over her chest. "He seemed rather proud of those deaths. I was there for the aftermath, Blake. I saw the victims."

"And what was a famous bounty hunter doing at the site of one of the galaxy's worst terrorist incidents?" Snidely seemed genuinely curious.

"That's classified," she retorted.

Bluebird took the cannon from off her back and shoved it nose-first into the sand so she could lean idly on it. She watched Nergal through narrowed eyes. He replaced his headgear. His shoulders heaved now and again, almost as if he were sobbing.

"There is more to his story," Bluebird said. "No man deserves what has happened to him."

Talisha turned toward her. "That's charitable. He mocked the genocide of your people."

"And I punched him for it. If he does it again, I will punch him again."

Talisha raised her eyebrows and gave a faint nod. "Fair."

Snidely shoved his hands into his pockets. "We have security footage of him attempting to evacuate some scientists off the station. Seems strange if his intent was to kill all of them."

"So he was framed, and then later started taking credit for the attack as a means of self-preservation." Talisha's voice trailed off.

"His fate is a pitiable one," Snidely said. "Exiled to this planet, quarantined for his condition; it might be necessary to have a reputation as a dangerous individual."

Cyrus finished scanning the Scorpion. "No sign of any pathogens. Vehicle's safe."

Engines roared in the distance. Through the shimmering haze, a cavalcade of armored jeeps could be seen hopping over the dunes and crags, coming toward them. Some had rust-colored flags streaming high overhead while the vehicle's occupants stood in their seats, rifles pointed at the sky as they screamed.

Nergal stood, a scowl forming on his face, fingers twitching. He reached into his apparatus and retrieved a long-barreled gun attached to a silver tube. He marched toward the approaching horde with seemingly no respect for his well-being.

"Bandits," Cyrus said, letting out a low chuckle. "Rogers had some fun earlier. Now let's show you hooligans what I can do."

The android tossed away the knitted poncho. Multi-barrel rocket launchers sprouted from his shoulders with a mechanical whir. He whooped and hollered, firing upon the approaching vehicles. The rocket left a spiraling trail of smoke in its wake, exploding into the first jeep in a massive ball of fire.

"He's an absolute fool," Talisha whispered. She cupped her hands around her mouth and shouted. "Nergal's still out there! Cool it with the explosions!"

Cyrus only laughed in response.

"And this is why I work alone," Talisha growled quietly.

The bandit cavalcade split formation—six jeeps to the left, and six to the right. Black shadows appeared overhead as two flying vehicles with long-barreled guns descended upon them. Cyrus had just enough time to swear loudly before ducking to avoid a hail of bullets.

"They've got wyverns, dammit!" he roared. "Where did these scoundrels get wyverns?"

Bluebird activated her barrier. She pounded against her chest once with her fist and the barrier's size expanded, wrapping both her and her companions in its protective semitranslucent bubble. Snidely cowered behind her while bullets battered against them.

Wyverns had been built and commissioned by the IGF military forces as tactical ground-and-air vehicles constructed for powerful strike assaults. How bandits on a backwater planet got hold of them was anyone's guess. Talisha made a note to focus on that later. For now, she needed a game plan.

She turned to Snidely and Bluebird. "I can keep the wyverns occupied. Big Blue, if I get them to land, can you finish the job? Cyrus's rockets aren't going to do us any good against their armor."

"Wh-what about me?" Snidely grabbed onto her arm. "Who's going to protect me?"

Talisha shoved him aside. "Protect yourself. We have a job to do."

"Barrier this size won't hold long," Bluebird said, raising her cannon high. "A direct blast will have limited range but should obliterate them. Hurry. Bring them close."

Talisha nodded and flew off. The wyverns circled around, focusing her with both guns. She was well within her element, deftly maneuvering out the way of their shots. The wyverns were made to be a hybrid of speed and power, but their bulky armor left her with the advantage.

The cavalcade circled around the scorpion. The barrier fizzled with each hit. From what Talisha knew about Ingle military tactics, those defensive barriers wouldn't last much longer under such heavy focus-fire. She'd have to hurry.

"Shoot them!" Snidely cried out to Bluebird.

Bluebird rolled her eyes. "Ethel and the barrier use the same plasma-energy packs. If you'd like to get shot at, be my guest."

Snidely turned his eyes on the scorpion. "Can you get me to the car?"

"Why?" She looked down at him with a befuddled expression. "What do you have planned?"

"The turrets! Put your barrier around the turrets!"

Bluebird smiled and hoisted him to her shoulders with a meaty hand. "You've grown a spine, company man! I like it!"

Talisha flew low, firing more blasts at the left wing of the first wyvern. Her arm cannon was capable of delivering small rapid blasts, or charging up for larger, more devastating shots. Aiming a big blast like that while dodging for her life would be tricky. She had to be controlled, to lead her shots.

The wyverns circled back around to strafe her, several bullets ricocheting off her armor and nearly knocking her off balance. Talisha winced. The armor could protect her from mistakes like that, but a full volley could damage her systems and send her crashing toward the earth. She screamed and sent a fully-charged blast as one of the wyverns came shrieking around to her front. The powerful orb of yellow light seared through its left wing with a loud crackle, sending the wyvern spiraling to the ground. It unfurled its legs, shakily orienting itself before turning its guns back to the sky.

"Big Blue! Now's your chance!" Talisha called out.

Bluebird hoisted Snidely into the turret and climbed after him. She laughed, watching the wyvern swivel its guns around to march after them. Her brows narrowed as she retrieved the cannon from her shoulders and swung its barrel in the direction of the rampaging vehicle.

"*Dasvidanya*," she whispered.

A searing sapphire ray blasted into the wyvern. The beam grew in intensity the longer it remained on target, pulsing and humming with every second. Screams inside the cockpit could be heard as the beam pierced its hull and melted the flesh of the pilots within.

The barrier around the turrets flickered. That shot drained it of all its energy. She turned to Snidely and patted him squarely on the shoulder, a light-hearted gesture that nearly knocked the tiny man over.

"It is all you now, company man. Knock 'em dead!"

He gripped both sides of the turret guns and swung them to face the nearest armored jeep. He roared and unloaded into the front engines of the vehicle. The occupants leapt from the vehicle in a panic as it careened into a ravine, where it exploded in a rush of flames.

With the pressure of the first wyvern down, Cyrus stood once more. Rockets shot out from his shoulders, homing in on several targets. Some of the bandits swung around, faster and more reckless than their compatriots, charging straight for the lone scorpion. Cyrus's rockets exploded behind them as they swerved, snaking patterns in the dust.

A shirtless woman with breasts sagging down to her navel scrambled to the front seat of the armored jeep. She unfurled a pole attached to a thick-headed spear spiked with flashing lights wrapped around the tip. Bluebird dove into the front seat of the Scorpion and threw it into first gear. Her foot slammed against the gas. The scorpion barely scraped along the spear's edge. Snidely had to grab onto the edge of the turret's guns to keep from getting thrown off.

"Are ya tryin' to kill us, woman?" Cyrus hollered.

"Bombs attached to those spears," Bluebird explained. "Typical bandit tactic."

The wyvern turned its attentions away from Talisha and darted toward the Scorpion, firing as it passed overhead. Several bullets pierced the hull. Blood dripped down Bluebird's chest and soaked the seat beneath her. She'd been hit. Repeatedly.

"Stop staring before I give you a black eye," she spat at Cyrus and Snidely.

Cyrus nodded and turned back to the convoy. He fired two more rockets. One missed, the other caught the back end of the cavalcade, sending two shirtless bandits into several gory pieces and heavily damaging the rear end of the vehicle.

Out in the desert, Nergal cackled. Talisha watched him march toward the convoy. Whatever he'd been working on down there was finally ready. He retrieved a hose and nozzle from the apparatus on his back, and, with eyes wide and manic, unleashed a forty-foot cone of emerald flames, engulfing one of the jeeps completely. The occupants dove into the dirt, rolling along the ground, flailing in horror. Some could only stare at their own exposed bones and scream.

"I'd call that a successful first test." He chuckled.

Bluebird pulled the scorpion to a halt, swerving in the dust. She stared, breathing heavily, fingers clenched tightly about the steering wheel. "Ma'am? What are you doing?" Cyrus looked down at her, a tinge of uncharacteristic concern creeping into his robotic twang.

"Sit down, metal-man," she said through tightly gritted teeth. "They shot my favorite boob. They must pay."

Bluebird shifted gears and slammed on the gas. Snidely whirled the turrets to face forward. His mouth hung open as Bluebird's plan dawned on him.

"Oh my god," he whispered, then screamed. "You're going to get us killed!"

Bluebird said nothing. Her face filled with fury and determination, each scar only making her scowl that much more intimidating. With a powerful roar she slammed the scorpion directly into the armored jeep. The veins on the side of her neck bulged as she leapt from the driver's seat and into the bandit vehicle. They barely had a chance to fire on her before she was grabbing them by the throat and slamming their heads bloody into the floor, hurling them around and bending their rifles into unusable pretzels with her bare hands.

"Sh-should we help her?" Snidely said, mouth hanging open.

Up in the skies, Talisha found herself growing weary. She kept finding herself stealing distracted glances down below. It was obvious even from her vantage point in the sky that Bluebird had been hit. She barely knew the woman, but her instincts demanded she do everything to ensure her safety.

More bullets rammed into her armor, sending several alarms screaming inside her helmet. Systems were facing extreme damage. Any further hits would cause the suit to shut down to begin self-repairs to preserve itself. She'd be left defenseless and stationary.

"All right, you son of a bitch," she whispered, charging another blast.

Direct hit. It went searing through the right wing of the wyvern, causing it to teeter and descend to the ground. She flew down to face it, readying another blast. She didn't get the chance to even fire. Bluebird had thoroughly finished thrashing and beating every passenger of the last armored jeep bloody and threw herself directly onto the front of the downed wyvern.

She pounded against the heavy armored surface with her fists, denting it. She found where the rivets nailed the plating together and pried them loose, digging her fingers beneath them, pulling the plating apart. Her fingernails were bloodied, and her skin reddened with the amount of effort. She looked on the verge of passing out.

With another roar, she managed to completely rip off the armored plating protecting the cockpit and shoved her fists in to grab the screaming pilot. He had a blaster in his shaking hands and managed to fire a few bullets into her shoulder. She didn't even wince as she gripped him by the throat and hurled him into the sand. The wyvern collapsed, and Bluebird tumbled into the dust, unconscious.

The bandit who'd been piloting the wyvern attempted to scramble away, planting his skinny little arms in the dirt. His eyes were wide as a frightened rodent, only eager to escape. He hadn't bothered looking where he was going, too fixated on the giant monstrosity who'd nearly killed him, so he didn't notice when he ran smack first into Cyrus's cold metal legs.

"And where were you headed off to, partner?"

Talisha hurried quickly to Bluebird's side, turning her onto her back and examining her wounds. "How is she still alive?"

Nergal hurried toward her, retrieving several bandages and syringes from within his coat pockets. "Please, allow me."

Talisha raised her arm cannon. "Not on your life, creep."

Nergal's brow furrowed. "As hardy as our bird of song is, without my expertise, she will die. Stand aside."

"I'm afraid he's right," Snidely said, stumbling his way toward them, looking more frazzled and tattered than ever. "I hired him not only for his capacity for violence, but also for his medical knowledge. It seemed fitting to have a healer on this expedition."

Talisha stood, keeping her cannon trained firmly at his throat. "If you hurt her in any way..."

Nergal rolled his eyes. "I know you may find this difficult to believe, madam, but I've never killed anyone without reason, and I don't intend to start now. Now, please. Let me save this woman's life."

Nergal knelt over Bluebird's body, surveying her wounds with quiet precision. It was the calmest Talisha had seen him. He injected Bluebird's veins with a syringe full of a neon-green mixture.

Nergal stood and turned to face them. "Help me carry her into the scorpion. The injection will stabilize her, but I need to remove the bullets and we're far too exposed out here."

Cyrus shook his head. "Bored now. I'll let the other guy take over while I nap and replenish my ammo. See ya, partners."

"Are you serious?" Talisha looked incredulous, but Cyrus had already gone.

The android went silent for several seconds before he placed a frazzled hand to his head. He looked to see the frightened bandit cowering at his feet, then to Bluebird's unconscious body. His systems scrambled for information, probing within the Cyrus subroutine's memory banks to figure out what the hell had happened.

"Mother Superior," Rogers scratched his forehead. "Sorry about that, fellas."

"Just help already! I can't carry this big lunk!" Nergal snapped.

"Right-o." Rogers turned quickly to the bandit. "Don't go anywhere, I'm a better shot than the other one."

The frightened bandit shook his head of mud-coated hair. "Okay."

Talisha looked down at the kid with pity. He couldn't have been older than nineteen. A scraggly unkempt youth so skinny you could see his ribs; likely turned to robbing and fighting other gangs over scraps of food, water, and fuel. There weren't bad people on Archimedes IV, just desperate people in bad situations.

Together, Rogers and Talisha managed to hoist Bluebird gently up to carry her into the back of the scorpion. She was too large to lie on the seats so they had to figure out the best position in which to not aggravate her wounds. In the end, they could do nothing but place her on her back between the seats on Rogers's poncho. Her shoulders still managed to be a tight fit, so she was propped at an awkward angle, partially on her side

Nergal stared, caught somewhere between legitimate concern and wry amusement. "If she manages to survive this, I'll consider apologizing to her for my remarks."

Talisha ignored his comment. She gave Bluebird another once-over to make sure the woman was still breathing and then went to check on the bandit. To the boy's credit he hadn't moved from his spot, still sitting there and shaking with terror. There were bruises around his neck from where Bluebird had strangled him.

"If she dies, it's your fault. You know that?" Talisha said, removing her helmet.

He shrugged his shoulders. "You fired on us first."

"And you wouldn't have?"

"Oh, we certainly would have. A scorpion would have been ace to have, but still. You fired on us first."

"All right, you made your point. How'd your people get a hold of a couple of wyverns, anyhow?"

"The Mother gives," the kid said with a shrug, as if it were the most obvious thing in the world.

"Please, get in!" Nergal called from the Scorpion. "I thought you were concerned with saving her."

Talisha nodded and grabbed the bandit by his arm, yanking him to his feet. "Gonna have to ask you to come with us, kid."

He made a passive blank stare in her direction, eyes devoid of any emotion. "Okay."

Talisha would have been unsettled had she not seen stranger things in her line of work. The Mother seemed to be a reference to a deity. She'd heard these kinds of platitudes before. Bandit camps devolving into religious cults was nothing new. Her more immediate concern was how a group of zealous scroungers had managed to get a hold of IGF property when this planet was far outside their jurisdiction. There were a few possible explanations, none of them comforting.

She hauled the boy into the scorpion and kept him sitting by her side. "Blake, got any provisions?"

"You didn't bring any of your own?" Snidely was examining the front end of the Scorpion, horrified at the initial damages caused by Bluebird's little stunt.

"'Course I did, but seeing as you're responsible for this trip, you should be responsible for feeding the prisoner."

"We're taking prisoners now?" Rogers said. "Can't say I approve."

Talisha sighed. "Only alternative is leaving him to die in the desert and that's not particularly humane either.

"All of that can wait! Let's get moving!" Nergal barked. "The serum will only last so long. You! Boy! Are there any caves nearby where we can find shelter?"

The bandit kid shrugged and pointed east toward a ridge of mountains. "Some caves out there, but I wouldn't. Lotta critters out and about."

"We are fully equipped to deal with *critters*," Nergal said bluntly. "Snidely, please. Take us to that ridge. We've wasted too much time chitchatting."

"Last time I checked, I was the boss here," Snidely muttered under his breath.

If the others heard him, they were clearly ignoring him. He grumbled a bit about that as he climbed into the front of the scorpion and made a course for the ridge. He rummaged around in his coat pocket for a pair of protective lenses as the sinking sun forced the searing rays directly into his eyes.

Talisha looked at the boy with the wild hair sitting next to her. "What's your name, kid?"

"Jefferson," he said blankly.

"I'm Talisha. Now, tell me about the wyverns. Where'd you get them?"

"I told you, the Mother—"

"Cut the crap, where did she provide them exactly? Those types of machines aren't exactly common around these parts."

Jefferson turned away from her. "In the woods, there was a crash-site, a gift to us from the Mother. We've been able to salvage most of it for scrap and oil, though the wyverns weren't damaged at all."

"And how the hell do you know what a wyvern is?"

"From the ship's database. It's still functional. No one was interested in it, so I make trips back there to check it out. I've learned a lot."

Talisha leaned back in her seat, rubbing her hand over her jaw. "Interesting."

Rogers turned his head in her direction. "Something on your mind?"

Talisha leaned forward, steepling her fingers. "The IGF were definitely on this planet. I want to know why. Jefferson, can you take us to these woods?"

"Got any food?"

"Of course."

"Then sure."

Snidely interjected quickly. "Excuse me, I am paying you lot for a specific extraction mission. The Temple? The key? We still need to secure the key, remember?"

Rogers leaned back in his seat and tipped his hat over his face, letting out a pre-recorded sigh to express his displeasure. "Those wyverns were a pretty nasty shock there, Blake. Don't ya wanna know if we're due for any other surprises? More we know, more we're all likely to walk away from this alive and a whole lot richer, comprendé?"

"You are a coolly logical one despite that ridiculous affectation," Snidely admitted.

Rogers tipped his hat politely and curled his legs beneath him, perching in a childlike manner.

"A strange lot we are," Nergal said quietly. "Never quite seen such a collection of misfits and freaks."

"Blame the company man," Talisha said. "He hired us."

Nergal looked at the driver, and his voice fell low so that he wouldn't hear. "I wasn't excluding him from that description. Did you see the way he manned those turrets?"

"Think he's in the wrong line of work?" Talisha smirked.

Nergal stared at her, his face grim. "It takes one to know one, and that man is a mercenary through and through."

"Not much difference between a mercenary and a corporate toady," Talisha said, shrugging her shoulders. "Capitalists with malleable ethics."

"And you don't put yourself in that boat? Too good for the likes of us?"

Talisha glared at him. "I'm doing what I can to help people. It's always been that way."

Nergal gave her a wide grin. "That's not what they said about your mother. Heard every mission left thousands of bodies in her wake."

She turned away from him, folding her arms across her chest. "Yeah well, I'm not my mother."

"So I've heard." Nergal leaned back in his seat, still smiling. "So I've heard."

Chapter Three

RED FLAGS UNFURLED from the schooners quietly skimming over the sand dunes like a vast ocean. Like the rest of Ching Shih's fleet, the sails were coated in the same nanite substance capable of transmitting a virus into any machine that dared photograph or scan them. Cutting-edge technology and unheard-of designs had once made Red Flag Solutions a devastating competitor in the corporate world. Those days had long since passed.

In those days, she'd worn fine gowns with large collars wrapped around her head like a halo. The back of her tresses would sweep along the floor in shimmering scarlet and gold to create a grand spectacle. The technology that now protected her fleet and opened their victims to attack had been used to line her clothes in brilliant holographic displays that wrested the attentions and pocketbook of everyone in the room. She was a much younger woman then, every bit as bold and daring, but her priorities had shifted.

Ching Shih was heavier now. She often wondered if getting fatter as you got older was just the weight of the years transferring itself to your body. She didn't mind it, of course. The way the fat had settled around her cheeks gave her the hardened jowls of a bulldog and made her far more intimidating than the waifish pixie look of her youth. It was a trade up as far as she was concerned.

She stood at the edge of the schooner and wrapped her birdlike talons about the railing and surveyed the barren wasteland. Her brow furrowed, remembering when she'd been here as a girl, back when it'd been covered in luscious green. Hard to believe it was the same planet.

Ching Shih still wore expensive gowns, but they had an altogether different function. She'd swapped out the brilliant colors for black silks threaded with protective armor. Even her makeup was intended to frighten and intimidate; pale and ghoulish, with lips the color of blood.

"Ching Shih, we're nearing the rendezvous point!" One of her officers barked over the comm-line.

"Keep straight ahead," she responded. "The only source of greenery left on this planet lies before us, crew. Be on your guard. The wars here left it vengeful and mean. The leaves themselves grew teeth and a desire to devour those who would destroy them. Sounds like we have something in common, eh, boys?"

That put a fire in them. Blasters raised high and a chorus of cheers echoed into her headset. She allowed herself a bemused smile watching the looming darkness of the trees near. Their branches were as gnarled and twisted as the stories claimed, rising into the sky like gothic cathedrals, and pulsing with their own unnatural heartbeats. She wondered if they really bled when you chopped their branches.

Black vines coated in ichor spilled out into the desert like veins. Ching ordered the schooners stopped before they got too close. Her eyes narrowed, watching the vines with repulsed fascination. She could see tiny motions of something being pumped through them. It looked for a moment as if cracks of red lights could be seen flashing angrily behind their pores.

Sounds of rumbling engines and crashing undergrowth filled the air. Several mechanical creations stumbled out of the forest with whirring saw-blades and flamethrowers. They traipsed about on multiple legs like giant metal spiders caring little for the terrors of the trees. Their blades cut the tongues that shot out from the cavernous maws of trunks and bark. Their flames purged the vines that sought to entangle them.

Ching Shih pursed her lips in silent approval.

The machines stopped just at the edge of the woods. Smoke from their exhaust pipes choked the air. The largest of these vehicles moved to the front and center of the line and a hatch opened in the top, allowing a burly white-skinned man with a beard the color of fire to emerge.

"Corporal Melanson," she said with barely a nod. "You've chosen a tactical venue for our meeting. I admire that."

Melanson was large in just about every sense of the word. He was a hairy portrait of old-world masculinity. His long ginger hair billowed behind him in a thousand different directions. His beard, dotted with several gray hairs, flowed all the way down to his hefty muscle-gut. His shoulders were just about as wide as he was tall, and he was well over six feet. He wore only a set of tight overalls, faded and tattered with time, and he smelled of grease and cinders.

His fat stomach shook as he let out a deep, rumbling laugh. "Corporal? Haven't heard that title in years. Guess what they say about you is true, you've a way with secrets."

"It was a compliment, Corporal." Ching Shih remained completely stoic, hands wrapped tightly behind her back. "My fleet outnumbers your band ten-to-one, so you've forced us to meet in territory where we're put to a significant disadvantage should you choose to retreat behind the trees."

Melanson's grin took on a menacing quality. "If you know my old post, then you must also know my tactics."

"I'm sure I read something about Melanson's Massacres somewhere." Ching Shih smiled. "But I hope it won't come to that. We've too much to gain and so little to lose. For now, though, as a sign of good faith in our partnership, I want to see the key."

His thick eyebrows furrowed together. "All right."

Melanson vanished inside the scrap-metal monstrosity. The night drew on while Ching waited patiently for his return, eyes locked on the other members of his party. One of her hands moved to the blaster on her hip. It wasn't a nervous or paranoid gesture. These bandits had little to fear from a fat old woman with a blaster on her hip. Just a reminder of where they stood, and who *she* was.

Melanson returned several minutes later, opening the hatch with a rusty creak. He held in his dirty palms an object covered with black sackcloth. He held it aloft for her to see aboard the schooner, then lifted the cloth to reveal a large black pyramid covered in the engravings and runic cuneiform of an ancient alien tongue. His hands were large enough he could hold it in his palm.

"I can't let you touch it of course," Melanson said, his eyes fixated on the pyramid. "No guarantee your people won't run off with it."

"Oh, I can assure you that's exactly what would happen," Ching Shih said with a cackle. "We'd wrest that thing away from you and be off in a heartbeat."

"Bit strange to be giving away your intentions like that," Melanson said, rubbing his chin. All the same, he covered the pyramid with the sackcloth and placed his arm behind his back.

"It's not strange at all. I respect you, Corporal Melanson. I respect you enough to establish the parameters of our relationship. You have made yourself a legitimate enough threat to my enterprise that I have to take you seriously, and in turn that makes you valuable as an ally. The second you stop being a threat, you stop being useful, and when that happens…"

"Our contract is terminated. You are as ruthless as they say."

"This isn't me being ruthless, Corporal." Ching Shih leaned forward so he could peer directly into her eyes. "This is me at my fairest. Pray you don't see ruthless."

"You make yourself pointedly clear, Captain." Melanson choked. "Though if you don't mind my saying, you talk too much. You have the coordinates to the temple, I take it?"

She straightened. "I do, but I will be withholding them until my men have gotten a chance to secure the site."

"Just 'cause you're likely to double-cross doesn't mean I am."

"Then you're a fool in the wrong game, Corporal."

Melanson let out another bout of belly-shaking laughter. "Well played, Madame. Very well, I take it we've come to an agreement. My men and I keep the key safe while you secure the Valran Temple. We split the bounty and go home richer than gods."

"Or we kill each other for the spoils," Ching Shih shrugged. "Either way, I look forward to it."

Melanson licked his lips. "If it comes to that, be sure to bring your best. You've yet to see the full might of my warband."

Ching Shih raised her blaster and pointed it at him. He stood before the barrel unflinching. She flicked the gun into the air and laughed.

"I would hate to tarnish our friendship by doing anything less," she said. "If I come to kill you, I will bring you the fight of your life."

"It's all I could ask for," Melanson said, shoving a finger behind the strap of his overalls. "Pleasure doing business with you."

Ching Shih bowed and barked a departure order to her sailors. The schooners roared to life and, with frightening alacrity, turned and zipped far across the dunes. Melanson watched, the hairs on his thick arms bristling.

"May the Mother protect us," he whispered to himself.

He'd never been a particularly religious man, but the platitude seemed to provide comfort to his war-band. He hoped it might instill some of that same comfort in him. It did not.

THE CRAGS AND caves formed strange shapes, warped by the harsh storms and wind. Some formed great pillars and spirals like some mad artist had spent his last remaining years sculpting them. Snidely pulled the scorpion to a halt outside the gaping maw of a domed cavern.

"I'll check inside first," Talisha said, locking her helmet into place. "Don't want to run into any occupants."

"Hurry," Nergal warned. He touched two fingers to the side of Bluebird's neck. "I need to operate soon."

Rogers stood and drew his pistol. "I'll keep an eye on things out here in case we get any visitors."

Talisha nodded approvingly and leapt out of the scorpion. She vanished into the darkness of the caves with her cannon aimed directly in front of her. There was a sweaty moment before she switched over to night vision lenses where there was nothing but an impenetrable blackness before her. A lurid purple flooded the lens as she scanned for heat signatures of anything crawling about in the caves.

The helmet had sensors that could pick up faint traces of scarcely audible noises. They were made apparent to her through a wavelength at the bottom right-hand corner of her visor. Other indicators flashed across her scanners, languages and symbols known to few in the galaxy aside from herself.

The Valran tongue was complex and nigh indecipherable. It'd taken her mother years of teaching for her to understand any of it. Her thoughts drifted to her mother.

Mom could be a real asshole. She'd spent years hammering everything about Valran culture, technology, and the language into her. She'd go on and on about how the task and responsibility of preserving their ways rested on their family, but no other could be trusted with it. Up until Talisha became a teenager, her mother seemed hellbent on passing on the mantle for her to take up the armor and carry on being a freelance agent for the IGF.

All that changed when Talisha came out of the closet. There'd been the telltale signs of course, such as when she'd dressed as a princess for a Halloween party several years prior and had been loath to change out of the costume. She'd been experimenting with makeup and the like, but most assumed she was just a pretty gay boy exploring the limits of gender expression.

When she came out as transgender, her mother's attitude abruptly shifted. She didn't even show up to her own daughter's graduation from the IGF Military Academy. It was like everything Talisha had been trained to do suddenly no longer mattered.

Their relationship only further deteriorated from there. Talisha kept in touch, asking for advice now and again. Mom was a jerk, but she was a smart jerk with a lot of experience. Besides, she'd lost most of her accumulated wealth caring for orphans and refugees, so she couldn't be all bad. It sucked, though, that none of the warmth or affection Mom showed those kids was ever once thrown her way.

Damn. Focus, Talisha. Get your head together.

Not like there was much present danger lurking within these caves anyway. There were flickers of noises showing up on the wavelength, but they were either too far or too faint to make any noticeable difference. That bothered her. It was fairly common to find some form of life dwelling within caves for shelter, especially in harsh climates such as this. Here there wasn't so much as a fungus.

She emerged from the cave several minutes later, visor raised. "All clear, folks. Let's get her inside."

Sometime later they managed to get Bluebird into the caves. Rogers kept an eye on Jefferson while Talisha assisted with prying Bluebird's heavy garments off her. The large woman's chest was bound in a thick plating of terracilium alloy, a highly rare metal.

"This explains a lot," Nergal noted, tapping the breastplate with a gloved knuckle. "Instead of flying straight into her vitals, the bullets were slowed. We just need to remove them before they burrow deeper and do any real damage. She should be fine."

"All the same, I'm going to be watching you," Talisha said.

He shrugged his shoulders. "You've no reason to trust me, but please stay out of my personal bubble. For your own safety, if anything else."

"Try and ease off him, why don'cha, Talisha?" Rogers called from the mouth of the cave. He'd perched on a rock and was staring out at the horizon, hand resting lazily over one knee. "Let the man work."

Talisha exhaled. "You're right. Starting to sound like my mother over here."

Snidely had been poking around on his datapad in front of the campfire. "I fail to see an issue there. She had a long and successful career before she retired. Brilliant woman, if a bit too generous for her own good."

"And what would you have done differently with those credits?" Talisha turned on him, a wry smile gradually forming.

"Invest them of course," Snidely shrugged as if the answer were so obvious that she was a fool for even asking. "With her contacts in the IGF, she could have set up a nice pension, sold the armor at an extraordinary price and lived off the residuals for years. Now she relies on the generosity of others and pity-money from her daughter every month. A sad end to the galaxy's greatest bounty hunter."

Talisha shook her head. "You're a piece of work, Blake."

He sighed and lowered the datapad into his lap. "Laugh all you like, that's the world we live in. A libertarian's wet dream of unfettered capitalism."

A chorus of groans from all other conscious persons caused Snidely's shoulders to tense and he resumed scrolling through the datapad. It became very clear to him that his philosophies would not be well received on this particular crowd. He chose the wisdom of keeping his mouth shut on any topics of business in the future.

Jefferson had curled up into a ball of skin and bones in a corner. He hadn't wandered off too far, just nearer to the mouth of the cave. He'd shown a great deal of apprehension about coming inside.

Ninety minutes passed. Nergal managed to pry the last shell casing from Bluebird's body and wrapped her wounds with clean bandages. He picked up one of the casings with a set of tongs and held it out for the others to see. Rogers let out a pre-recorded whistle.

"How many of those shells were in her?" Rogers asked. "How is she even alive?"

"Several," Nergal said, throwing the casing back into the bloody pile with the others. "She's an extraordinary woman, I'll give her that. Now all that's left is for my serum to do its work. She should be fine by morning."

"Bullshit." Talisha folded her arms over her chest. "Those wounds will take days to heal."

Snidely looked up from his datapad. "Dr. Isaac is telling the truth. It's why I hired him. While his unique condition is a point of interest for us at Plymouth, his research is far, far more appealing."

"When one is riddled with as many diseases as I am," Nergal said. "The eradication of all bodily ailments becomes a priority."

Rogers paused for a moment. He then turned to Snidely. "Talisha's armor. Nergal's research. Blue's cannon…"

"And your unique consciousness," Snidely said, nodding. A smile crept onto his face. "Yes, you were chosen for more than your particular talents on a relic-hunt. My superiors thought it risky bringing you all together like this, especially with the Valran artifact taking top priority."

"But you thought getting to study us all up close would give us a better means of reverse-engineering the technology for yourselves," Nergal whispered dryly. "You've been recording us."

"From the instant you set foot on Archimedes IV," Snidely said. A panicked look suddenly came over him. "You're not upset, are you?"

"The IGF has been doing the same thing to me for years," Talisha sighed, lying on the ground, arms propped behind her head. "Least with your people it's par for the course. Can't get mad at a snake when it bites you. It's just doing what comes naturally."

"More than that," Nergal sniffed. "This one is hoping to get a hefty promotion once this is all over."

"You've a remarkable talent for the obvious, Dr. Nergal." Snidely rolled his eyes. "Any more shocking revelations you'd care to share with the class."

"Just one." Nergal stood opposite the campfire, arms shoved into his coat pockets as a smug expression formed over his features. "Your superiors see your ambition and haven't quite decided if that makes you an asset or a liability. You've got a real knack for running your mouth when you shouldn't and don't know well enough when to play your cards close to the chest. At this point, no one can tell if it's guts or stupidity. I reckon you've skirted by on luck and determination for so long that they want to know how much you've got to offer them before you do something really foolish and bring the whole company down with you.

"Any other time they might have had you monitoring the situation from a comfy shuttle, orbiting the planet and sending messages all covert-like, but they wanted to know if you could survive with the gang of lowlife's your ambition hired. You're so prone to gambling their pieces on the board they thought you'd like to know what that felt like. Frankly, I can't tell if you're being tested...or punished. Getting warm, Blake?"

Snidely's nostrils flared. He stood and marched angrily toward the mouth of the cave. Talisha snorted, watching his pathetic attempts at conveying furious indignation. It was too adorable to bear, and she soon was doubled over, hands clutching her stomach laughing till she was red in the face. Rogers joined in with his own mechanical laughter. Even Nergal giggled at Snidely's expense.

"Should someone go after him?" Rogers said, still jovial.

Talisha shook her head. "I highly doubt he'll find anything out here. Like I said, the cave's pretty much devoid of life—"

She was cut off by the sounds of panicked screaming. All turned startled eyes toward the mouth of the cave. Jefferson stirred quickly to wakefulness. He stared wide-eyed, bottom lip quivering.

"Critters," he whispered.

"Impossible." Talisha lowered her visor.

Only Snidely could be seen through her thermographic visor, and, according to her sensors, he was dangling six feet in the air. Talisha's shoulders tensed and she moved for the sounds, arm cannon raised. Rogers and Nergal followed behind, drawing their weapons.

"What's going on? Whaddya see?" Rogers pressed.

Frustration crept into her voice. "Not a damn thing. That's the problem. Whatever this thing is, it's not putting out a heat signature of any kind."

Snidely's screams grew louder and they picked up the pace rushing toward the terror. There was something there all right, gripping the company man in muscular humanoid arms coated in long bristling fur. It looked like a fifteen-foot-tall maggot with a hundred spindly cockroach legs to support its bulbous white body. The distressingly humanlike arms were pulling Snidely's flailing body closer to a set of chomping mandibles. Teal-colored slime dripped from their jagged edges, pooling in a goopy mess about the creature's lips and chin.

"What are you waiting for? Shoot it!"

Rogers waved his gun, struggling to find the creature. "Y'all better tell me if I'm aiming at whatever's got the boss."

Nergal stared at him, visibly concerned. "What's that supposed to mean?"

"This creature doesn't appear on radar," Talisha barked. "It's invisible to him!"

Talisha raised her visor and launched herself into the air with her jetpack. She flew around the creature's side to fire wildly at its arms and bulbous body, searching for a weak spot. The creature let out an ungodly hissing noise before dropping Snidely to the cave floor, and it turned to crawl on its human arms toward her.

She wanted to wretch just watching the way the critter moved. She thought she could see long wispy strands of hair atop a round protrusion from its head. It was a brief and fleeting vision, but it almost looked like a human head with a blank lump of flesh where its face should be.

"Okay! That's new!" She panted, flying away from a lunge of its powerful arms.

Nergal retrieved the hoses from his apparatus. "Heard of these monsters before, from a bandit whose insides had been completely warped by its venom. Hair falling out in clumps, fascinating business. He'd started growing weird white lumps on his back, same color and texture as that thing there."

"What are you trying to say?" Talisha flew out the way of another lunge and fired on the creature again.

Nergal allowed the fires in the apparatus to heat up before stepping forward. "I mean don't let it touch you. My theory is these things are looking for new hosts for their eggs."

A wide arc of flame shot from Nergal's guns and consumed the critter. It groaned and shrieked, coiling in on itself in a vain attempt to put out the flames. Nergal smiled wickedly, watching it scream its last.

Snidely rushed to his feet, stepping in front of Nergal to gaze down in open-mouthed horror and fascination at the creature. "Is there any part of it you left intact, you brute?"

Talisha leaned against the cave wall, panting heavily. "You're welcome. He saved your life."

Snidely stamped his foot. "This creature has the capability of cloaking itself from all scanners. Those implications are huge! Dr. Nergal, as a scientist, surely you could understand the need to-"

Nergal popped the edge of the gun directly into Snidely's little nose. "The bandit was beyond saving. His body underwent a fascinating metamorphosis before I decided it was in my best interest to kill him. Didn't want something let loose rampaging about inside my lab. If you'd seen what I'd seen, you would not suffer such a creature to live. The harm such a thing poses to our little party is simply too great."

Snidely grabbed Nergal's gun and threw it out of his face before leaning in close, spittle flying from his mouth. "This is *my* expedition! I'm in charge! I will decide what to risk, not you!"

Nergal wrapped his fingers around the back of Snidely's throat and pulled him closer. "No one has ever dared get this close to me. Always afraid of what they might catch. Are you stupid, Blake Snidely? Or just suicidal?"

Snidely grabbed onto Nergal's collar. He'd gone completely red and his entire body shook. His screams were nigh unintelligible. "I! Have! Vision! You are just a quarantined...*fff-freak*!"

Nergal's resolve never broke. "There it is. That's the special word I was looking for. Feels good to bring things out into the open, doesn't it?"

"Break it up," Talisha said, rubbing her temple with her fingers. "Try not to let him get under your skin like that, Snidely."

Nergal smiled. "Oh, we're just clearing the air. I like to know where I stand with people."

He turned his back on the flummoxed corporate man and sauntered toward the campsite. Rogers watched silently. He shook his head and made the sound of a tongue clicking against the roof of his mouth.

"Do you think the same thing about the doctor?" he asked, turning to Talisha.

"Excuse me?"

"I didn't see you stopping our boss from laying into him before. Way I see it, Dr. Isaac was just retaliating."

Talisha exhaled. "Nergal was clearly antagonizing him, but I can get why you wouldn't see that."

"And why wouldn't I see it?" A tense edge crept into the robotic Southern twang.

Talisha gave him a hard look. "Calm down, cowboy. I didn't mean anything by it."

He'd had one hand casually leaning against the butt of his pistol. He sighed and relaxed his stance, turning away from her. "You think you're better than us, don't you?"

"That's not—"

"Don't lie to me. I get it. You're human, law-abiding. Got your shit together, don'cha? Rest of us must have done something real awful to wind up where we are, 'cause the system's been so damn fair to you."

"All right, I get it." Talisha covered her face with her hand. "I didn't mean to offend you, and I apologize."

"Can't kill a steer with intentions, now can ya?" Rogers sniffed and moved on.

There's not too many feelings worse than guilt. A broken heart, sure. Betrayal is definitely up there. Losing someone you care about, probably top of the list, but right below that is pissing off someone whose opinion truly matters to you.

She groaned and turned to follow him back into the cave.

As she neared the campfire, she heard a soft voice singing a Karstotzkiyan hymn. Bluebird was conscious and holding Jefferson against her chest, stroking his hair. Her wounds seemed to have healed quite a bit. Her eyes were closed in a serene expression of motherly tenderness. She looked up, having noticed Talisha's approach.

"I thought Karstotzkiyan songs were meant to be sung loudly," Talisha said with a wry smile.

"That is mostly true, but the Hymn of Belegor is special," Bluebird said. Her voice was quiet so as not to disturb the sleeping bandit youth. "It is about a great battle that occurred outside the home of a lonely widow and her five children. She took them below to a bunker she had prepared to keep them safe, and, while the bombs raged outside, she sang to them so they'd be less afraid. It's a reminder to our people not to forget our loved ones and families. They are worth more than all the glory in the universe. It is meant to be sung in the same voice of Belegor to her sons and daughters, a lullaby to soothe them to sleep."

"Thank you," Talisha said, sitting next to her. "For being so kind to him."

"He is a lost little lamb," Bluebird said, and stroked Jefferson's hair. "A victim of circumstances, no different than any of us. When I woke, he was shaking and hiding, so I sang to him."

"There's got to be something we can do. Maybe something in the temple might find a way to put this planet right." Talisha lay down, folding her arms behind her head. "Valran technology is something else. They might have a way to fix things."

"That would be nice wouldn't it? But I do not trust things will change for any of these people," Bluebird sighed.

"What do you mean?"

"Ever been to Phebes? It is a city on the planet Felkor. Full of poverty and corruption. Back when I was with the Sapphire Knights, I was part of a troop meant to oversee new order. Funds were diverted to the city in an effort to stimulate economic growth, provide new jobs, better education."

"Isn't that something that should be done anyway?"

"Of course, but shut up." Bluebird said. "New money encouraged businesses to set up shop in Phebes once more. Rich shits bought homes for cheap and their presence caused landowners to hike their prices so no working person could live there. They either died homeless and begging in the streets or fled to find shelter elsewhere.

"From an outside perspective, Phebes looks like a smashing success. The city's grown, it's beautiful. It's unrecognizable from the hellhole it was, but that aid was never offered to the people living there."

"Planet becomes livable again and the corporations come swooping in and turn it into a tourist trap," Talisha said, eyes lowered. "Everyone living here loses."

"Many wind up incarcerated. Many like poor Jefferson here. Have you ever seen an IGF prison?" Bluebird leaned back. "The problem is systemic, little bounty hunter."

"Didn't realize you were so political."

She closed her eyes. "I'm not. I just pay attention. Good night, Talisha Artul."

ABOARD THE MAYFLOWER, Madame Inspector paced behind a row of programmers plugging nervously away at their monitors and keyboards. She would occasionally stop and stare at one of the little code-monkeys. They'd squirm and start sweating as the stench of her cigarette smoke filled the air behind them. She did this not to prevent any wrongdoing or errors, but to remind them of a universal truth. Madame Inspector was always watching.

Her eyes fell over a communiqué that'd been sent to the planet's surface. She leaned over a poor woman's shoulder, causing her to flinch and remove her hands reflexively from the keyboard. Madame Inspector glared sideways at her.

"Pull up that message," she said in a threatening whisper. "I want to see who sent it."

The woman squeaked and hastily opened the message to display its full contents on the monitor. It was directed at Blake Snidely, but that's not what troubled the inspector. It was the name attached to the sender.

"You sent this?" the poor confused woman said, voice quivering.

Madame Inspector stiffened. "So it seems I have. I want you to monitor any communications sent back and forth from the planet's surface, especially if the messages have my name attached. "Is that understood?"

"Yes, Madame Inspector. Of course."

"And what was your name?"

"Kayleigh."

"Kayleigh, if you whisper of this to any other soul I will have you thrown out an airlock."

"Yes, Madame Inspector."

Madame Inspector pulled the long cigarette holder from her mouth and exhaled. Her eyes narrowed as she briskly exited the room. Someone was attempting to undermine her authority. That was clear. Mr. Snidely had allies aboard the Plymouth with no respect for protocol or orders. Her goal now was to find them and have them terminated.

MORNING ARRIVED WITHOUT incident. They'd all slept in shifts to avoid any more run-ins with the critters. There'd been some disbelief and shock when Rogers insisted he also have a time of rest. He remained miffed even into the next morning that it'd been assumed he would take watch all by himself. It was necessary for him to power down for a few hours to regain his energy and replenish ammunition.

True to Nergal's word, Bluebird fully recovered. Talisha watched as the Karstotzkiyan double-checked the energy cells on her suit and cannon. She carried additional cells in containers strapped around her waist and in separate compartments on the weapon itself. Replacing a cell seemed to be a lengthy process. The plasma cannon was likely designed to be a stationary weapon manned by multiple people with a quarter of Bluebird's strength.

"Have you ever considered taking a smaller weapon along with you, for when you run out of energy?" Talisha asked. "Just seems like all that firepower is useless if you run out in combat with no backup option."

"Oh, you haven't noticed? I always have backup weapons." Bluebird gave her a wicked grin. She dropped her cannon to flex both arms. "These guns!"

Talisha's mouth fell open. She pressed her face directly into her palm. "Oh my god."

"And we're off to the races." Nergal sighed. No one heard him over the sounds of Bluebird's raucous laughter.

After rations were eaten and everyone's guns were considered fully stocked, they loaded into the scorpion. Snidely attempted to climb into the driver's seat. He was stopped by Bluebird's mighty hand coming to rest upon his shoulder.

"You got to drive yesterday, let someone else have a turn," she insisted.

He stared at her incredulously. "What are you, my mother?"

Bluebird's brow furrowed. "Share. Why don't we let Rogers go?"

The android twisted his hat around his head and looked up. His voice came out in a distinctive growl. "Cyrus reporting for duty. 'Fraid I'm gonna have to turn you down on that one. I'm a bit lazy and if it ain't a fight, I'll just be popping my keester up in the back seat if ya don't mind."

"Cyrus. Right." Bluebird placed her hands on her hips and sighed. "Dr. Isaac, you should go. I bet you are fantastic driver."

Nergal stared at her for a good second and then laughed. When he realized no one was laughing with him, he froze. "Oh god, you're serious. No, no. I shall not be driving today, nor any other day. See, I took an oath to do no harm and that would surely violate it."

"You're responsible for the deaths of nearly a million people!" Talisha shrieked.

Bluebird smiled. "Talisha then, you drive!"

Talisha's shoulders slumped. "Yeah. Sure. Why not?"

She climbed into the front seat. A part of her was mildly interested in piloting a scorpion. That old itch for messing around with machinery was tingling at the back of her head again. She really wanted to dig around under the hood and see what made this baby go. Scorpions were famous for their speed, making them useful for hit-and-run tactics.

"You okay, partner?" Cyrus asked.

"Yeah." Talisha let her fingers run over the steering wheel. "Why's that?"

"Saw a starving dog once two seconds before he tore into a steak someone threw his way," Cyrus said with a shrug. "You had that same expression."

"Never driven one of these before," Talisha admitted. "Little excited. Snidely, how fast can these things go?"

"Try not to get us killed. I'd greatly appreciate it," came the clipped response.

Bluebird patted Talisha on the head as she climbed in. Jefferson was perched on Bluebird's shoulders. He clung to her head like a wide-eyed, gangly lemur.

"Go as fast as you like, little bounty hunter," Bluebird said. "We have places to be after all."

Talisha removed her helmet so she could feel the wind rushing through her hair. She stomped her foot against the gas pedal and left a trail of dust in the desert behind them. Her face was manic as she pushed the scorpion for all it was worth.

Snidely gripped onto the sides of the vehicle for dear life. His cheeks puffed as the scorpion flew into the air coasting over one of the dunes. It thudded and jolted violently upon landing on its wheels.

Nergal clutched the bottom of his seat, eyes full of mortal terror. "Talisha! Darling! You are making me sick! *ME!* Do you realize how redundant that is? *Slow down!*"

Only Bluebird and Cyrus seemed to have any sort of relaxed expression during the ride. Cyrus lacked the ability to express any kind of emotion whatsoever, though his posture appeared calm enough. Bluebird's scarred face showed nothing but glee and pride.

Jefferson remained stoic through most of the ride. It wasn't until the third time the scorpion went flying through the air as it hit the peak of a dune that he actually broke into a weak smile. That smile grew wider and bolder, and he raised his arms high into the air and let out an exuberant holler. Bluebird held his tiny legs extra tightly, so he didn't fall from her shoulders.

Cyrus turned his gaze to the east. There were a series of small black shapes moving quickly over the horizon. "Talisha, hold up a minute."

Something about his tone of voice broke her from her reverie. She slowed the scorpion to a halt. Snidely was grateful she hadn't slammed on the brakes. His neck couldn't take any more thrashing about in the passenger seat.

"What is it?" Talisha turned to face Cyrus.

Cyrus zoomed in with his scanners. "Schooners looks like. An entire fleet of 'em."

Snidely turned quickly in his seat. "Cyrus, quit scanning them immediately. The Red Fleet is here."

Cyrus turned to stare at him. "How do you know that?"

"I received a communiqué this morning from Plymouth. Their ships were spotted heading toward the planet's surface. I'd hoped they would be stopping to refuel and move on. If they've brought out the schooners, I fear they're searching for something."

"Ching Shih," Talisha whispered. "You gotta be kidding me."

"Think they're after the temple?" Bluebird mused.

Snidely returned to his seat, facing forward. "Obviously. There's nothing else on this god-forsaken rock. We have even less time now than I thought."

"We still need to know how that bandit warband managed to get a hold of wyverns," Talisha insisted.

"And do you want the most fearsome pirate in the galaxy to lay her hands on ancient Valran technology?" Snidely retorted. "Your little pet issues can wait, Miss Artul."

"No more comfortable with pirates getting that technology than I am with you, but I'm not one for backing out of a job." Talisha turned. "Give me a heading?"

Snidely handed her his datapad. "We managed to track the key to Melanson's Raiders several miles from here. They tend to roam around these coordinates. They prefer ducking into the woods and emerging to attack travelers between settlements. Likely they grabbed the key during one of their raids."

"Well, with any luck they won't know what it is they've got," Talisha said. She put the Scorpion back into gear and headed in that direction.

Cyrus leaned back in his seat. "The traveling bandits and nomads of this planet aren't just a buncha ignorant yokels, y'know. Why're you always acting like everyone's beneath you?"

"Well, this ought to be good," Nergal said under his breath.

Talisha just about stopped the vehicle. "Why does everyone think that? I don't think I'm better than anyone."

Cyrus shrugged his shoulders. "Oh, I don't particularly care what some IGF lackey thinks of me no-how, but damn, Rogers was fit to be tied. Ever notice he only tends to bring me out whenever something has him really pissed off?"

She relaxed her grip on the steering wheel. "Well next time you boys have a chat, let him know that I'm sorry. I've a lot of respect for him. I get what he's going through."

Cyrus let out a mean chuckle. "Really? Do you really know any of what we've been through? Ever work your ass off for people who don't give a shit? Work hard for acceptance, only to get treated like property."

"Actually, I do," Talisha said, raising an eyebrow at him. Her shoulders softened. "Lots of places in this galaxy don't treat folks like me right. Only reason my services are even called for is 'cause this ancient piece of tech I'm wearing and my mother's reputation. Even that doesn't come close to giving me equal power or privilege. Always walking a tightrope these days."

"It's not the same thing," he grumbled. "Not the same thing at all."

"I'm not going to play a game of who's got it worse, Cyrus. This isn't the oppression Olympics. I know our experiences aren't comparable." She sighed and pinched the bridge of her nose between her fingers. "I am sorry, though. I mean it."

The android fell quiet for a long while. "I'll let him know you said that."

Nergal made a retching noise. "And here I was hoping for some delectable bickering."

"We've too much in common to be at each other's throats," Bluebird chided, punching him in the shoulder. "Even you, green man."

"I'm going to throw up my breakfast and dedicate it to you," Nergal spat. He rubbed his shoulder where she'd punched him. "How's that for common ground?"

"Your attempts at being unpleasant change nothing," Bluebird said, still smiling.

Minimal conversation passed between them for the next six hours. It grew too damn hot to talk. Even Talisha was bothered despite her armor's internal cooling systems. Without them she'd be roasting. The worst was the angry red brightness of the sun in the bleak apocalyptic skies. She was forced to lower her helmet before the garish rays blinded her completely.

They drove beneath the crisscrossing bridges of a broken and crumbling freeway. It stood adjacent to the grayed-out remnants of a city decimated by a generation of warfare. What buildings remained were husks of mortar and crooked steel beams. Skeletal bodies watched from the bridge as the scorpion zipped beneath them, driving farther toward the great expanse of trees on the horizon.

Jefferson latched his fingers around tufts of Bluebird's matted hair. He squinted as the trees of the woods came into view. His arms begin to shake. His chapped lips slowly parted into a smile, and he kicked at her shoulders like a five-year-old.

"We're approaching the Mother," he whispered. "I feel her."

"In there?" Cyrus asked. "Place is a damned death trap. Meat-hungry plants and the meanest trees I've ever seen."

Bluebird held Jefferson's legs steady. "How did you survive?"

"He's part of Melanson's warband," Talisha said. "Isn't that right, kid?"

Jefferson nodded. He retrieved a half-eaten bar of rations he'd stuffed down the front of his ratted pants and took a large bite out of it. Every crunch was accompanied by a dead-eyed stare.

Snidely grimaced at the kid's expression, then turned to Talisha.

"I demand you tell me what's running through your head," he said in a quiet voice.

"You don't think it's strange we ran into a portion of the very same warband who's holding the key we're after?" Talisha said, brow furrowed in a pensive expression.

"You're not afraid, are you?" Snidely's voice cracked a little.

Her fingers gripped the steering wheel just a little too tightly. "Fear is useless. I'm cautious. Caution is telling me that this job is about to get more interesting than either of us would like it to be."

"What are you thinking then?" he asked.

Talisha fell quiet for a bit. "Not sure yet."

"Might wanna think faster, cowgirl." Cyrus pointed toward the blackness of the woods. "We've got company."

Three wyverns flew from the tops of the trees followed by several spider-like machines pouring forth from the branches. Underbrush crunched beneath treads as six tanks wheeled behind them. Talisha pulled the scorpion to a halt.

"How much storage capacity do these things have?" Talisha grabbed Snidely's arm.

"Not much."

"Big enough to hold Bluebird and our cowboy?"

"What?!" Bluebird yelped. "Bounty hunter, I will not be stuffed like luggage."

"And if shit goes south, a surprise attack from you and Cyrus might be the only thing to save our asses," Talisha said through gritted teeth.

"I can clear out some of the supplies and rations," Snidely said. "It's not the worst plan, but I'm open to suggestions."

Bluebird folded her arms over her chest and sniffed. "I will suffer this indignity but once."

Cyrus shrugged. "Still one more hitch. Jefferson here heard the whole thing."

"Oh, he won't be any problem," Nergal said.

He retrieved a syringe from his coat pocket. He pulled Jefferson from Bluebird's shoulders and had him pinned to the floor of the Scorpion. The needle was in the boy's arm before anyone could stop him. It all took less than six seconds.

Talisha yanked Nergal off the floor. "What is your damage?!" she shrieked.

Bluebird snatched him from Talisha by his throat, lifting him off the ground. "What did you do to him, you green prick?"

Nergal gasped, prying at her fingers in vain. "Let me loose, mad woman! It was only a sedative!" Bluebird released him. He coughed, falling to the floor next to Jefferson's crumpled body, then looked up at her scowling face. "We can pretend we're returning him to the bandits. It's a great cover."

Bluebird reached down and helped him to his feet. "You think almost as quickly as you move, doctor."

Nergal rubbed his throat. "One has to be spry when so often they find themselves manhandled by their compatriots."

"Womanhandled," Bluebird corrected with a smirk.

Cyrus groaned. "So glad I don't have a stomach. That joke was terrible."

"Focus!" Talisha barked. "Melanson's Raiders will be on us soon. I don't doubt we could whip these guys in a fight but I'd rather not risk it."

"It's even more likely that at the first instance of trouble they'll head into the woods. At that point the key will be lost to us," Snidely added sorely. "This transaction must be delicate."

Chapter Four

MELANSON'S RAIDERS HAD stopped to set up camp for the evening, erecting tents and watch-posts with lightning efficiency. A scout spotted the lone Scorpion several miles away from the camp. Melanson barked out orders, demanding all men ready to bear arms in case a group of desperate idiots were hoping to steal from the Raiders. The bandits accepted that explanation and hurried quickly to their posts.

Melanson knew better. He had never seen a scorpion in person before, but he was part of the team that came up with their initial design. That was years before he'd been left abandoned on this hell-planet. Seeing that reminder of his past literally driving up to meet him sent shivers down his spine.

His first thought was that the IGF had returned to the planet specifically for him. That was wishful thinking; they wouldn't come back for him, and certainly weren't the type to send in a lone scout. He'd been a part of enough incursions on hostile planets to know deployment policy involved a massive drop-ship full of tanks and infantry, and that was only after well-timed drone strikes had thoroughly laid out the welcome mat. There was no comforting explanation as to why a lone scorpion would be out here in the desert. He made sure his assault rifle was fully loaded, then locked an additional grenade into the harness strapped to his chest. When the hairs on the back of his hands prickled like this, it meant violence.

Melanson was well-acquainted with violence—over a decade's worth of service in the IGF military. He'd seen flesh melting off bone from laser cannons, crops withering under the effects of weaponized radiation, and he'd smashed his boot heel against the faces of violent uprisings. After that, he'd moved off the field and took his brilliant mind to engineering, where he drew up the blueprints to craft the ultimate weapons of war. It was little surprise that he'd take to life on Archimedes IV so voraciously. A lifetime of killing is never done.

Melanson snagged a set of high-tech binoculars from one of his scouts as he journeyed to the edge of the camp. He zoomed in close to see three passengers disembark from the Scorpion. His mouth fell open when he saw the woman in the Valran armor among them.

"Talisha Artul," he sputtered. "Can't be. She's gotta be pushing sixty. What the hell is she doing out here?"

That's when he noticed the unconscious teenager being carried in her arms. Jefferson. He belted sharply to his snipers to lower their guns, then unleashed a string of curses under his breath. All this but a day after his deal with the Red Fleet left him jittery. He'd not the stamina for this kind of intrigue. He much preferred the simplicity of murder.

The thin little man in the suit waved a white strip of cloth over his head as they approached, a meaningless gesture. Melanson smirked, hoisting his gun back over his shoulder. He folded his burly arms over his chest and watched the trio approaching the encampment. Now that he could get a better look at the woman's face, he could see there was no way she could be the same Talisha Artul he'd known from his days in the IGF. She was much too young, and her features were harsher. This woman looked deadlier, meaner even.

"Oi!" He bellowed. "You've got something that belongs to me!"

Talisha nodded as she entered the camp. "He's passed out cold. Had a bad run-in with a critter the night before."

"I knew a woman who wore that same armor, years ago." Melanson took a thunderous step toward them. "Do you know a woman named Talisha Artul?"

"That's my name, but you probably knew my mother."

"Holy shit-balls, I'm getting old," Melanson laughed heartily. "Please! Please! Come in!"

He turned his back on them and marched into the center of camp. The closer they got to the woods, the more at peace he felt. Building the machines to survive the brutality of the trees had been his idea. Where others had seen only an impenetrable bastion of horror, he saw the only real shelter on this planet. Only way to be safe is to make yourself at home with the monsters.

As he led them past a procession of powerful machinery put together from the scrap retrieved from the wasteland and ripped from other vehicles, pride swelled within him. He'd taken a couple terrified youngsters and some forgotten elderly and made them into an army. They'd found a way to take the hell on this planet and thrive.

TALISHA HATED THAT she had to be the one to carry Jefferson. In the case of a fight breaking out, she could certainly drop the kid in a heartbeat, but a heartbeat can separate life and death. That fraction of time lost could get them all killed. Her pulse ran just a bit higher. This entire mission had been just that; control slipping steadily out of her fingers and building its way toward the ultimate clusterfuck.

Her eyes scanned the camp. Melanson wasn't an idiot. He was showing off. There was a bandit stationed by every spiderlike vehicle, and no doubt the wyverns were loaded and ready for takeoff at a moment's notice. He was using this moment to intimidate her with his power. It was working.

She felt the stares of each bandit and had to quell the hateful thoughts running through her head. She'd spent too much time around the IGF. All the language about bandits and refugees on backwater planets over the years had tainted her perspective. It was so easy to see these people as less than human, as nothing other than scum to be blasted away by her arm cannon. It was an unpleasant train of thinking, one that made her physically ill. She'd have to work better at keeping her prejudices in check. A bandit with a gun was just as likely to kill her as a guardsman.

Melanson's name seemed familiar to her, but only in the vaguest of memories. Her mother had been pretty tight-lipped about her encounters with the IGF. Talisha was still certain the name had been brought up elsewhere. Still, if this guy knew her mother, it might explain where the wyverns had come from. It also gave her a good cover story.

Melanson led them to a large rust-colored tent in the center of the camp. He pulled open the flap and gestured inside, allowing them to walk past him. Talisha caught him staring at Jefferson with a glowering expression. Soon as he noticed, he broke once more into that fatherly, boisterous smile.

"Give me the boy," Melanson instructed.

Once Jefferson was in his arms, he walked toward a small cot near the back of the tent and laid the boy gently down upon it, caressing the back of his head. Nergal's eyes narrowed.

"He's your son," Nergal observed.

Melanson's shoulders lowered. He sighed. "Not quite. The boy's father was very dear to me. I loved him. He died some time ago."

"Then he must be very precious to you," Talisha said in a quiet voice.

Melanson nodded. "He's a good kid. Smarter than most would give him credit for. He just has a different way of being."

Nergal snorted. "That's one word for it."

Melanson scowled. "Talisha. Who is your rude, green friend?"

Talisha stepped forward. "These are my associates. I was investigating a rumor about Wyvern sightings on Archimedes IV. That's IGF exclusive technology so there was worry they might have fallen into the hands of pirates."

"Interesting." Melanson stroked his beard. "Your mother preferred to work alone, you know. Always hated when the IGF sent along a troop of guardsman. Felt like we'd get in her way. She might've been right, but it was always a privilege to watch her kill people. Woman made murder an art."

Talisha winced at that. "So you're former IGF, I take it?"

"Corporal Melanson, 3rd Battalion. Got a chance to work with your mother during the rebellion of Weyland Prime."

"How'd you wind up stranded on this rock?" Nergal asked.

Melanson leaned in close. "About a decade ago, the IGF deployed here and I was part of that task force. We landed in the woods just behind us. I'm the only one who made it out alive."

"Who is this Mother that Jefferson keeps referring to?" Talisha pressed. "He said it's where you got the wyverns."

"The wyverns were looted from the base of the drop-ship. The AI unit in the ship's mainframe still works, no clue how. Didn't take long for an entire cult to spring up around her. Figured these people needed some sort of hope, so I didn't question it."

Snidely spoke up then. "What was the IGF doing out here?"

Talisha could have strangled him. She tried not to show any signs of panic on her face but was certain Melanson had seen her eyes flash with fear and anger. That'd be all it took to convince him that she lied about working with these people. He knew a lone wolf when he saw it, and she was more similar to her mother than she cared to admit. He'd see that and see that she had lied about everything else. She should have made the entire party hide in the scorpion and handled this by herself.

Melanson paused, licking his lips. He twiddled his thumbs, then pulled on the strap of his assault rifle. Talisha eyed his body language, her fingers tensing and readying to fire a shot from her arm cannon. She needed to relax. An itchy trigger finger would get them all killed.

"Recon work mostly," Melanson said in a careful voice. "Just because the planet's outside jurisdiction doesn't mean the IGF doesn't deploy troops every so often to oversee the state of things. It's always good to see potential threats to the sector if they crop up. But why are you lot really here?"

"Pardon me?" Snidely said, stiffening.

"Especially you," Melanson glowered down at him, causing Snidely to gulp audibly. "Delicate hands you've got there. Fine suit, if a bit dusty from a few days travel on this planet. You strike me as a company man. If this Talisha's anything like her mother, she hates your type even more than scum like me and that green thug over there."

"Snidely's a representative of our employer," Talisha's voice came out in that perfect manner of apathetic irritation. It communicated a presence of low stakes.

Melanson turned toward her, shoulders softening. "Is that so? Someone out there has an interest in the wyverns, is that it?"

"They are top-of-the-line military technology," Talisha said. "My client is hoping to salvage one to reverse-engineer the technology and sell it at a lofty profit. Dr. Nergal here is accompanying us as a guide on a hostile planet. He's been quarantined here for years."

Melanson smiled. Talisha could have cheered. He bought it. He bought the whole damn thing.

"Maybe we can cut a deal," Melanson said. "Cut me in on some of the profits, and I'll happily take you to see Mother. The blueprints to the wyverns are still in her database."

Talisha huffed. "What guarantee do I have you're not leading us into the woods to get killed?"

"People these days, so untrusting." Melanson let out a chuckle. "Very well. I'll let you borrow one of my tanks. It's equipped with enough flamethrowers to keep the plants at bay."

"I'd also be interested in taking a look at one of those eight-legged horrors you've built," Talisha said. Her love of mechanics took over for a second.

Melanson snorted. "And let your people start selling those off too? No, the spyders belong to the Raiders alone."

"We would happily compensate you for the design, of course," Snidely interjected, always the opportunist. He scratched his left hand absent-mindedly.

Melanson shook his head. "I'm too sentimental. The spyders were Jack's idea."

Nergal's eyes drifted toward the boy. "Jack. That was the name of the boy's father, yes?"

"Aye." Melanson's eyes softened.

"What did this man mean to you?" Nergal said. He stared into Melanson's eyes, brow crinkling. He looked pained.

Melanson turned to face Jefferson, stroking the boy's hair idly. "There are those who make life less unbearable. When you're down in the shitter, it's hard to hate it 'cause you get to wake up every morning and be with them." He turned back to face Nergal, stone-faced. "That's who Jack was, satisfied?"

"Satisfaction is for those who lack ambition," Nergal said, mouth dry. "But your answer will suffice."

Nergal still had that faraway, wistful look on his face. His hands clenched into fists as he silently walked toward the entrance of the tent. Talisha contemplated whether or not she'd want to later ask him what the hell this was all about.

Melanson folded his arms across his chest. He raised an incredulous brow. "And you said he's a doctor?"

Snidely scratched his left hand again. "He came highly recommended."

MELANSON SHOWED THEM to the tank. He held Jefferson up on his back with the boy's arms wrapped securely around his neck. The kid was still out cold.

The tank was your standard model used by the IGF military, though it'd been heavily modified to suit the needs of Melanson's Raiders. Three sizable flamethrowers had been fixed to the sides to drive back the forest's attacks. The front end was equipped with two saw-blades to clear a path before them. Each tread had been carefully aligned with mean-looking spikes capable of crushing anything beneath them.

Talisha whistled as she climbed inside. Melanson laughed at her pestering questions about the various alterations to the vehicle's design and inner workings. A lot of the tech-talk was well over Snidely's head, and Nergal seemed far too wrapped in his own thoughts to care.

The plan was that Melanson and a group of his Raiders would escort the tank into the woods, and then serve guard while Talisha investigated the wreckage of the IGF drop-ship. Everything was going well.

Talisha hadn't relaxed completely. The next few steps of the plan were their most dangerous. She'd left a comm-link with Cyrus and Bluebird and would signal them to steal into the camp to try and secure the key to the Valran temple. With Melanson's forces split this way, he'd be cut off and unable to swiftly respond to an outside attack.

She hadn't bought Melanson's story about the IGF investigating planets outside their jurisdiction. Hostile planets were sanctioned off by the IGF, denied resources and aid. Their hostile status was only ever revoked when the planet proved ripe for colonization.

The IGF had specific plans for Archimedes IV. Talisha had a hunch it'd something to do with the Valran Temple. Part of her hoped that her foray into the drop-ship's AI unit would net her a chance to see what the military database had on the Valran.

She took a deep breath and took a moment to familiarize herself with the tank's controls. Snidely watched through narrowed eyes as she fiddled with the knobs and levers and quickly picked up on what did what. By the time Melanson was leading them into the woods, she was driving the tank and operating its flamers as if she were an experienced pro.

"You take to technology like a fish to water," he mused. "Plymouth could use a woman of your talents full-time."

Talisha's face wrinkled in disgust. "Uh...thanks?"

Nergal turned to him sharply. "Could you not do that-that *thing* for five minutes?"

"What thing?" Snidely looked genuinely confused. "What did I do?"

Nergal leaned in close, his voice acidic. "Sometime I'll have to tell you the circumstances that led to my unique condition."

Snidely blanched and turned away, scratching his hand feverishly. "Understood."

Talisha ignored the brief little spat and made a call to Bluebird and Cyrus. "Look alive, you two. We're headed into the woods with a gathering of Melanson's Raiders. Defenses will be split. I want you to scout out the camp and snag the key. Try the big tent at the center of the camp. Avoid getting spotted if you can, but if not, you know what to do."

Cyrus must have switched back over to Rogers sometime during the wait. No doubt he hadn't been too keen on being stuffed in the trunk with Bluebird. "Loud and clear. We'll wait a few moments longer for you to get a good distance away from the camp in case things go ape-shit."

Bluebird's angry voice came hollering into the comm-line. "But not too much longer! I am ready to explode like biscuits in a can!"

Talisha smiled. "Good luck. Both of you."

The procession of tanks and spyders smashed their way into the woods. Talisha kept her eyes fixed on the screens in front of her, each showing a camera feed from all sides of the vehicle. One monitor had a motion tracker installed, keeping her abreast of the other vehicles in the convoy, as well as any attacks from the nearby trees.

Melanson's voice crackled into the tank's comm systems. "We shouldn't have too much trouble while inside the vehicles. The trees are smart. They don't bother us. We don't bother them."

"What happens once we step outside the vehicles?" Snidely said, nervous.

Melanson laughed. "Then things get interesting."

Snidely turned a pale shade of green. "Oh goody."

BLUEBIRD ABOUT TORE the hinges off the trunk when she threw it open. Rogers was hauled off her and hurled unceremoniously out into the desert sand. His metal limbs crumpled beneath him like a discarded puppet. Bluebird emerged, swearing in her native tongue. Strands of her bright blue hair clung in sweaty clumps to the sides of her face and neck, both the color of an angry tomato. She fell to her hands and knees, gasping.

Rogers was quick to her side. He tried to help her up, but she shoved him away and staggered for a minute. It was everything she could do to keep from screaming.

"I have endured much in my time!" She spat, pointing a shaky finger at Rogers. "I have had my loved ones ripped from me, held the faces of comrades as they died in my arms, and endured false imprisonment. But this? This is a new low!"

She collapsed onto her ass, hands splayed out in front of her.

"I need..." she said, then laughed. "I may need to rethink my life."

Rogers placed both hands on his hips, waiting for her to calm a bit. "Way I reckon it, there's two ways go about stealing this key. We sneak in all quiet-like, which quite frankly is beyond our skill-set."

"I am as quiet as a church mouse," Bluebird said, and then threw back her head in a laugh. "Hah! See? I made a funny."

Rogers groaned. "The other way is a full-frontal assault, and that'd be ill-advised."

Bluebird stared at him. "You have another plan?"

Rogers retrieved his hat and Bluebird's cannon from the trunk of the Scorpion. He tossed the cannon into her outstretched grasp. His fingers twirled the wide-brimmed hat around before resting it squarely just over his brow.

"Why yes," he said confidently. "Yes, I believe I do."

IN THE HOUR or two that it took for the sun to set, the temperature drastically shifted. Days on Archimedes IV were a blazing hellhole, but at night everything turned frigid. It's part of what made it damn near impossible for anything to grow outside the mutant carnivorous plants in the forest.

Most of the encampment had finished setting up their makeshift barriers and watchtowers by the time Bluebird and Rogers deemed it safe enough to creep close. The moonless night kept them shrouded in darkness. She was almost impressed with the efficiency at which the Raiders had erected a wall of scrap metal and towers in a thirty-foot radius.

She hoisted the cannon over her back and scaled the far-reaches of the southern wall, just out of sight of a watchman. He was too busy staring down the sights of a sniper rifle to see the threat rapidly clamoring toward him. He had a split second of terror as her fist obscured his vision and he was knocked unconscious. Rogers joined her in the tower a few seconds later.

"Keep your head low," he instructed. "Yer a mighty imposing sight, missus. They'll spot ya in a second."

She pinched the rifle between her fingers and deposited it into his hands as if getting rid of an unwanted insect. "Use this pitiful looking thing. It will be quieter than your six-shooter."

"Thank ya kindly."

He took the rifle and stared down the scope. While Cyrus might have had access to his more explosive weaponry systems, Rogers excelled when it came to precision. He lined his sights carefully and pulled the trigger. The rifle barely twitched as it moved between targets; three shots, three kills, and all within the span of a single second.

"Well done, cowboy." Bluebird rose, causing the tower to complain beneath her weight. "Now there is no one who will spot me."

Rogers stared at the groaning beams of the watchtower. "Yeah well, all the same, let's clear off before your magnanimousness brings this whole thing down."

"Good idea."

They kept to the outskirts. Bluebird had to crawl along on her hands and knees just to stay in shadow. Rogers's smaller frame was able to navigate the darkness with ease. She trusted his robotic eyes, occasionally stopping on his orders to avoid a patrol of guards.

One of the bandit guards clearly had been drinking a bit too much and staggered away from the rest of his buddies, rubbing his crotch through his jeans. Rogers stared from his hiding spot in the corner of the wall, silently praying the bandit wouldn't come any closer. Bluebird's massive form would be instantly spotted.

The bandit guard stepped into the darkness and unzipped to take a piss. He turned to the side, mouth drooping a bit. He hadn't a chance to call attention to the bright blue streak hurtling toward him. *WHAM!* Another bandit's clock cleaned from one of Bluebird's devastating punches. She gave Rogers a thumbs-up and they continued their silent trek toward the center of the camp.

Two of the wyverns had been left behind to set watch over the camp, but fuel was too scarce and expensive to simply leave them hovering. They'd been left grounded in an open area of the camp. A few guards and pilots huddled near them, hands open over a burning barrel to stave off the bitter cold.

Rogers hurried to stand behind one of the wyverns. "All right, Cyrus. Time to strut your stuff."

He rested a hand flat against the back leg of the vehicle. His entire body jolted and then collapsed. Bluebird hurried to his side to catch him.

"Will this work?" she asked.

"Never tried splitting our consciousness like this before," Rogers said, a tinge of nervousness creeping into his voice. "Reckon it was worth a shot."

A moment passed. Then, one by one, the lights behind the wyvern's panels flickered on. Its legs groaned as they shifted from side to side, like a newborn calf learning to walk. The guards turned around, startled by the wyvern's sudden movements. Their arms shook as it rose to its full height and trained its guns on them.

Cyrus's familiar gruff twang emerged from the vehicle. "Woo-hoo! Time to shoot, Luke, or give up the gun! You varmints are about to get a serious wake-up call!"

"Mother preserve us!" one of the bandits screamed. "It's possessed!"

"Shut yer cock holster." Cyrus fired the guns, sending a stream of bullets into the group of fleeing onlookers.

Bluebird laughed, patting Rogers on the shoulder. "Well done, cowboy. Go find the key. Cyrus and I can keep these losers distracted."

She hoisted Ethel from her back and charged the second wyvern before it had a chance to lift off. The plasma beam sliced it into melted bits while she cackled. Rogers had to take a minute to watch the chaos as gunfire and screams filled the night.

"I miss being a sheriff," he murmured to himself, shaking his head as he hurried to Melanson's tent.

THE DARKNESS OF the trees loomed all around them. It wasn't Talisha's first time venturing into inhospitable territory, but this forest caused the hair on her arms to stand on end. The trees pulsed and bled, their bark covered with pus-filled tumors and strange growths that set off scarlet vapors. Those same vapors coalesced into a thick scarlet fog that covered the ground, creating an unwholesome atmosphere of dread and horror. Every plant was like a set of beastly organs sprouting up from the ground.

Talisha could see the broken wing tip of the drop-ship coming into view. It was almost hard to believe that they were looking at what was most assuredly an outdated model. A large vessel capable of holding up to a hundred troops, several vehicles and a year's worth of rations. A single drop-ship could deploy an entire army and alter the tide of any battle with surprise reinforcements.

"Wasn't expecting it to be so big," Nergal said after a moment's pause.

"Would you believe they're even bigger now?" Snidely said with a wry smile.

Snidely scratched at the flesh around the top of his hand again. Nergal noticed. The skin had been rubbed raw. He watched the little corporate man dig at his own skin with his fingernails.

"Is that so?" Nergal asked, brow furrowed.

"Yes." Snidely caught Nergal's staring and hastily shoved his hand into his pocket. "The IGF military represents one of the largest and fastest-growing armed forces in the galaxy. The drop-ships had to be scaled up to compensate."

Nergal lunged forward, gripping Snidely's wrist despite protest. Nergal inspected Snidely's hand closely before releasing it. There were traces of white spots all along the skin spreading down to his wrist.

Snidely stared, mouth agape. "What is your problem?"

"The critter," Nergal said coldly. "You've been infected."

They'd barely a chance to react to that statement when Melanson's voice broke through the comm-line. "Disembark, people. We're here."

Each of the vehicles backed into a perfect circle surrounding the drop-ship. It created an ideal line of fire for a near impenetrable defense. Didn't make Talisha feel any safer as she left the safety of the tank to approach the ship. The doors seemed to have fused completely shut, though holes large enough for several people to crawl through had pierced its sides.

Talisha kept her arm cannon trained in front of her, making sweeping motions about the area.

"You'll be completely safe to do what you need in there," Melanson said, laughing quietly. "I assure you, we have nature beaten."

"With all due respect," Talisha snipped back. "I've been on plenty missions where people died after making statements like that."

Melanson laughed again. "Well hurry it on up and get in there."

Talisha lowered her cannon. She was grateful that her helmet completely obscured her facial features. Melanson wouldn't see the open-mouthed look of distrust. She didn't like her life being left in the hands of a man she was ultimately trying to rob.

"Snidely. Nergal," she said quietly into her comm. "I want you two back in the tank."

"I can't drive that thing," Snidely protested.

"I'm sure there's an instruction manual in the glove compartment," Nergal sneered. "We'll figure something out."

"Thanks," Talisha said.

Her voice fell quiet. She wasn't used to Nergal actually being accommodating. She added it to the list of things bothering her about this place.

Inside the darkened hall of the drop-ship, Talisha did a quick heat-scan. No life signs detected, but her encounter with the critter last night left her skeptical. She crept cautiously forward, one arm fixed to her cannon to keep it steady as she swept the hallways with it. Her boots made clanking sounds against the rusted metal grates beneath her feet.

Overhead, several exposed wires still flickered with electricity, even after all these years. She turned the corner and saw the skeletal corpse of a former IGF Guardsman slumped against the door panel. A decorated medical officer, looked like. There was a dusty datapad still clutched in his bony grasp. She took a quick moment to scan and download its contents. Most of the data was corrupted and irretrievable. Talisha was able to find one bit of relevant information, a final log entry.

"Been on this planet several days now. Can't escape the woods. The trees here have a mind all their own. They won't let us leave. We've lost so many of our men. Melanson's still missing. Coward deserted us most like. Opportunistic bastard. Would like to join him though, anything to get out of here.

"More complaints of noises at night from the men. I've prescribed everyone sleep-aids to help with the jitters, but I'm starting to hear it too. Terrible moans coming from outside. They sound human, unholy cries of the damned."

The datapad also contained a map of the inner workings of the ship that she scanned directly into her helmet. It'd give her a better route to the location of the ship's AI unit. She left the datapad in his lap and continued moving down the corridor.

Talisha froze at the end of the hallway. A meter that measured soundwaves flashed at the bottom-hand corner of her visor. She could hear the skittering clatter and skritches of rapid movement across the hull.

Reflexively, Talisha charged the beam on her arm cannon. She used the glowing particles of energy to light the way in front of her. A looming shadow appeared at the end of the hall, then vanished. According to her visors, there was nothing there.

"You have to be kidding me with this shit," she muttered.

The skittering grew louder and louder, until it was directly over her head. She darted her gaze upward, bringing the cannon to the ceiling. A woman's face stared down at her with wide pupil-less eyes and gray bits of stringy hair rotting out of her head. The creature screamed, opening her mouth into multiple distended jaws. Talisha fired the fully-charged blast from her cannon causing the woman's face to explode into several gory pieces. They fell and splattered against the ground on either side of her in chunks.

Breathing heavily, Talisha was able to get a good look at the thing that'd tried to jump her. It had the same maggot-shaped body like the critter from last night, but was otherwise completely different. This one had a pair of human legs, and only one human arm, and its underbelly was coated in a padding of thick black hair.

Furthermore, the stomach seemed bloated, bulging outward. Talisha gasped and peered closer. Each strand of hair was connected to a small white sac that wriggled and moved with a life of its own. This thing was readying to lay a nest of eggs. Even more were still lodged within its belly.

"Oh to hell with this," Talisha muttered and charged another blast of her cannon.

She continually fired at each egg until she was certain there were none left. She then blew open the Critter's stomach releasing a wave of noxious gases and blue bile that spilled across the rusted grating. Even after the creature's bloated corpse had been thoroughly scorched and splattered across the halls, Talisha waited breathlessly for it to clamp its jaws at her. Nothing happened. The Critter was dead.

It occurred to her that her previous missions had left her in some need of psychological therapy. She sighed wearily and continued on her way. Her nerves were fried. If the payout for this job was as much as Snidely promised, she deeply considered taking it and using it to invest in work a little less bonkers.

The danger was nothing. Guys with guns, bandits, armed insurrection? All that was just par for the course in a galaxy torn apart by poverty and war. It was the really weird shit that was starting to get under her skin. Psychic jellyfish, bug monsters that assimilated and mutated humans into propagating its species, and that wasn't even the half of it. The universe had opened up to her in the last few years and given her a taste of true horror. She'd half a mind to turn the other way and run.

It's what she would do if she had any damn sense. Part of her wondered if it was why her mother quit hunting bounties. Maybe she'd seen something too strange and frightening to handle and decided to hang it all up. It certainly wasn't the killing. The first Talisha Artul had no problems with that.

Finally the doors to the ship's central control room opened. Inside were a set of monitors that made a semicircle around a dimly-illuminated console. The screens flickered on as she entered the room, revealing a bald computer-generated head staring blankly at her. Talisha removed her helmet and waved half-heartedly.

"Sup. Mother, I take it?" Talisha said, sidling over to a chair in front the computer and collapsing in it.

An artificial female voice responded, its tone friendly and warm. "It is the name designated to me by the current users of this unit. How may I be of service?"

Talisha leaned forward. "I need everything you've got on the Valran."

Mother blinked. "One moment please...that information is highly classified. You do not have access permissions."

"'Course it would be."

Talisha leaned forward and opened the command console on the machine. It hadn't been the first time she'd have to bypass security restrictions on an IGF system to access crucial mission data. They were notoriously secretive, even on intel that would have made it necessary to do her job with minimal casualties. The visor within her helmet had scanned several IGF databanks in the past and memorized thousands of security protocols making entry into their systems a breeze. A few clicks of the keyboard and the code was cracked.

"All right, lay it on me," Talisha said, smiling.

"Access granted," Mother chimed. "The Valran were an ancient species of nomadic humanoid aliens with distinctive avian characteristics, such as powerful wings, beaks, and talons. Documents indicate that they once prospered and thrived on the planet Avem, but fled a great catastrophe, details of which are unknown.

"The Valran people continued to move from planet to planet bringing with them unparalleled growths in technology and education. The calamity that befell their planet, however, seemed to have followed them as many grew sick and died. Their population dwindled, and those that survived entombed themselves deep within temples scattered across an untold number of worlds.

"The last time a Valran was ever seen alive was when a messenger visited a child formerly orphaned upon the planet Jyrraxis. A ship was reported entering the sector and docked in front of the Noble House of Artul. It left within a few hours of having made contact. The child was reportedly adopted into the Artul family but a year earlier."

"Mom," Talisha whispered. "Are you saying the Valran knew my mother?"

"It is currently believed within the IGF that prior to her adoption, the bounty hunter Talisha Artul had been raised by the last living remnants of the Valran people."

"That's a lot." Talisha exhaled. She placed a hand on her forehead and wiped the sweat from her brow. "All right, what do you know about the temple?"

NERGAL AND SNIDELY sat next to each other in cold silence. Snidely kept staring at the white spots along the back of his hand, scratching intermittently. The itching had grown worse in the last half hour.

"If you like," Nergal said, pausing a bit. "I'd like to experiment with my serum. See if it helps stave off the infection."

"I thought you said there was nothing that could be done." Snidely's brow furrowed. He drew away from Nergal, covering the infected hand.

"My previous encounter with the critter-infection was before I'd perfected my serum," Nergal explained, calmly retrieving a vial of the glowing green liquid from his coat. "As a physician, it'd delight me to have defeated it."

"That serum can't possibly be a magic cure-all." Snidely snorted, skeptical. "I've seen it heal wounds, but curing an infection you've hardly tested or sampled?"

Nergal smiled, holding the vial to his face. Snidely was unsettled by the way it cast its eerie light over his gruesome features. It was one thing to let this strange doctor medicate the mercenaries under his hire, another entirely to find himself an experimental subject.

"That's where you're wrong, Mr. Snidely." Nergal caressed the vial with a loving finger. "This vial contains the essence of life itself. Trust me, I'm a scientist."

Snidely inched away from him. "Only the desperate and the crazed would trust someone like you."

With frightful speed, Nergal grabbed Snidely's arm and pulled the sleeve of his shirt all the way up his arm. The white spots had spread, the skin having nearly changed color completely A series of raised bumps had spread across his flesh. Snidely whimpered, turning his face away so he wouldn't have to look at it.

Nergal leaned into Snidely's face, licking his lips. "The next stages of the infection will be more painful than anything you could even imagine. I'd say desperate is just about right."

Snidely's mouth contorted into an ugly grimace. He didn't know whether to throw up or cry. He took several deep breaths as panic took hold.

"This assignment has gone all wrong from the beginning," he gasped. "I shouldn't even be down here. My own body turns against me. It's all so fucked!"

Nergal's eyes softened. He gripped Snidely's wrist. The two men looked at one another as silent understanding passed between them.

"I understand," Nergal said, his voice quiet and sincere. "Please. Let me help you."

Snidely's fingers gripped the folds of Nergal's coat. "All right. Do it."

Nergal drew the contents of the vial into a syringe. He pulled Snidely's arm forward and gave him an almost apologetic look before inserting it directly into his veins. Snidely threw back his head and howled.

"Wh-what's happening to me?" he managed to scream.

Snidely clutched his stomach. The burning sensation spread from his arms and intensified within his gut. His entire face became drenched with sweat as he shook and gasped for air.

Nergal reached within his coat for another syringe. "The mutation within your system has already begun. My serum is trying to counteract it. It will get worse before it gets better."

"And here I thought we were...*nngh*...sharing a moment," Snidely grunted through his spasms.

Nergal retrieved a third syringe and injected it into Snidely's neck. The spasms slowed until the company man fell completely limp in his lap. Nergal held his shaking body close.

"Something for the pain," he whispered.

Already most of Snidely's skin had turned the color of milk. There were four raised knots just beneath his shoulder blades. Nergal looked over Snidely's unconscious form, tracing his fingers along the back of the company man's spine. The serum's attempts to counteract the infection might have sped up the rate of mutation. He'd need to keep an eye on his patient in case the treatment failed.

Nergal ran his hands through Snidely's hair. Holding the man in his arms like this brought up too many painful memories. He'd every impulse to shove the corporate creep to the side, but he didn't. How long had it been since he'd held anyone? A lifetime, probably.

"Dalton..." The name slipped from his lips almost unconsciously.

He rolled Snidely over onto his side and shoved him to the opposite end of the tank in disgust. Nergal bore no ill will toward the man at this point, only a profound sense of self-loathing and bitterness. He was repulsed by his own trauma. If he could fry those particular parts of his brain he would. They served him little.

Nergal sat, wrists resting over his knees as he stared off into the nothingness. Snidely's body still shook and quivered even as the man passed in and out of consciousness. Nergal couldn't help but steal occasional glances his way. He swore at himself for his weakness and grabbed Snidely to cradle him once more.

"Who's Dalton?" Snidely groaned, barely awake.

"Go to sleep," Nergal ordered.

"Please...I need something to focus on." Snidely's voice was weak and hoarse.

"Fine. He was my partner. Another scientist." Nergal sighed. "Real idealistic fool, he was, but it was the worst foolishness, the infectious kind. He had big dreams and big ambitions and wanted to help people and dammit if listening to him didn't make you want to follow.

"The whole project was his idea. We were going to cure diseases. All of them. An end-all drug that could be cheaply produced and sold to those who couldn't afford more expensive treatments.

"We'd discovered an enzyme on one of the rumored Valran home-worlds. Any virus that came into contact with it evaporated. Just had the problem of completely rewriting the DNA of all test subjects, killing them. We were on the verge of a breakthrough. A million scientists all working toward a common goal of ending sickness. We just didn't count on our biggest sponsor pulling the plug.

"Shouldn't have trusted a company that thrives off keeping people sick to adequately fund our research. Black Pharmaceuticals did us a nasty. Bombs were planted across the station by their elite swat teams, and we were executed. Our research was destroyed. I had to watch a firing squad murder my colleagues. Dalton was the first to die.

"In the confusion, I'd been infected by the test samples of the various diseases we were working with. A slew of pathogens from every planet in the galaxy. Injected myself with our serum to try and counteract the symptoms before they killed me. Serum worked, but not without consequences. It turned me into this ugly, green *thing*.

"So I killed them. I killed all of them. Anyone associated with Black Pharma got exposed to my sickness. After that the IGF arrested and quarantined me on this rock."

A minute passed. Then Snidely managed to croak out a faint whisper. "How lonely that must have been."

Nergal's eyes blazed with hate. "It was pure hell."

The comm-line crackled with static as Melanson's voice poured in. "Look alive people. Trees are sending their minions after us."

Nergal slid Snidely out of his lap and moved to the controls at the front end of the tank. His eyes scanned the monitors. A group of figures were briefly illuminated in the darkness by warning puffs of fire from Melanson's flamethrowers. They stood, crouched among the leaves, swaying eerily in the crimson fog.

"Minions," Nergal breathed. He swallowed hard. "Right."

TALISHA EMERGED FROM the control room. Her gait was swift and purposeful. Her helmet lowered onto her face as she rushed through the halls of the drop-ship.

She alerted Nergal on her comm-link. "Hey, Doc. How ready are you to get us out of here?"

The line crackled. "I'd stay put if I were you, Miss Artul. It's a bit of a fiasco out here."

"I don't like fiascoes," Talisha snapped. "What the hell is going on?"

"Oh nothing that unusual, just that the dead walk the earth." His voice sounded uncharacteristically shaken.

Talisha's pulse quickened. "Zombies? Again? Really?"

"Again?" Nergal almost shrieked. "You were actually serious about that whole jellyfish thing?"

"How many?" Talisha now ran through the halls readying for a fight.

"No idea."

"What type of undead are we dealing with? Virus? Psychically controlled?" Her words were clipped, direct.

"There are different categories for this?" Nergal spat. "I'd guess something to do with the spores in the area. They seem to be piloting the dead bodies of former IGF personnel."

"All right, I've got an idea."

"Feel free to let me in."

"I've seen spores that animate corpses before, usually insects. It's both a defense mechanism, and a means of reproduction."

"To pilot a human body would require some rather complex evolution," Nergal replied. "What are you thinking?"

Talisha held her arm cannon to her face and opened a holographic panel just over her wrist. She flipped through several buttons marked by the Valran tongue before nodding satisfied. She clenched her fist, charging the beam. Instead of the yellow ball of energy that formed at the tip of the cannon, there appeared a crackling blue orb.

"Electromagnetic pulses," she said gruffly. "Fry their brains. Just need a second to charge up a wide enough blast to cover the whole area."

"These tanks aren't protected against an EMP! You'll fry our equipment, you numbskull!" Nergal protested.

"The blast should only short them out for a hot-second," Talisha insisted. "But be ready with your flamethrower in case the trees get feisty."

Nergal let out a long sigh. "I hate this planet."

Talisha said nothing. She marched to the edge of the ship and flattened her back against the wall to peer around the corner. She saw them, the shambling corpses of a hundred soldiers.

They had bits of vines growing out their shoulders and legs, some with roots piercing out their eyes and poking through the tips of their fingernails. A few dozen had bark growing over their exposed rotting skin. Where their bodies had decayed, plant-growth had taken over to fill in the gaps as best it knew how.

The tanks and spyder vehicles trampled and battered the zombies, only for them to stand once more. Limbs were torn asunder to be re-attached by the vines. Even as the flames scorched their bodies they still charged forward, heedless of their own survival.

Talisha kept the blast charging, willing the blue orb to grow. Charging a blast this size usually wasn't her style. It took too long and was generally too damned risky. There was no telling how much devastation she could cause if she focused long and hard enough. Stories of some of the things her mother had been able to accomplish with this same suit still intimidated her.

Talisha wasn't satisfied till the orb had become about the size of Bluebird's fist. It swirled and crackled angrily. At times its form rippled and threatened to come undone. It took everything she could to control it.

"All right, this is as good as it gets," she muttered and raced into the throng.

The eyes of the plant-zombies turned on her. They tripped and fell over each other in their scrambling rush. Bones cracked as heavy feet trampled over fallen limbs. Talisha leapt into the air with a thrust from her jet pack. She aimed the sparkling orb of electricity below, watching them claw for her with hungry hands. Vines shot out of the trees attempting to wrap around her ankles. She could barely aim while dodging. Fortunately, they were all clumped up nicely enough that she was certain to hit them all in a single blast.

"Lights out," she said.

The sound of a thousand shrieking birds filled the air. For a brief moment the entire area was illuminated in a blinding blue light. Soon as the orb hit the first zombie it detonated, sending a pulse that rapidly expanded and covered everything. Visible blue fizzles of electric bolts could be seen quickly snaking over every zombie and tank around them before vanishing.

Talisha nearly collapsed. The blast felt like it'd taken something out of her, like knives pricking at the base of her skull. The zombies all collapsed into a pathetic, lifeless pile. The flamethrowers on the tanks halted and the spyders groaned on their legs as they all but collapsed. For a moment all was still.

Then the trees retaliated. Vines eagerly shot toward the spyder's legs and yanked them apart. Doors were torn violently from the tanks and screaming bandits hurled into the open maws of trees. The next six seconds were filled with gore and carnage as fresh corpses were added to the forest floor or eagerly devoured by the local fauna.

Melanson was pulled from his tank. The slimy vine squeezed around his gut even as he thrashed and reached for one of the grenades on his belt. He pulled the pin with his mouth and roared, hurling it into the den of trees. A large explosion shook the forest and the vine recoiled, releasing him. He fell to the ground and pulled out his assault rifle, firing wildly at anything that dared move or approach him.

"Kiss my fat, hairy ass!" He bellowed. "I will fuck all of you!"

Talisha took that opportunity to fly toward the tank with Snidely and Nergal. She fired off several energy blasts to fend off the attacks of the nearby trees before hurrying through the door. She flipped several switches once inside, starting the flamethrowers. Several vines that had attached themselves to the tracks of the tank let out an abominable screeching noise before slinking off into the darkness.

She collapsed into the pilot seat and removed her helmet. She took a cursory glance about the tank. She saw Snidely curled up and shivering in the corner, and that was all.

Talisha made a call on her comm-line. "Nergal, you there?"

He responded quickly. "Doing just fine, Talisha. Go on without me."

"Nergal, dammit. What are you doing?"

"Taking out an insurance policy. Trust me. Everything will work out just dandy. Keep Snidely sedated for me. Unsure how well he's doing with the creeper-infection. Would hate for you to survive all that just to get ambushed from behind."

"What?!" Talisha screamed into the mic.

"Toodles!"

Nergal disconnected from the comm. There'd be no reaching him now. Talisha could have screamed and flipped at least a half-dozen tables, maybe more. She wheeled around in her seat and took a concerned look at Snidely.

"How you holding up?" she asked.

He responded by giving her the middle finger.

Talisha nodded. "Got it. Let me know if you need anything."

She turned back to the controls and began the trek out of the woods. She was eager to leave this creepy place behind. She hoped she'd never see Melanson or his Raiders ever again.

Chapter Five

NOTHING REMAINED OF the Raiders's camp but the acrid stench of smoke and seared metal. Those that survived Cyrus's rampage had long since fled into the night. Bluebird had kept her plasma cannon focused mostly on dismantling the tanks and additional wyverns in the encampment.

Talisha drove the tank toward them. She was greeted by silence. She emerged from the tank, surveying the torched encampment with an open mouth. Bluebird was reloading the energy cells in her plasma cannon. Talisha approached her.

"Some infiltration mission," she said, flabbergasted. "Did you leave any of them left alive?"

"Most ran like cowards when Cyrus took over the wyvern," Bluebird said. "They thought it was possessed by demons."

Cyrus wandered over, still in his wyvern body. He lifted one leg to make a waving gesture. Talisha raised an eyebrow.

"Not too inaccurate," she said. "So did you get the key?"

Rogers joined them, folding his arms over his chest and shaking his head. "Not a gosh-darned thing. Melanson must have it on him."

Talisha stifled a groan. All that risk for nothing. One of the spyder units came lumbering out of the forest. Bluebird dove in front of Talisha, aiming her plasma cannon at the mechanical horror.

The hatch atop the spyder raised and Nergal climbed out, raising both hands in surrender. "Lay down your weapons, you fools. It's me!"

Bluebird kept her weapon trained on him, lip curled. "Where have you been?"

Nergal reached into the spyder and dragged Jefferson out by his arm. The boy was just conscious enough to struggle, though not by much. Nergal pulled him close and pressed the visor of his protective suit against Jefferson's face, causing the boy to squirm uncomfortably.

"I got us some leverage," Nergal said, smiling. "We'll get that key. Won't we boy?"

"Nergal. What the fuck." Talisha almost spat.

"Don't get so self-righteous," Nergal hissed, turning on her. "You could have warned Melanson and his raiders about the EMP, but you didn't. You rendered their vehicles useless and let them be slaughtered. If I hadn't intervened, the little brat here would have been plant-food."

Bluebird lowered her cannon. She turned to Talisha. Her brow furrowed in an expression of stunned disappointment. Her stance parted and she tilted her head to the side.

"That true, bounty hunter?" she said.

Talisha folded her arms over her chest. "If you knew what I knew about Melanson..."

"Those people were fighting to survive!" Bluebird insisted. "The boy is innocent."

"That *boy* piloted a powerful piece of weaponry that nearly killed you," Talisha retorted. "My sympathies notwithstanding, these people are still dangerous. Thought you understood."

"I fight with honor!" Bluebird yelled. "With dignity! I don't lure people to their doom to stab them in the back! I thought you a proud warrior, Talisha Artul. I was wrong. You are a coward."

Nergal screamed at the both of them. "Hey! As much as I love watching like-minded individuals tear each other apart over their own hypocrisies, we have work to do. We can still get what we came for."

The earth shook, rattled by an explosion. They heard the echoes of gunfire coming closer and closer. There were screams and raucous laughter, then Melanson emerged covered in blood and bruises. He held a machete in one hand, and his assault rifle in the other. He'd tucked the gun into his armpit so he could wield it single-handedly while hacking away at the vines. He appeared to have hurled every grenade he owned.

Nergal smiled down at him. "Corporal Melanson, delighted you could make it."

"You treacherous mercs!" Melanson roared, stumbling toward them. "Ya filthy flapjacks! I ought to skin you alive!"

Nergal dangled Jefferson's skinny body over the edge of the spyder. Melanson froze. His expression shifted into wide-eyed terror.

"Easy," Nergal soothed, then chuckled. "Your boy here could wind up injured if a fight broke out. I'll take care of him though." His voice lowered to a threatening octave. "I'm a doctor."

Melanson threw his rifle to the ground. "What do you want?"

"The key to the Valran Temple," Nergal spat. "Where is it?"

Melanson's shoulders shook. "Should have never taken the damn thing in the first place. It's in my tent. Now give me back my boy and leave us in peace."

"Liar!" Nergal's tongue passed over his teeth. "My associates have lain waste to your entire camp and its nowhere to be found. Tell us the truth."

Melanson's eyes widened. He was actually pleading this time. "I'm telling you the truth. I left it there, thinking it'd be guarded."

Nergal bit his lip, clearly in deep thought. Talisha stared nervously. She thought about how much Nergal was desperate to get off this planet. Melanson could be telling the truth, but that didn't get him what he wanted. He wouldn't want to believe that. Getting into this temple was his last chance to escape, and he wasn't about to let his only lead go without a fight. Nergal removed one of his gloves.

Talisha's eyes widened. She threw off her helmet and flew to meet him. It was too late. Nergal had a bare, green finger hovering just inches over the boy's neck.

"Cool your jets, Miss Artul," Nergal said in a threatening voice. "You've led us well enough, but I'm taking over for now. These negotiations are going my way."

"This is ridiculous, Nergal. Please!" Talisha yelled.

Nergal smiled.

"Cool your jets, Miss Artul." Nergal warned. "Want to further compound your guilt by getting this boy killed? Back away."

Bluebird glared at the both of them. "Do as he says, bounty hunter."

Talisha complied, even as her stomach churned. She slowly drifted to the ground. Her shoulders shook as she stared, open-mouthed and sweating.

Nergal turned to Melanson and called out. "Do you know why I was quarantined on this planet? They were going to have me executed but couldn't safely dispense of my corpse. I'm a carrier for just about every nasty virus and pathogen in the galaxy. It'd take but a single touch to kill your boy. A gruesome fate, but you can save him. Give me the key."

Tears ran into Melanson's beard. His large hands shook as he fell to his knees, crying. "I don't know where it is. Maybe Ching Shih took it. I don't know. Please, don't hurt my boy."

"And why should I believe you?" Nergal said.

"Because," Melanson sputtered through his tears. "He is all I have left."

Nergal stared. His expression was full of pain. Talisha recognized that look, one of pure loneliness. How many years had Nergal spent here, isolated, cut off from anyone who might have loved him? She'd undergone a similar transformation, one that had killed off every relationship she'd ever valued. Her heart quaked with fear as she recognized with that loneliness came desperation and the ability to do the unthinkable.

Don't do it. I know you're hurting, but don't do it. For all that's inside you that's still good, don't hurt this boy.

"I believe you, Melanson." Nergal pulled his hand away from Jefferson's neck.

"I'm certain Ching Shih has the bloody key," Melanson said "I'll help you find her. Just let me have him back."

Nergal took a deep breath and lowered his eyelids.

"I'm going to give you a gift," he said. "The freedom that comes from having nothing left to lose."

Melanson's eyes bulged. "No!"

Talisha screamed, knowing what was coming next but powerless to stop it. Nergal clamped his fingers over Jefferson's face and shoved him from the spyder. All watched as Jefferson fell, the telltale green marks of the infection already spreading across his face where Nergal had touched him. Melanson rushed to catch him. Jefferson fell into his arms, coughing and sputtering. Melanson brushed his hair aside, shaking and quivering in horror.

"No, no, no," he pleaded. "Don't do this. Don't leave me alone."

Boils appeared alongside the areas where Jefferson had been touched. A black and green discoloration spread from his face quickly overtaking the rest of his body. Blood trickled from the sides of his mouth. His body went into ugly, violent spasms. All the while, Melanson held him close.

"I'm scared," Jefferson said, his voice weak and hoarse. "Make it stop."

Melanson raised his machete high over his head. "Go. Be with the Mother."

With a painful roar, Melanson brought it down on Jefferson's neck, decapitating him. It was a better fate than leaving him to suffer Nergal's disease. Melanson's shoulders heaved and with a mighty sob he grabbed his assault rifle and aimed at Nergal, showering him with a spray of bullets. Several shots pierced Nergal through the chest and shoulders and he fell back into the spyder vehicle, full of holes and covered in blood. Cyrus marched forward, gunning down Melanson before anyone had a chance to react.

His body riddled with bullets, Melanson took a slow step in front of Jefferson's corpse. He'd barely the energy to kneel down and cup the boy's head in his hands. He fixed Talisha with a pained, weary look before collapsing into the dust. Nergal's spyder rose on its legs and retreated into the night. Talisha almost flew after him. Bluebird stopped her, placing a strong hand on her shoulder.

"He's critically wounded," Bluebird said. "He will not get far. There has been enough killing today."

Talisha turned her back on the dead bodies in the sand. "I'm going to check on Snidely. He wasn't doing so well when I last left him."

"You do that."

Bluebird's face was still as stone. It was the only sign that the events had left any impact on her. Her large boisterous smile had been replaced by a frightening stillness. Talisha placed her helmet back on her head and flew toward the tank. She wouldn't let the others see the horror in her eyes.

Rogers knelt in front Melanson's corpse. He removed his hat and pressed it against his chest.

"We should bury the dead," he said. "Least we can do."

"No." Bluebird stepped close behind him. "I am just as responsible for this. Melanson died like a warrior. We will erect a funeral pyre."

Talisha returned, shoulders stiff. Bluebird and Rogers stared as she approached. Her fists were clenched.

Bluebird's brow furrowed. "Now what?"

Talisha looked at them, and said in a tight voice, "Snidely's gone."

BLAKE SNIDELY HAD been due to check in with Plymouth for the past three hours. Per his assignment, failure to comply with this arrangement would mean he had died or failed in his mission. Madame Inspector elected to give him another three hours before considering his position terminated.

She'd not managed to pinpoint his allies aboard the Mayflower. That annoyed her more than anything else. She wasn't accustomed to having her authority challenged. Someone on this satellite had balls. It was her every intention to rip them from their scrotum.

Still, with Snidely out of the picture she no longer had to waste time indulging his ambitions. Madame Inspector could focus on rooting out this mole and getting inside the

Valran Temple. Her spidery fingers tapped quickly over the console in her office. She leaned back and took a drag from her long cigarette, the gears turning behind her eyes.

There were many who wanted to know the name of the Inspector. They dared not ask. She preferred to be represented by her title. A name meant she could be seen as a person, and not the face of everything her position of power presented. A person can be usurped, thwarted. Faceless power represented so much more.

Truth was, Madame Inspector had gone so long without so much as hearing her name uttered or using it in any conversation that it was almost lost to her. She was certain she hadn't forgotten it completely and that if compelled, could restore it from the buried cobwebs of her mind. She had no need of it, and so it remained buried, just beyond reach.

Memories of her childhood were beyond her grasp, as well as any personal relationships she might have had. She was certain at one time she had been loved, but what was the point in thinking on it? Even memories were useless to her now.

A face appeared before her in lights hovering over her desk. It was the Chinese pirate. Madame Inspector made no attempt to mask her disgust.

"Madame Inspector," Ching Shih said, tonelessly. "I'm impressed you were able to contact me."

"We reversed the tracking on your little virus. There's a chink in your armor."

"I see. What do you want?"

"A chance to negotiate peacefully. I've no reason to destroy you just yet."

"Negotiations that begin with threats are far from peaceful," Ching Shih said. Her stoic expression never faltered. It was the ultimate sign of contempt.

Madame Inspector leaned forward. "Just assuring you of the parameters of the dialogue."

"They're noted."

"Good."

"You want access to the Valran Temple."

"You're very astute," Madame Inspector said. "If my people are correct about what lies inside, there's no reason for us to fight."

"If *my* people are correct, you have every reason." Ching Shih smirked. "I'd be a fool to treat you as anything other than hostile."

"So there'll be no negotiating, I take it."

"Once upon a time, I was the type to cut deals. I was the best of them," Ching said. "Then everything I loved was taken from me and I realized the true nature of diplomacy."

"And that is?"

"It's used by those who don't have the means to take what they want." Ching smiled, revealing a set of yellow and blackened teeth. "Madame Inspector, if you could truly take what you need from me, there would be no contact. Only death."

Madame Inspector stood from her chair. She placed both hands flat on her desk. Her eyes were cold and vicious.

"I will give you a chance to back away from an otherwise fatal mistake," Madame Inspector snarled. "I'm interested in one thing and one thing only, profit. Minimizing loss, while maximizing gain, *that* is profit. Don't let your pride lead you into doing something foolish."

Ching Shih actually laughed at her. No one had ever laughed at her before. She wasn't entirely sure how to react. All she knew was an unpleasant sickness boiling deep inside of her, and a desire to make that laughter stop at any cost.

"I am familiar with profit," Ching Shih's voice was drenched in malice. "I would never negotiate with you. Eat shit and die, Madame Inspector. When we meet face to face, I will cut your tongue from your mouth."

The line went dead. Madame Inspector had a second of staring at the old pirate's face, frozen in laughter before it and the screen turned to black. She dug her fingernails into her desk and dragged them across the surface. It would be better to delegate these next steps to someone less emotionally compromised. If they failed, she could terminate them and keep moving down the line until she finally got what she wanted. That'd be the smart thing to do.

But no one had ever laughed at her before.

Madame Inspector had put her entire life into this company. Those who managed to climb so far didn't just retire. They knew too much. They vanished. She had no intention of vanishing.

She leaned back in her chair and took a long deep drag of her cigarette. Every potential year left of her life flashed before her eyes as she exhaled. Clouds of smoke billowed around her head. She'd allowed herself so few indulgences. The thought that she might be willing to throw her entire life away both frightened and excited her.

She called for her secretary. "Make an announcement to ready the fleet. We're going to war."

Never before had Plymouth declared open war on a planet. Never before had the entirety of their fleet been summoned. Such a colossal disregard for protocol would bring down the fury of her superiors. She smiled. Her career and her life were over. She was free to kick-start the apocalypse.

No one would laugh at her again.

CHING SHIH STOOD at the port bow, face stern and calculating. One of her crewmen approached her holding a datapad. She retrieved it from him wordlessly.

"It's just as you said, Captain," he said. "Plymouth cruisers are flying in from all across the galaxy. The full fleet should be here in a day or two."

"And the others?"

"The IGF military have already been contacted about a heavily armed presence heading toward Archimedes IV. We expect their arrival shortly."

Ching Shih's lips curled into a terrifying smile. "Everyone should be proud of their hard work. Bring out the flagons of Aurelian Whiskey. The revenge of the Red Fleet is at hand. Tonight, we celebrate. Tomorrow, we kill."

TONIGHT, WHEN BLUEBIRD sang, nobody stopped her. Her voice was loud, guttural, and full of pain. She stood in front of a pyre erected for Melanson and his fallen raiders, her tears glistening in the light of the flickering flames.

Talisha sat several feet away, legs curled to her chest. She idly flicked through Snidely's datapad, idly scanning the contents into her helmet's database. Her knowledge of how to hack systems like the IGF's hadn't been enough to crack the encryption codes so Rogers helped get her into its files.

Plymouth had kept Snidely's information access to a bare minimum. Most of what she'd been able to uncover were coordinates leading to the actual location of the temple. If it was true that the Red Fleet had taken the key, she doubted their fragmented team could do anything about it now.

"Mind if I pick your brain about a few things?" Rogers said, sitting next to her.

"Go right ahead."

"Electromagnetic blast, huh?"

"Yeah. Disrupts psychic feedback."

"How many types of blasts you capable of?"

"Depends. I don't really understand how the technology works, but there're sequences that manufacture the generation of different energy types."

"All right." Rogers nodded. "Weird alien shit, I get it. What I wanna know is why you didn't do the same thing with the wyverns the other day?"

"Wouldn't have worked," Talisha said. "Wyverns were commissioned specifically to embark on a planet constantly covered in electromagnetic storms. Needed something that wouldn't short out. Anyway, it might have damaged your systems."

"So you're not an uncaring person normally," Rogers said. "You actually give a damn about who's in a squad with you."

Talisha looked at him. Her eyes were sad. "Always."

Rogers turned his face to the sky. "So what was different with Melanson's Raiders?"

"Melanson was no innocent." Talisha turned her attention back to the datapad, pursing her lips. "The IGF are responsible for the destruction of this planet. Melanson orchestrated the whole damn thing."

Bluebird turned to face her, stopping mid-song. She moved toward Talisha with a perplexed expression. "What?"

Talisha nodded. "Yup. They knew about the Valran Temple but were afraid the megacorps would discover it if they launched an expedition. They worked to destabilize the governments here on Archimedes IV. Funneling weapons to rebel insurgents, staging a coup, eventually inciting the war that tore this planet apart."

Rogers whistled. "Ain't that beat all. So, when the dust settled and they finally came back to claim their prize, it gobbled them up."

Talisha stared into the flames. "They destroyed this planet. I thought it'd be fitting that it destroy them. Melanson especially."

"You dealt justice as you saw fit," Bluebird said, folding her arms over her chest. "And innocents got swallowed by it."

"I'm sorry," Talisha said, her voice low. "I was so angry I couldn't think."

Bluebird sat between them. She then surprised both Rogers and Talisha by wrapping her arms around them, pulling them close. She squeezed gently.

"I cannot discourage violence as a solution to injustice," she said. "But it's powerful, and once you start, you cannot stop. Be sure it's channeled in the right direction."

"You don't hate me?" Talisha sniffed.

"I have little use for hate," Bluebird said. "It takes too much energy."

"Don't you hate them Ingle fellas?" Rogers asked.

Bluebird's face turned to stone. "That is different."

They fell silent for the next several minutes. Bluebird kept their bodies warm in the harsh cold of the night air, occasionally rubbing their shoulders affectionately. No one had ever been so readily familial with Talisha, not even her own mother. It was nice.

"Cyrus has, uh, really taken to that body, hasn't he?" Rogers said after a minute, watching the wyvern patrol the edges of the camp.

"I am certain he appreciates not having to share for once," Bluebird said with a smile.

Rogers shook his head. His voice had a twinge of concern. "Cyrus never liked sharing much of anything if I'm perfectly honest. He's more the type to take what he likes. Giving him a body like that, damn. Might lead to trouble."

"He didn't seem so bad when I talked to him." Talisha shrugged. "A sentient wyvern though? Not sure the galaxy's ready for that."

"He wouldn't have to keep the wyvern," Rogers murmured. "Not really. I didn't think about it at the time, but we could inhabit any piece of technology we wanted."

"No wonder Snidely was so eager to get his hands on you," Talisha said. "You're something completely new, cowboy. What are your plans?"

"Pardon?"

Talisha sighed and leaned forward, rubbing her shoulders. "Snidely's gone. Likely dead or gone full mutant-bug-thing by this point. That's our only contact with Plymouth. I know missions like this. No liaison, no paycheck."

"You don't seem ready to leave the planet yourself," Bluebird noted.

"Money or not, I want to know what's inside that temple," Talisha said. She gazed at her gauntlet, then clenched her fist. "I'd like to know more about the Valran. Figure out my legacy, I guess."

Bluebird smacked her on the back. "A worthy quest for a fine warrior. I'll accompany you. What about you, Sheriff?"

"Not a sheriff anymore," Rogers corrected. He sighed and shrugged his shoulders. "Thought about trying to get off this planet. Not sure where I'd go. I'll hang around a mite longer I guess. What'cha think, Cyrus?"

The wyvern turned slowly around to face them. "So long as I get to kill more people, I'm in."

Rogers turned to Bluebird and Talisha. "See what I mean by how creepy that guy's getting?"

"I'll keep an eye on him," Bluebird said, brow furrowed.

"Still, having him on our side is gonna make things a bit easier," Talisha said. "The Red Fleet won't be as easy to bamboozle. If the rumors about Ching Shih are true, she's a ruthless and calculating opponent."

"Thank you for the compliment," an amplified voice boomed over the desert.

All of them looked in the direction of the speakers to see a fleet of ships and schooners decloaking several feet in front of them. They were ambushed on all sides by red sails. Talisha had heard of such technology but had never seen anything like a fleet of a hundred vessels suddenly materializing before her. One of the schooners drifted closer. An old Chinese woman stood on the bow with her hands wrapped behind her back. She stood tall and imposing with her armored robes billowing in the wind.

"I assume I warrant no introduction," Ching Shih continued. "You've slaughtered my allies. You will take their place, or you will die."

They were led aboard Ching Shih's schooner at gunpoint by several long-barreled, high-precision rifles. It wasn't the first time Talisha had been taken prisoner. The rising surge of adrenaline within her had to be controlled, not suppressed. Adrenaline was useful for keying her focus, allowing her mind's eye to take snapshots of important information. She'd chosen to bide her time and ride this out, see where things took her. She hoped Bluebird and Rogers would be smart enough to do the same. They seemed to be following her lead.

Cyrus was the only one she worried about. That wyvern body he'd acquired could let him do some massive damage on the Red Fleet, but they outnumbered him a hundred to one. He'd be destroyed in minutes. Even now he looked like a cornered animal, growling at the ship's cannons aimed in his direction.

Ching Shih's personal guard were nearly as threatening as she was—warriors in golden power armor illuminated by red neon lights around their chest and helm. In one hand they carried powerful lances with small blasters at the tip, and in the other, shields made up of a crackling electric barrier. There were only the four of them, an elite squad that kept her surrounded with their impenetrable might. Two moved to disarm the new passengers. Ching Shih stopped them with a raised hand.

"No," she said. "They are allies. Not prisoners."

"Sure as heck feels like it," Rogers said. "No disrespect intended."

Ching Shih bowed solemnly. "Security precautions. You are dangerous folk."

"Would we still be alive if we weren't?" Talisha raised an eyebrow.

She smiled. "Of course not. You would have been shot instantly. Come into my quarters. We've much to speak about."

"What about our other metal friend?" Bluebird gestured to Cyrus.

"My office is impressive, but it's not *that* big. He'll have to wait outside."

"I like her sense of humor," Bluebird whispered to Rogers.

Rogers shrugged. "You do have a fondness for *big* jokes."

Bluebird's cheeks puffed from having to contain a hearty guffaw. What released was an undignified squeaking sound as air spilled out the sides of her mouth. Talisha buried her face in her palm. There went her last hope of matching Ching Shih's imposing dignity.

Ching Shih beckoned to them, drawing to her captain's quarters at the edge of the schooner. "Hurry, my crew has a celebration planned for the evening. I won't want to keep them waiting."

"Celebration?" Talisha raised an eyebrow.

Ching Shih's fingers rubbed the hilt of a sword tucked into her scarlet sash. She licked her lips, and locked eyes with each of her guests.

"This is a special night for us," she said. "And I am feeling generous."

Two of her guards remained stationed outside, while the other two followed them into Ching Shih's chambers. Along the walls were decorative weapons and various banners and silks. A suit of ancient Chinese armor was displayed regally in a glass case on the right side of the room. Just adjacent to it was a small prayer shrine and Buddhist altar.

Ching Shih gestured to a set of chairs around a table. "This room is only private during times of meditation and prayer. Any other time it is a place for me to seek council among my most trusted advisors. That you are even allowed to look upon it should be taken as a sign of great courtesy. See that you reciprocate."

Talisha nodded, taking her seat. "Understood."

Ching Shih waved her hand over the table as the lights in the room dimmed. Lights shimmered over the table's surface, creating a holographic representation of the planet. She pointed to a massive satellite orbiting the space around the planet.

"You should be familiar with the Plymouth Corporation," she said. "They hired you to get them access to the Valran Temple. Given that Blake Snidely is no longer with you, it's safe to assume that's no longer on the table."

"You do your homework, that's fer sure," Rogers said breathlessly.

Ching Shih continued, "What you are looking at is a representation of a cloaked satellite they've had circling the planet for some time now. When the IGF became aware of the Valran Temple, so did Plymouth. This is their final solution should anyone but themselves enter the temple, a doomsday weapon capable of destroying all life on this planet."

"Do you have access to its design?" Bluebird asked, rubbing her jaw.

"We have detailed blueprints," Ching Shih said, flicking her fingers across the image to change the display to that of a schematic. "Do you know something I should?"

Bluebird stood and reached across the table. She pointed to the weaponry at the center-end of the satellite. The circular shape for funneling vast amounts of plasma was unnervingly familiar to her.

"It is the same design as Ethel, my plasma cannon," she said. Her jaw locked. "I am certain of it."

"If Plymouth really does own Ingle, that'd certainly make sense," Talisha said.

"This goes beyond that," Bluebird fumed. "Securing the rights to produce that cannon for Ingle's paramilitary division was my last assignment for the Sapphire Knights before everything went to hell. They never once produced any cannons. Mine is all that exists in galaxy."

"Agda Valencia," Ching Shih cooed, reclining in her seat. "I thought you looked familiar. You don't look like your old picture anymore with your hair and facial scarring, I must say. You were a war hero, if I recall. I'm sorry about your wife."

"They killed her," Bluebird fumed. "Dragged her into the streets and beat her to death."

Talisha stared, open-mouthed. "Big Blue...I'm so sorry."

Bluebird had drifted into her own little world, eyes glazing over. "Ingle's higher-ups feared my reputation as a war hero would fuel Sascha's political career. There were multiple death threats if she didn't divorce and denounce me to the public. She was originally against it, but I made her go along. In the end, while on assignment, my own squad attempted to assassinate me. That was when I found out what had happened. That's when I came home to find her butchered just outside our house.

"Corporate greed destroyed my life, and ended hers," Bluebird said through angry tears, her shoulders shaking. "And these cowards are at the heart of it!"

She pounded her fist on the table, leaving a sizable dent in its surface. Two of the guards motioned forward, but Ching Shih waved them off. They returned to their positions.

"Plymouth's crimes against humanity are innumerable," Ching Shih said in a quiet voice. "Their weapons have devastated entire worlds. Their wars have earned them endless profits while destroying countless lives. They make even the horrors of the IGF look saintly. It is for this reason that they must be destroyed."

Talisha stared as the pirate's words dawned on her. "That's what this is all about," she said. "You're not interested in the temple at all. This is about revenge."

"You aren't listening!" Ching Shih bellowed, rising swiftly to her feet. "It is about removing a threat to every man, woman, and child in the galaxy. That very same weapon destroyed our planet, our livelihood. It decimated our people. Imagine what they would do with the technology of the Valran."

"They already have a planet-destroying weapon. How much worse could it get?" Rogers said. "Not to belittle anyone's pain here, but they seem pretty untouchable."

"Plymouth demands absolute secrecy in order to maintain its hold on the galaxy. If dragged into the public eye, they would be forced into open conflict with every armed force they've attempted to strong-arm and blackmail over the years." Ching Shih sat down once more and flicked through the projected images. "They are mobilizing their fleet upon this planet in light of Snidely's failure. The IGF has also begun to arrive in this system."

"They've been monitoring the planet," Talisha said. "Of course they'll be here. Everyone is after that temple."

Ching Shih drew up a detailed plan of a projected battle between three large armies, "Plymouth believes I have the means to enter the temple, which means that the Red Fleet will be the first to draw their forces, but once the IGF see them attempting to break into the temple, they will surely join the conflict."

"You want us to break into the temple for you," Bluebird said. "Uncover what's inside while you keep the outside forces distracted."

"It's a win-win situation," Ching Shih explained. "Provide a service to the galaxy by decimating a corrupt militaristic force and destroying a vile shadow corporation, then we profit off ancient alien technology."

"Yeah we made a similar deal with Melanson's people early this evening and it didn't go so hot for anyone." Rogers shook his head. "Not sure I like cutting deals where this temple is concerned. I'd like just as much to clear on out of here."

"You don't have a choice in the matter, robot." Ching Shih said threateningly. "Melanson and his raiders were going to be my task force assigned to infiltrate the temple. You killed him. Now you will take his place."

"I assume that means you have the key?" Talisha asked. "Melanson didn't have it on him."

Ching Shih raised an unconvinced brow. "He never gave it to me. Wasn't the trusting sort. Wonder why?"

Talisha rolled her eyes. "He insisted you took it. Given the circumstances, I'm inclined to believe him."

"Undermining my alliance with him was not in my best interests," Ching Shih said, frowning. "I didn't let him on to that, of course. It would have been bad business. My people did leave a tracker on the key. It's how I was able to find you. You're lying to me."

That last bit was added with a flick of her talons. Her body language had shifted. She'd adopted a parted stance, as if readying for combat. Talisha watched one hand dip below the table, likely ready to draw her blade.

"I am not lying, I swear it." Talisha's voice rose an octave. "There's nothing I could take from you. You are holding all the cards in this negotiation."

"That's what Melanson thought and look what happened to him," Ching Shih snapped. "You're a clever one, Talisha Artul. What's more you're as ruthless as your mother. I'd be foolish to treat you as anything less than a threat to my enterprise. Where is that key?"

The two guards stepped forward, brandishing their lances. Bluebird whirled around, hands locking around their weapons. Talisha retrieved her blaster from her hip and stood, her cannon aimed at Ching Shih and her blaster at the guards. Ching Shih's sword was drawn in an instant.

"Aw heck with it!" Rogers yelled.

He reached beneath his poncho and slammed a large black pyramid onto the table. All weapons relaxed as every eye darted sharply to the object. Talisha stared first at the pyramid, then turned her look of confused betrayal onto the cowboy.

"What've you done, Rogers?" she whispered.

Rogers collapsed in his seat, slamming his hat next to the pyramid. He wiped his brow and shrugged his shoulders. He never looked more human than in that moment. He seemed utterly exhausted.

"How many folks got killed over this thing?" he said. "Sure seemed like a lot. Now, I've seen some pretty bad humans in my time, but lately, seems to me like y'all just can't be trusted with this shit. You'll end entire worlds over it. I thought maybe we oughtn't open the temple. Stop folks from killing each other."

Ching Shih sheathed her sword. She walked around the table and snatched the pyramid in her grasp. She turned once more to Rogers and laughed in his face. He looked away, unable to meet the harshness of her gaze.

"You really are sentient," Ching Shih mocked. Her smile vanished. "Capable of human ignorance *and* arrogance. Your programming is something else, cowboy."

"Jefferson died..." Talisha's words were quiet. "And you could have stopped it."

"I'm not sure it would've," Rogers said. "You saw the look in Nergal's eye. He wanted blood—just like everyone else in this room, even you. All you humans wanna do is kill each other. I was just foolish enough to think that you needed this friggin' rock to justify it."

He looked at Ching Shih.

"Might I be excused?" he asked, grabbing his hat. "I'll fight in your battle. Ain't gotta spend extra time convincing me, I ain't got no choice in the matter. I'm just another weapon to you people. It's all I'll ever be."

"Show him to a cabin," Ching Shih instructed one of her guards. She smiled as Rogers was escorted from her quarters. "Penchant for melodrama, that one. Probably learned it from all those old Western films."

Bluebird slumped into the chair, propped her elbows on the table, and dug her fingers into her hair. "I am very tired. It has been a long day."

Ching Shih sighed. "Very well. You may go for tonight. Talisha, I'd like a chance to speak to you privately before you depart."

"Yeah. Sure. Whatever." Talisha laid a weary palm against her forehead.

Bluebird gently touched Talisha's shoulder before sauntering out of the cabin.

Ching Shih directed her guards to leave them. She and Talisha sat across from each other in apprehensive silence. Ching Shih had her hand coiled around her face, staring at Talisha, appraising her. Talisha wanted to turn away from those eyes. "What do you want?" she asked.

Ching Shih stood. "Do you know how I was able to take the refugees of a fledgling empire and forge them into the galaxy's most feared criminal enterprise?"

"If I say yes, will you get to the point?"

Ching Shih turned her back on Talisha and stared at the suit of armor on the opposite end of the room. Her voice took on a withered tone, ill-suited for a terrifying space pirate. It sounded more like a reminiscing grandmother.

"Information, Miss Artul." She returned to face her with a somber expression. "It is the only currency that matters. When you venture into the temple tomorrow, I want you to keep whatever technology you find, or better yet, leave it there to rot."

"But you said?"

"My people are expecting a treasure trove of guns and jewels," Ching Shih muttered, rolling her eyes. "But introducing something new like that to the galaxy changes the game. If we carry bigger guns, so will our enemies. We may not look it, but we are a fragmented people. An escalation of armaments would destroy us."

Talisha squinted. She struggled to understand this woman's motivations. "So what is it that you really want?"

"I'm no fool," Ching Shih said, pacing about the room. "The galaxy is on the verge of a new arms race. Our only chance at survival is by choosing our role within the new era. I want everything you have on the Valran Empire: their history, their language, their religion, and culture."

Talisha cringed. "I don't even have access to all of that with years of information stored into my helmet. Why would I give it to you?"

"I've nothing to bargain with," Ching Shih admitted, her shoulders slumping. "I could threaten your life again, but I've a feeling that'd get redundant. I'm going to do something I've never done in my life. Talisha Artul, I humiliate myself before you. I'm begging you...help us."

Talisha stood quickly. "Excuse me?"

Ching Shih laughed. "I'm sorry. You must think me a silly old woman. You might be right."

"I don't understand how knowing more about the Valran will help you," Talisha said. "People have begged me for this shit before, lady. Some were just trying to manipulate me."

"Do not insult my pride," Ching Shih snapped. She calmed a bit, taking a deep breath. "I'm sorry. Let me explain myself."

"Yeah." Talisha folded her arms over her chest. "I think you had better."

"That temple is opening," Ching Shih said, leaning against the table. "If not us, then Plymouth or the IGF, or someone else. Other temples will be found. Information about the Valran will become high in demand. If my people can control the flow of that information, we can retreat to our own private corner to hide from the oblivion that will come to the galaxy."

"You really think it's going to be that bad?" Talisha murmured.

Ching Shih fixed her with a harsh gaze. "I've made a long career out of predicting worst-case scenarios, child."

Talisha sighed. "It's not that I don't feel for your plight."

"But you don't trust me." Ching Shih nodded. "I understand."

Talisha walked to the cabin door. She froze in front of it, then lowered her head, shoulders heavy. "I'll think about it. All right?"

"Then that is all I can ask," Ching Shih whispered. "Good night, bounty hunter."

Talisha left. Ching Shih stumbled into her seat at the table, fingers brushing over the panels. The holographic map vanished, leaving her in dim darkness. She removed the decorative crown from her forehead. It'd become so heavy these past few years.

Chapter Six

NERGAL DROVE THE tank far into the desert. He did his best to bandage his wounded body along the way, hoping the serum would begin to heal him. It seemed that over the years he'd developed a resistance to its curative properties. He could feel the wounds closing, but they were agonizingly slow, and the process torturous.

Eventually the tank ran out of fuel, coming to a creaking halt. He swore loudly, banging his fist against the controls. It'd all gone to shit. Sometimes it felt like the universe itself were conspiring against him, making a mess of all his plans. All he wanted was a place off this barren hellhole. Was that so difficult?

Clutching at his wounds, he clamored out of the tank and stumbled into the frigid winds. He'd been forced to discard most of his protective suit in order to bandage himself with tattered fragments of his shirt. He kept the coat he'd stolen from the tavern wrapped about his skinny shoulders as meager protection from the harsh atmosphere.

He'd tried to carry the rest of his weapons and chemical apparatus, but they proved burdensome, and were soon abandoned. All he had left was a vial of his precious serum. It'd be the last till he could find a working laboratory again.

The serum had kept him alive, but only just. The disease still churned and grew and multiplied within him. His lips cracked and peeled, and his gums bled fiercely if he gritted his teeth too tight. His thin gangrenous limbs protested this desert trek. He suffered every moment he was alive.

It would be so easy to collapse into the dust and rot here, leaving a vengeful corpse for some unlucky bandit to loot. His nest of diseases would live on infecting others long past his death. His suffering would at last be at an end. If there was an afterlife, he might see Dalton again.

Yet Nergal fought against extinction. He was still alive, after everything he'd been through and all he'd suffered. A withered husk of a man to be sure, but somehow still breathing, still capable of wreaking havoc to any who crossed him. He swore under his breath that if he died here and now, he'd find the high courts of the universe and sue.

For Doctor Isaac Nergal, death was always a possibility, but never an option. He was a festering sack of pestilence and death living an unlife full of torture and regret. More than that he was pissed. Anger and hatred are unpleasant emotions, but they provided the fires that sustained him, and kept propelling him forward through the darkness.

When he finally collapsed three hours later, it was with his fists clenched, still struggling to pull himself forward. He'd managed to crawl several paces, even after his legs had stopped carrying him. He kept his eyes open until weariness forced them closed. The last he saw before surrendering to unconsciousness were hands white as a corpse reaching down to grab him.

NERGAL'S EYELIDS FLUTTERED open. He was covered by a blanket and lying next to a warm furnace. Two scents filled his nostrils, baked beans over an open stove and the stench of death and carnage. Each left him nauseous. He rose slowly, letting the wool blanket fall from around his shoulders. He'd been stripped naked, and he hurried to cover himself up again.

It was a small house, barely insulated from the outside elements. It'd suffered the planet-side wars over the years, but somehow still stood intact. A host of survivors had taken shelter here over the years, leaving all manner of waste and refuse and the occasional graffiti to mark their passing. Their remains were scattered across the living room floor.

Nergal surveyed the bodies hurled across the room. The first body was a middle-aged man lying directly across from where the front door had been ripped from its hinges, then haphazardly shoved back into place. His intestines were spilling into his lap. The next body was a young white woman holding an empty carbine. She was left pinned to the wall by a chair leg protruding from her chest. There were three more corpses stacked in a pile just a few feet away. Their features were indistinguishable after someone had smeared their faces against the hot surface of the furnace.

From the bloody trail leading from the living room to the hall, Nergal could only assume there were more bodies scattered throughout the house. He rubbed his eyelids and hoped that whatever had wreaked all this mayhem wasn't interested in coming for him next.

"Oh good, you're awake." The voice was familiar, and yet different. The vocal chords had shifted, grown coarser and meaner. "I was worried I might have to force-feed you."

Nergal stared hard as a figure stepped into the room. He wore a pair of tattered black pants and heavy combat boots clearly stolen from one of the many corpses left strewn across the house. His skin was white as paper, and there were four insect-like legs bound in a black hairy carapace protruding from his back. There was no color to his eyes, just an unending blackness.

Despite all its mutations, the face was unmistakable. Blake Snidely smiled, revealing a row of sharp pointed teeth and the hint of mandibles growing along the inside of his mouth. Nergal shook his head in disbelief.

"Your serum," Snidely said. "It had some rather interesting effects."

"You dressed my wounds," Nergal noted. "Took my clothes."

"They were dripping wet from ice," Snidely said. "You would have frozen to death."

"That's not what concerns me." Nergal's eyebrows furrowed. "You should be dead."

Snidely brushed a strand of gray hair away from his face. Something about the mutation had shifted Nergal's perceptions of the man. He was still a frail, bone-thin figure, but he seemed so much more at home with it all. His hips swayed with sensuous confidence as he approached, fingers brushing along Nergal's bumpy cheek. Nergal almost recoiled instinctively.

"I'm immune to your disease now," Snidely whispered. "Isn't that a hoot?"

Nergal's gave an uneasy smirk. There was nervousness in his eyes. "Previous occupants had some issues with letting you stay?"

Snidely chuckled. "If you saw a pale white monster approaching your door holding a naked green plague man, what would be your first reaction?"

"Shoot on sight," Nergal said with a casual shrug. "I'm guessing the critter infection has left you with some added benefits."

"I'm very fast," Snidely said. "And well, the strength speaks for itself. Exciting part is they never even see me coming. I was nary a blip on their radar when I shut out the lights to this place. I crawled about on the ceiling to rip their heads from their necks."

"I thought you had a proclivity for violence." Nergal licked his lips. "It's nice to see you coming into your own. What do you intend to do now?"

Snidely sat on the bed next to him. He took Nergal's hands in his own. Their fingers touched and Nergal's breath caught in his throat. He stared into Snidely's eyes. Physical contact after so many years of isolation, it was almost frightening.

"My time with Plymouth is over," Snidely said. "I'd be an experiment to them at best. More likely a liability to be expunged. I'm naught more than a monster now."

"Being a monster..." Nergal's voice fell to a timid whisper. "It isn't all terrible. I've found that at times it can be quite freeing."

Snidely wrapped an arm about him and slowly pressed Nergal against the bed. They stared at each other surrounded by filth and death. A macabre bond formed between them, one that can only be shared by the desperate and the unwanted, the hideous and reviled.

"It's a new world for me," Snidely said, pressing his forehead against Nergal's. He straddled the other man's legs. "Don't make me walk it alone."

Nergal laughed. "And to think when we first met, I hated you."

"A lot has changed," Snidely said with hissing laughter.

Nergal reached with both hands clamped around the back of Snidely's head and kissed him. The strange jagged teeth cut along the inside of Snidely's mouth as blood ran down the back of his throat. That made it all the more freeing, to abandon themselves into the twisted copulation of their own abhorrence.

"There will be no place in the universe for us," Nergal said breathlessly.

"We'll make our own," Snidely responded, caressing his cheeks. "The Valran were once the most powerful force in the galaxy. That power should be ours."

TALISHA WAS ESCORTED to a cabin on one of the schooners. The general carousing and sloshing drinks outside left most of the bunks empty. Only Bluebird and Rogers shared the room with her. She waved half-heartedly to them before falling with a slump into a bunk nearest them.

"What did the pirate want?" Bluebird asked. She was lying on her back with her hands behind her head, staring at the ceiling.

Talisha shrugged. "My culture."

Bluebird raised an eyebrow. "What does a pirate want with the disgraced house of Artul?"

"I think she means the Valran, ya big dummy," Rogers muttered. His voice was muffled through his hat resting over his face as he lay with his legs propped up against the wall.

"Yeah, that." Talisha exhaled wearily. "I meant the Valran, sorry. She thinks if I tell her their culture and history, she can sell it off in the coming years to the highest bidder. She's convinced it's the only way her people will survive."

"Sounds manipulative," Bluebird sniffed. "You have no responsibility to these people, Talisha. You know that right?"

"I don't owe anyone anything," Talisha said, and laughed a bit. "Doesn't mean I don't have, well...ethical issues."

"I'll give you some simple ethics," Bluebird said, propping herself up by her elbow. "Reciprocity. What has she done for you?"

"If everyone acted like that no one would do anything for anyone." Talisha removed chunks of her armor.

"That's how the world operates, youngin'," Rogers said. He rolled over in bed. "Aw, don't mind me, I'm just feeling sorry for myself."

"It's shit," Talisha spat back. She removed the rest of her armor, save for her arm cannon. She refused to be left completely defenseless."Anyway, weren't you all about protecting innocent and poor folks?"

Bluebird groaned. "This is not same thing. You are one woman. This is heavily armed fleet of pirates with some of the best technology and software in the entire galaxy. I do not think they are hurting for aid."

"That's not how Ching Shih made it sound," Talisha said, throwing her hands in the air in frustration. "But you might be right."

"That brings me to another thing." Bluebird stood and folded her hands over her chest. "What she asks of you is no small favor. She wants to use your culture for capital gain."

"But it's not mine," Talisha groaned. She clutched her hands to her head and wanted to scream. "Am I being selfish? I feel ownership of this shit."

"The Valran aren't with us," Bluebird said. "True. But they entrusted your mother with their heritage. She passed it onto you. It's your choice. You shouldn't let some stranger bully you into thinking you owe them something you don't."

"About that," Talisha said. "Outside of Mom and me? Not many people actually believe the Valran exist, and those that do aren't concerned with their culture or religions. I might be letting it die with me if I don't share it."

"I'm going to bed. Y'all are making my head hurt," Rogers called out and rolled over onto his side to face the wall.

Bluebird whistled and scratched the back of her neck. "You have a lot to think about, little bounty hunter. It is your decision after all. You want to do the right thing, and I respect that, but it's not always so cut-and-dry. You have to choose the avenue of least harm and live with those consequences."

"If I make the wrong choice?"

"If you do? Don't whine about it. Fix it." Bluebird moved back to her bunk and climbed in, causing it to creak noisily under her weight. Her feet reached well over the edge of the mattress. "Get some sleep, little one."

TALISHA'S NIGHT WAS miserable. There were times when her body burned and she had to throw the covers across the room, only to retrieve them moments later as ice gripped her from the inside out. Her mind had trouble differentiating whether or not she was asleep or awake, drifting in and out of an uneasy state of half-consciousness.

Jefferson's face flashed through her dreams, bloody and weeping. She stood amidst the burning wreckage of a vast city surrounded by corpses while the looming specter of her mother's face held sway over all. Talisha ran past a horde of the screaming dead until the bodies clamoring for her aid grew too numerous and she had to fly above them.

Rising high into space she saw a gradient vision of amber and orange. Fading into view was the Plymouth satellite with its orbital cannon pointed at the planet below. Talisha screamed at it, even as a massive hand dragged it out of the sky. It melted into the form of a familiar arm cannon, and she saw the distinctive shape of a Valran helmet appear in the atmosphere. The helmet lifted, and it was her own face staring back at her. Talisha held her hands protectively in front of her eyes as her giant doppelganger fired the cannon at the planet, incinerating all.

She woke midscream.

Rogers had a steady hand on her shoulder. "Easy, darlin'. Bit early for screaming."

"Sorry." She placed a quivering hand against her forehead. "My cocktail of issues has gotten irritating, to say the least."

"That being said," Rogers said. "Might ya get that cannon out of my face?"

Sometime in the moment it'd taken him to shake her from her nightmare, she'd charged her arm cannon and had it placed directly under his jaw. She swore and lowered her arm, apologizing profusely. He stood and scratched his forehead.

"I'm sorry," she said for the third time. She took a deep breath and ran her fingers through her hair. "I could've killed you."

"You need to get a grip, cowgirl." Rogers turned his back on her and went back to his bunk. "They're promising a war today."

"I know. I know." Talisha began putting on her armor. She stole a glance at Rogers. He was sitting on the edge of his bunk with his head buried in his hands. "You all right?"

"Thinking I know why I got drawn to old Western types," he said. "Men. Human men, they cry. Real life people cry. Even when they don't wanna admit it. Ya need to release all that horribleness somehow.

"I can't. I wasn't built to. I was built as an enforcer. Ya know there were supposed to be others like me? Some planet with a police brutality problem thought that maybe robots could police without prejudice."

"I've heard the story." Talisha moved closer to him. "The project was scrapped wasn't it?"

He nodded. "Yuppers. Turns out my progeny shared all the prejudices of those who programmed them. Whole line had to get scrapped. It's how the good folk of Dover Town were able to get an enforcer model so cheap.

"Now folks in Western films, least the men-folk, they don't cry. They feel and love, but they don't cry. It ain't realistic, 'cause human men cry."

"You saw them as machines," Talisha said. "They were like you."

"Like me," Rogers repeated. "Or like someone I wanted to be. I think those men could all feel pain, but they didn't know how to express it, save for by up and shooting someone. They took all that mess inside them and went and protected people with it. Thought that's what I wanted to be."

"There's worse things in life to aspire to," Talisha said, sitting down beside him. "You're not a bad person, Rogers."

"I'm not a person," he growled. "And if I was, I don't wanna be like the folks in those films. Even the best of them, they know nothing but killing. The more I become like my heroes, the less I wanna have anything to do with them."

"I know exactly where you're coming from," Talisha said wincing. Her shoulders drooped, like a heavy weight had crashed against them.

Rogers chuckled a bit. "Can only imagine. Living up to the legacy of the great Talisha Artul's gotta have its drawbacks."

"You spend your whole life trying to be like someone," she said. "Then one day, you look in the mirror and realize that you've succeeded in every way imaginable, but somehow you still hate yourself."

"Took the words right out of my mouth, but at least you can cry."

"Which leads to dehydration-induced headaches," Talisha countered. "Tears aren't all they're cracked up to be."

"No," he shrugged. "I guess not. Listen, about yesterday..."

"Don't worry about it," she said. "We both made mistakes. I think, I'm also learning I'm not the hero I've always wanted to be."

"I don't believe in fate," Rogers said, rising to his feet. "But it's a humdinger of a coincidence us being two souls coming together like this."

Talisha returned to her bunk to begin putting on the rest of her armor. She turned to face him. "Sure is. What do you think it means?"

He retrieved his hat from his bunk and placed it over his head. "I dunno. Reckon maybe if we don't like becoming the people who inspired us, we should become something else. Maybe we've just outgrown our heroes. Think it's high time we stepped it up a notch?"

Talisha's smile faded. "I'd like to, but I'm not sure how."

Rogers shrugged his shoulders. "We'll figure it out. Hopefully. Maybe we can look out for each other. Keep the other honest."

"Accountability," she said. "Maybe that's what I've been missing. Mom hammered into me the lone-wolf mentality so hard that I never thought about what I might be missing out on."

"And what's that?"

"A friend."

She stretched out her gauntleted hand. He clasped it heartily. Then his fingers braced hers for a moment. He swayed, staring at her hand.

"What's the matter?" she said.

He shook his head. "Sorry. Just...when you've got your armor on like that, your fingers are metal. Just like mine."

Talisha tightened the handshake. "No matter what happens today, I'll be watching out for you. Bluebird too."

"I'll be the wind at your back, cowgirl," he said. "You can count on that."

Chapter Seven

THE IGF HAD never mobilized so quickly. The fleet was ordered to depart under the command of Ajar Mattu. Their orders had come directly from the Council of Thirteen, the highest authority in the galaxy. He flexed his fingers into a tight black fist, taking only the briefest of comforts in the crinkling sounds of his leather gloves.

Commander Mattu had served sixteen years in the IGF Navy before being promoted as a high officer and lieutenant, eventually assuming the lofty command rank. There were few actions the IGF took without his direct knowledge or say-so. His practicality and intelligence had made him an ideal fit for the job.

The IGF higher-ups were so mired in bureaucracy and senseless political squabbling it'd made an inept laughing stock of the largest military fighting force in the galaxy. It'd take them months to deploy to a routine distress call, often too late to be of help to anyone. Mattu had spent most of his command post railing against unnecessary restrictions and red tape in an effort to speed the process and deliver critical aid. Many of his peers blamed him for the consistent reliance upon outside help from bounty hunters and mercenaries, after all, it was he who'd first called upon the services of the first Talisha Artul. He'd argued that if the IGF were free to offer assistance to those in need of it, then all bounty hunters would be driven out of their profession, as there would be no need of the government to rely upon them for aid.

Mattu was a tall dark-skinned man with graying hair kept wrapped beneath a black turban. He had a closely trimmed beard and goatee along the sides of his narrow, angular jaw. Most distinctive about his appearance was his left eye. It'd been shot out two decades ago in a firefight, and he was later fitted with a mechanical replacement. While his wealth and status gave him later access to more human-looking upgrades, he'd come to prefer it as a symbol of his fighting experience. The intimidating red glare it cast over a darkened room when he entered suited his flair for the dramatic.

He was handed a request to attend a private holo-screened meeting in his office to debrief him on the situation developing on Archimedes IV. He thanked the officer who delivered the message and retreated from the balcony, saluting his troops before he left. The rapid deployment of such a vast fleet had left them equally alarmed. It was important to at least instill some form of confidence. He would not let them see their commander so rattled.

Pale lights flickered off his shiny leather boots as he stormed through the halls of the drop-ship en route to his office. Nervous men and women under his command darted to and fro alongside him, rushing to their stations, carrying datapads and map coordinates. There was a general nervous atmosphere. The unprecedented had occurred.

Mattu's office doors swooshed open allowing him entry. He ducked into the door and sat at his desk. He took a moment to adopt a knowing, casual posture before answering the call from his superiors. With a hand tucked under his chin, he looked thoughtful, dangerous.

"Ajar Mattu, Commander of the 497th reporting."

A series of faces on different screens flickered into view, hovering just a few inches over his desk. Every time they appeared the same joke ran through his head. They really ought to warn people before popping into view like that. The sea of whiteness could blind somebody.

"A situation is developing on Archimedes IV that warrants the immediate attention of the Intergalactic Peacekeeping Force," the talking heads droned.

"A planet that was deemed hostile and out of our jurisdiction am I correct?" Mattu said with a raised eyebrow. "While I am all too eager to provide aid to the suffering souls that still live there, I've reasonable doubts that's why we're going."

"Your petty insolence wastes our time."

He shrugged. "No disrespect, just a question."

"What you're about to be told is to be kept top secret. If any evidence is found that you have leaked this intel to an outsider, you will be tried for treason and executed. Is that understood?"

Mattu blinked. He sat forward. "This is about the Valran, isn't it?"

"It's always about the Valran. For many years we have been aware of and guarded the sites of their many temples scattered across the galaxy. The one on Archimedes IV is most important to us, our operations upon the planet have been...delicate."

"You mean it's the only one you're interested in and every mission has resulted in a colossal failure."

"Shut up. Our scientists have confirmed that our detailed scans indicate dormant technology capable of inter-dimensional travel. The rumors that the Valran were a warp-capable species are true. As such it's been within the IGF's best interests and yours for us to gain access to this technology before one of the corporate goons has a chance to turn it into a marketable product."

Mattu scoffed. "My interests? We have the fastest ships in the galaxy. Using alien magic isn't going to get us deployed any faster when it's not within the Council's interests."

"Ease your tongue, Commander. Your reputation alone is all that keeps you in that seat. You can still be supplanted."

"I'm just jerking you around fellas." Mattu gave a good-natured smile. If he thought kissing up to them would have worked, he'd have laid it on a tad thicker, but it suited their egos more to believe he was a wild card that they could keep tamed. "So what's the situation developing on the planet surface? What's changed?"

"Twelve hours ago, the IGF received an anonymous report that a large fleet had begun to head toward the planet. Satellite imagery from the space around the planet confirmed those reports. We don't recognize them from any of the known corporations or licensed fighting forces within the galaxy."

"Extragalactic?"

"Unlikely, the speed isn't any faster than our own current vessels, nor are they capable of warp travel. We must assume for now that the force has been amassing in secret, beneath our very noses."

"Shadow corporation," Mattu said with a gravelly voice. "So I was right."

"Indeed."

"In that case I want a larger army to be deployed to the planet's surface. We have no idea what we're facing, and I'd like to avoid unnecessary casualties."

"Out of the question."

"But you said—"

"Protecting the Valran Temple is a priority, and an emergency one, which is why you've been granted the clearance to assemble an immediate deployment of forces. A larger force will raise questions as to why the Council approved the decision to deploy armaments on a planet deemed hostile and no longer under our protection.”

Mattu fumed. “You’re sending our men in with no intel. No aid or backup. This is a clusterfuck in the making!”

“You’ll only be setting up a defensive perimeter around the temple. You will handpick a squad of your finest men to make an excursion inside and recover the warp-technology.”

“A squad?” He shook his head in disbelief. “We don’t even know what’s in the temple. You’re asking me to split my forces from a perimeter when we’ve still no clue the size of the enemy force we’re to defend against. This is outrageous.”

“It is the will of the Council.”

Mattu stood. He pounded his fist against the desk, causing the coffee cup to rattle and spill several drops across the slick metallic surface. “Get your wrinkly white heads out of your wrinkly white butts and listen to me! I will not be held responsible for this shit-show.”

“Are you saying you wish to resign your post?”

There it was. They would never formally discharge him from his position, but they’d certainly obstruct his proposals and make his life hell, see how far they could press until he finally quit and they could have their way with the IGF military. Every other time he was content to give it right back to them, fighting tooth and nail over every table scrap of progress. His vision for the IGF was a force that helped people, while the Council saw only fit to help themselves. Like hell he’d resign.

Still, he had to reconsider the current situation. They were testing him again, certainly, but they had a vested interest in this planet. For the first time in all the years of battling with the talking heads, they had something to lose. He’d be a fool not to take this opportunity and press them for an advantage.

"I refuse to take part in condemning these men to their deaths," he said, straightening his shoulders. He clasped one hand behind his belt buckle and stood, legs parted. Even at his age, he was still an imposing figure. "You will give me no choice but to turn in my resignation and file a complaint against the courts for gross negligence."

"Negligence? No one will believe you." The statement betrayed the concerned looks the talking heads were giving each other.

"The Council of Thirteen specifically sends a fleet of the IGF military to disembark on a planet that they themselves declared hostile? Defend against a fighting force of unknown power with inadequate resources, and then issues the order to split said forces on an excursion for military gain? I think I have a case here."

"Very well, we will take your complaint and resignation under advisement. Though, as a gesture of goodwill, perhaps you'd like to know the status of an individual who might be of some interest to you is on the planet."

That startled him. Their attitude had dramatically pivoted from off guard and frantically scrambling for ground again into that of confident card-sharks. He'd heard rumors that the talking heads were all psychically linked upon getting sworn into office. He hadn't ever wanted to believe such stories, but experiences like this gave them an unnerving credence.

Mattu attempted to look casual. "Goodwill? From you? Thought you never touched the stuff."

They smiled. "The bounty hunter Talisha Artul has been sighted on the planet's surface. Weren't you acquainted with her mother?"

Mattu paled. He stared at the screen as a satellite image showing that all-too-familiar armor. The image had her frozen midair blasting a set of wyverns with her arm cannon.

"What's her business on Archimedes IV?" he asked, returning to his seat, eyes fixed on the screen. He clenched his hands into fists to keep them from shaking.

"She has a hunting license," the talking heads said purred. "We don't keep track of all her activities. She's a free citizen with all her permits in order. There've been attempts to track down her current employer to ensure there'll be no unnecessary losses to key assets."

Mattu placed one hand behind his back and tried not to look nervous. "What've you found?"

"Absolutely nothing. It's as if her employer doesn't exist. We can only assume she's working for the enemy. She probably doesn't even know it. If she attempts to enter that temple, whoever assumes command in your place will have no choice but to fire on her."

"That won't be necessary," Mattu barked. "I worked with her mother, she was always completely reasonable. I'm sure her daughter will listen."

"It's likely, but whoever replaces you might not share your optimism. They won't risk their men getting shot by some bounty hunter over negotiations."

Mattu sighed. "I get your point. I'll command the fleet."

"Are you sure? It is after all completely your choice in the matter."

"Am I free to go?" His eyes narrowed dangerously. They'd pissed him off, and he couldn't hide it.

"Good luck on your mission, Commander. The fate of the Intergalactic Peacekeeping Federation is in your hands. Remember that."

Mattu closed the call and withered into his seat. His office darkened without the glowing lights from the holo-screens. He pulled up a fresh screen and swiped through it several times until he returned to the satellite images taken of the bounty hunter. He stopped on one that showed a clear image of her face. His eyes softened. His mouth hung open. He lay back in his seat, fingers clamped over his mouth in stunned silence.

He'd become aware that Talisha's daughter had taken on the famous armor and followed in her mother's footsteps. He'd read the reports of her excursions with the military but had never actually seen the young woman. Mattu had deliberately avoided looking into anything regarding the second generation Talisha Artul. That chapter of his life had closed long ago when the senior bounty hunter made it abundantly clear she never wanted to see him again. His newfound suspicions changed everything.

He hoped he wasn't being sent to kill his only daughter.

BLUEBIRD HAD LEFT the cabin early in the morning, before Talisha or Rogers had awoken. She'd barged across the schooner. The guards only briefly attempted to stop her making entry into Ching Shih's quarters. They were silenced by her weary voice calling from inside. Bluebird gave the guards a curt nod before barging through the door.

Ching Shih was sitting at the table, hand pressed against her forehead. She held a tall emerald bottle with a thin neck. It was uncorked. There was a glass sitting on the table, but she'd long since abandoned its use in favor of chugging directly from the bottle.

"Apologies," Ching Shih said. "This is no way to greet you, and my guards are rather enthusiastic."

"You look terrible," Bluebird noted, pulling up a chair next to her.

"You're one to talk." Ching Shih smiled and offered her the bottle. "Baijiu? It's a rarity in the galaxy these days."

"Sharing drinks before battle is Karstotzkiyan tradition." Bluebird raised the bottle in toast before taking a hearty swig. She took a big gulp and licked her lips. "It's quite dry. Have you slept at all?"

"No. I'll be dead soon enough. I can sleep plenty then. Best to use my time wisely."

"Nights drunk with worry is wise?"

"Don't be an ass." Ching Shih snatched the bottle from her. "Give me that. What'd you want to see me about?"

"To accompany the fight against Plymouth."

"Your services wherever you choose to offer them are valid, but don't you think your friends will need your protection?"

Bluebird sighed. Her shoulders heaved. "Talisha is a good person. She wants to do the right thing but is filled with doubts. Rogers is more bitter and lonely than even he understands. They are powerful warriors, but both so very lost."

"So it is not your strength they need, but your guidance."

"I have experience. I've suffered same as they, but there is distance between my suffering and theirs."

"Perspective is a gift. Lets you see things you might have missed."

Bluebird smiled. "You sound awfully sentimental for a hardened pirate."

"I am a sentimental hardened pirate," Ching Shih corrected with a smile. She passed the baijiu to Bluebird.

Bluebird took another hearty swig. She pounded on her chest with her fist before letting out an ungodly belch. Ching Shih winced visibly but said nothing.

"The taste grows on you," Bluebird said with a nod. "I will not abandon my new friends for a quest of personal vengeance. Sascha would never approve. Feels like shit though. Like I am giving up a sense of closure."

"You place duty before satisfaction." Ching Shih raised her brow high, then took the baijiu back. "I drink to your sense of honor."

"I have but one favor to ask."

"Name it."

Bluebird reached into her pockets and retrieved a silver chain and oval pendant. It'd been heavily scratched and damaged over the years. She opened it, revealing a picture of a woman with dark hair and fierce brown eyes.

"She looks powerful," Ching Shih commented.

"I want you to take it with you, when you assault the satellite." Bluebird closed the pendant and placed it on the table. She slid it toward Ching Shih, her fingers lingering for a brief moment against the chain. "She should be there when you destroy them."

Ching Shih took the pendant. She stared at it with a furrowed brow. Her shoulders drooped. With a sigh, she clenched it in her fingers and tucked it safely beneath her robes. She'd been carrying the burdens and dreams of so many over the years. One more wouldn't break her.

"I'll ensure it gets back to you."

"Just kill them." Bluebird's eyes flashed. "I want her to hear their screams in the next world."

Ching Shih smiled. "Consider it done."

She rose slowly, removing her crown from the table and placing it once more upon her brow. All semblance of a weary old woman vanished. Though she had spent the entire night lying awake and drinking, she looked once more a frightening display of dignity and power. Ching Shih walked to the door of her cabin, hands clasped in front of her. She waited calmly for her guards to open the door. Bluebird smirked and followed shortly after.

An unexpected scene awaited the blue-haired mercenary upon leaving the cabin. A man and a woman were being dragged from their quarters onto the deck of the schooner. Ching Shih's eyes narrowed as she stepped forward, fingers locking around the hilt of her sword. The other ships flew closer, their decks packed with watchful occupants.

Rogers and Talisha exited their cabin to see the display. They stopped just short of rushing into the gathering crowd. Talisha lifted her visor to give Bluebird a bewildered expression. Bluebird could only shrug in response.

Both the man and the woman were forced to their knees by the guards. Their heads were lifted so they were forced to stare into Ching Shih's disapproving gaze. She drew her sword and pointed it at the man's throat.

"What are your crimes?" she demanded icily.

"We were caught stealing from the private servers," he confessed through tears. "You're leading us to our deaths, you bitch! I wanted out!"

"Yes," Ching Shih whispered, kneeling down to his level. She gripped his jaw in her hands, scraping her long fingernails across his cheek. "I am a bitch, but you weren't stealing from me, you twit. You were stealing from her! And him! And him! And every one of your comrades."

She stood and gestured widely. "Theft from this vessel is theft from you all. It is theft from the hardworking people who help us restock and refuel when we land on their planets. It is a violation of the systems we have put in place to ensure our survival."

Once more she aimed the blade at his throat. "As such, I will let your crew decide your punishments. What shall it be? Shall I show mercy on one who would deign to steal from his brothers and sisters?"

She waited for their response. She knew what it would be. She'd given the same offer many times in the past, and in the past there'd always be the same response.

A sweeping cry rose from all sides. "Death! Death! Death!"

Talisha watched, mouth hanging open. A grimace formed across her face. Ching Shih ignored it. She cared little for the opinions of others.

Ching Shih raised the sword and brought it down on his neck. The sword glowed hot for a brief second as it made contact. Smoke rose from the wound and his head fell cleanly from his shoulders leaving an acrid stench.

She turned the sword on the woman next. "Do you renounce the actions of this man? I am not without mercy."

"Just let me go," the woman pleaded. "Don't kill me."

"Do you renounce him?"

"Yes! Yes! I let him talk me into it. I'm sorry."

Ching Shih gripped the woman's hair in her fist and yanked her face upward. She brought the sword against her throat and squinted. "That you would sell out your comrade so easily ensures that you know nothing of loyalty."

The woman's eyes widened in panic. She struggled against her captors in vain. "No! Please! Don't! I didn't—just please, don't kill me!"

Ching Shih's lip curled in disgust. "Die with some fucking dignity."

The sword came down. Again, the blade burned hot and her head lopped against the ground and rolled along the deck. It sent a smear of blood across the metal surface.

"Clean this up!" Ching Shih barked to her crew. "Then prepare for battle! We have two armies to fight this day."

While the rest of Ching Shih's crew rushed to obey her orders, Talisha moved to confront her. "That was unnecessarily cruel."

Ching Shih tucked her sword into her sash. "I didn't ask for approval of my methods, bounty hunter."

"No, but you asked for my help."

"And that suddenly gives you the right to question my authority? It is not enough that I humble myself before you, but now you must challenge me in how I command my crew?"

"I've no right," Talisha said, exasperated. "But I won't hand over my culture to vindictive pirates. You had me believing you were about more than this."

"You believed that all on your own. I've made no attempt to hide my true self from you."

"But you wanted me to see you as desperate, as someone who needed my help."

"And my harsh commands negate that somehow? Talisha Artul, I am who I am. Perhaps you ought to find out who you are before passing judgment, hmm?"

Talisha pressed further. "I get it. You're doing what you have to do. So do I. I have to protect what's important to me. I'm sorry."

Ching Shih frowned. "Do not apologize. This is the first thing you've said since we met that was with absolute surety."

"I wish your people the best."

"You should prepare for your excursion into the temple." Ching Shih turned her back on her.

"I understand."

"And Talisha?"

"Yes?"

Ching Shih turned back to face her, retrieving the Valran key from her garments. "I've no anger over your decision, but you let me humiliate myself before you. You will pay for that someday. Pray that I do not survive this fight."

Ching Shih clutched Talisha's wrist and forced her hand open. She shoved the key into her fingers, then turned away. Talisha stared, mouth gaping. For the pirate queen, this had been a business transaction turned sour. The possibility of a violent confrontation would be nothing more to her than an inevitability.

Chapter Eight

PREPARATIONS WERE MADE, and battle plans were drawn. Given Talisha's relative unease with spending any more time with the Red Fleet, she would be piloting her own ship to the Temple. She pulled up a holographic panel over her gauntlet and typed in the appropriate coordinates. The ship's autopilot would track her down and begin charting a course in her direction.

While they waited for its arrival, Rogers turned to her, arms folded over his chest. "Is this thing battle capable?"

"Yes, but I've a feeling it wasn't designed for military purposes," Talisha said. "It's Valran, just like my armor, so it has some of the same beam and energy-shifting technology, but really it's built for speed. More useful for hit-and-run tactics than full-on fights."

"Still, wondering why you didn't call it down in our previous encounters." Rogers shook his head. "Feels like an additional asset that might've saved us some headaches."

Talisha chuckled nervously. "This ship has a bad habit of failing when flying in planetary orbit."

"Faulty mechanics?"

"No, nothing like that. Just bad luck. Lightning storm on one planet, freak accident involving the climate on another. One time, a weird dragon monster tore a good chunk out of the wing as I made entry onto the planet's surface. Left me stranded there for a good several weeks."

Rogers stared. "You have seen some serious shit."

Talisha made an ugly laugh. "You have no idea. Ship should be here in a few minutes, you should probably tell Cyrus we're gonna head out soon. He'll have to fly himself. No room on my ship for a wyvern."

Rogers scratched the back of his neck. "Yeah about that."

Her expression soured. "Oh no. What happened?"

"One of the pirates told me he flew off early this morning. Just skedaddled. Said he didn't want any part of us anymore."

"Oh jeez. I'm sorry to hear that."

Rogers sighed. "Feels kinda crap, yeah. I used to see him as being kind of my id, ya know? He had control of a lot of my weapons systems that I don't hardly use, so it feels like a piece of me just flew out without saying so much as a goodbye. Oh well, prolly for the best."

"Maybe, but I'm here for you." She placed a hand on his shoulder and gave it a squeeze.

"Thanks, cowgirl."

The ship took about a half hour to arrive. It was larger and roomier than the scorpion, though clearly designed for only a small squad of passengers. It had the same faded sunset colors of amber and gold as Talisha's armor, with many similar avian-inspired trappings along the wing tips and frontal nose area. The ship seemed to lack doors or windows. Its shape was completely smooth all across the surfaces. There was a raised bubble across the top of the ship where Rogers supposed a turret or some other form of weaponry might be stored.

He let out a pre-recorded whistle sound. "That's a heckuva machine ya got there."

Talisha gave a half-hearted smile. Her fingers brushed across the holographic display on her gauntlet. A whooshing sound emerged from the ship followed by a presence of steam as a panel appeared, forming seemingly organically from the ship's left side. The panel raised itself upward into a door and a short runway ramp slid into view.

"I'll be cow-kicked, ain't that something?" Rogers shook his head and made a tongue-clicking sound.

Bluebird bounded past them, hoisting her cannon onto her shoulders. She had to duck and turn to the side just to squeeze in the doorway. She turned around and stuck her head out the door and gave a thumbs-up.

"This is a fine vessel," she called. "A bit small, though."

"I don't think it was meant for Karstotzkiyans," Talisha replied with a smile.

Bluebird shrugged. "I will not hold it against them."

They climbed into the ship to find claustrophobic quarters to the back and a few chairs near the cockpit in the front. Rogers had to wonder where the engine room or thrusters were located. He couldn't accept that such a seemingly powerful vessel could fly without one.

Talisha hurriedly rushed across the ship, grabbing clothes and blueprints and folders that had been left scattered across the cockpit and seating area. Rogers chuckled, watching her. There were all the telltale signs that this had been a makeshift home to her for some time. He smiled, strangely pleased by her messy habits.

"Sorry. Not used to having passengers." She bundled a pile of clothes in her arms and brushed past them to hurl the pile into her cramped quarters.

Rogers wandered over to what appeared to be an antiquated jukebox sitting in the corner. His fingers brushed across the surface. They'd had one like it in the Dover Town saloon, but it hadn't functioned in years. This one appeared to have been kept in proper working order. Talisha slammed the bedroom door shut behind her. Rogers looked at her and jerked a thumb in the direction of the jukebox.

"Mind if you help me get this thing to work?" he asked. "Bit embarrassed to say this, but always wanted to hear one. My memory banks don't have much access to music."

Talisha winced visibly. "You're not gonna like it."

"It's a jukebox right? They play jazz records and country and stuff."

She crossed over to the jukebox, shaking her head. "Yeah. Stuff."

"No stalling!" Bluebird called, leaning against the back wall of the ship. "Let us hear your joyous melodies."

Talisha's shoulders drooped and cringed visibly.

"Just remember," she said, before pressing play. "You were warned."

What followed was the heavy thud-thudding of aggressively distorted guitars and guttural wailing into a microphone. She had unfortunately neglected to lower the volume on the ship's speakers first. That first guttural scream rattled poor Rogers, who'd had his head dangerously close to the speaker output. His entire body vibrated. He tried to scream at her to shut it off but found he couldn't raise his voice louder than the angry din.

Bluebird's face illuminated into immediate delight. She clenched her hands into fists and pumped at the air, making flailing motions and stomping in rhythm to the drums and distorted bass. Talisha made a quick effort to drastically lower the volume. Rogers nearly collapsed against the jukebox, keeping his hat pinned to his brow with a shaking hand.

"This music! It is for warriors! You'd fit in with Karstotzkiyan culture!" Bluebird shouted, continuing to thrash about in tune with the beat.

"I've heard some selections of music in films and holovids, and that most certainly is not music," Rogers managed to pant. "What the hell was it?"

"Earth stuff. Heavy Metal. This is some really old junk though," Talisha said sheepishly. "Helps me think."

"How can you process thought with this racket?" Rogers said.

Bluebird grabbed him by the shoulders and swung him around in a circle. "How can you not dance to it?"

His voice came out in a distressed hiss. "Darlin'! I'd love it if you put me down!"

Talisha cut off the music. "Sorry, Rogers. You wanted to know. Bluebird, c'mon. We gotta focus."

"Oh-ho! I am focused and ready for combat!" Bluebird deposited Rogers onto his shaky feet.

"Well, hopefully it won't come to that," Talisha said.

Rogers shook his head. "You can't even understand the lyrics to that mess."

Talisha looked at him kinda sheepishly. "Well for me, the lyrics don't matter too much. It's just about filling the room around me with something as angry as I am. Feels a lot better to throw it out into music than just let it stew, ya know?"

He thought about that for a moment, then chuckled. "We have very different uses for music, I guess. But I appreciate ya tellin' me."

Talisha made her way to the pilot seat. She sat down and moved her fingers over the Valran symbols across the touch panel. The ship hummed quietly to life and was soon shooting into the sky. It reached an altitude above the clouds in a manner of seconds. A screen appeared in front of the cockpit revealing a detailed look at the planet below. She quickly plugged in the coordinates to the Valran Temple. They were sure to reach the temple's site before any of the approaching armies. With any luck, they'd be able to get in and get what they need before the conflict even began.

THE SHIP FLEW along at a steady pace, soaring on autopilot. It gave Talisha plenty of time to think about the trials ahead. She didn't share Bluebird's excitement for more battles ahead. She'd seen enough violence and bloodshed that week. She'd killed before, but she'd never put that much thought into who was at the other end of her guns. It left every other one of her missions in question.

These were survivors, refugees of a system that had destroyed their world and then abandoned them. Any violence they committed was in response for survival. She was the invader, upholding the very same corrupt laws and systems that had turned those individuals to violence in the first place. Her mother had been the same.

Talisha's eyes widened and she groaned out loud. She swore and kicked the dashboard in front of her repeatedly in her own frustration.

"Hey." Rogers grabbed her by the shoulder. "You okay?"

Talisha turned to him. "I think I get why Mom hung it up so suddenly. I get why she didn't want me doing this."

"Why's that?"

"She figured it out," Talisha said, staring off into the distance. "Working within the law is only right and good when the law is just. She put down rebel uprisings, dooming those planets to more decades of suffering and degradation. I've been just as complicit. I thought I was the hero just like she did. Really, I'm just a heavily armed destruction tourist."

No one had a response to that. Talisha was glad. She didn't know what she would have done if they had tried to console or contradict her in any way. She needed to focus.

They disembarked at the edge of a barren cliff overlooking a canyon. It was a gray area, utterly devoid of life. There were no visible trapezoidal structures as indicated on the scans Snidely had shown her. She almost believed for a second they were in the wrong place.

"Where is it?" Rogers asked. "I don't see nothin'."

"Gonna do a quick scan for any Valran technology in the area," Talisha said. "Might give us a better read on where to touch down."

The screen turned black for a brief second before revealing a constructed grid outline of the surface below. Sure enough there was a massive underground structure with adjacent piping and structures stretching up just beneath the planet's surface. Closest detection to an entrance was deep within the heart of the canyon.

Talisha pointed at the screen. "All right, looks like there's our way in. Let's go."

She pulled the ship lower, delving deep within the heart of the canyon. A heavy green fog covered the area, and the ship seemed to vanish beneath it. Her scanners indicated a poisonous atmosphere, harmless to the skin, but dangerous if ingested. She gave Bluebird a spare gas mask from a compartment just over the cockpit.

The ship docked in a wide-open area on the canyon floor. They stepped out into an eerie quiet. The fog was so thick down here that it obscured even the canyon walls.

"If I hadn't seen the scans myself," Rogers commented. "I'd say we were in the wrong place."

Bluebird shook her head. "Do not trust your eyes, metal-man. Feel it? This place is marked by death."

"Gotta agree with Big Blue," Talisha said, taking in a quick retinal scan of the surrounding area with her visor. "More important the ancient thing is, the creepier and more desolate its surroundings are gonna be. It's like a rule or something. All right, I found it. Over here."

She suddenly rushed forward, almost vanishing within the soup-like fog. Bluebird and Rogers had to run, switching to thermographic vision just to be able to keep track of her. She finally stopped a yard away, dropping to her knees.

"What did you find?" Bluebird stood over her.

Talisha's fingers brushed along the ground. There were lines here visible only to the tracking technology in her visors. Her fingers traced them till she found a large enough indentation within the ground for the key.

"We've got it," Talisha said. "Step back. I don't know what's going to happen."

She retrieved the key from her pack and shoved it smaller side down into the triangular indentation. The key turned all on its own, making an audible click. Bluebird could now see the lines for herself as they glowed and revealed a series of esoteric alien symbols in lights all along the ground. Talisha stood quickly and backed away from the key, putting protective arms in front of Bluebird and Rogers.

A rumbling was felt from deep beneath the earth. The canyon walls shook, and ancient boulders were dislodged, falling into the canyon and smashing against the rocks below. A black structure thousands of feet in height and width slowly rose from the planet's surface, uprooting ancient vines and scraping along the sides of the canyon walls.

The structure was made up of a slick ebony material, with small traces of amber-colored grooves and inlets all across its surface. Talisha recognized the symbols as Valran, but even with her mastery of the language couldn't place or translate them. This was completely alien to her.

A massive set of stairs and pillars led up toward a gaping sixty-foot-wide entrance to the temple. Two great statues guarded the opening, each a hundred feet in height and facing the other. They were powerful bird-like creatures standing upright and wearing robes masterfully carved to give the illusion of fabric. In their outstretched talons, they helped each other hold aloft a large dark orb.

"I don't think anyone is going to have a difficult time finding this place now," Talisha said, her voice shaking.

That was an understatement. The temple noticeably jutted out still several hundred feet above the canyon walls. It'd be a black blot on the horizon for hundreds of miles.

"Then we best hurry," Bluebird said, taking the lead.

Talisha nodded. She quickly typed out some commands on the holographic panel on her gauntlet. Her ship closed its doors and took off into the skies. She'd programmed it to circle the perimeter and feed constant updates to her helmet.

Inside the temple was a wide-open chamber with a long hallway that seemed to stretch on into infinity. A set of stairs on either side led into dizzying passages all spiraling upward. Lining just about every wall were displays of piping and plaques with incomprehensible writing. It looked nothing like the style and make of Talisha's ship or armor. That slick organic feel and the avian flourishes were completely missing. This was an industrialized nightmare of a building.

Directly in the center of the room was another statue, about half as large as the two guarding the entrance. It was another Valran, this one gangly and naked from the waist up. It wore only a set of black robes made from the same dark material as the building's slick walls. The eyes were inset with red crystal and its beak was open in a permanent, threatening roar.

"Where do we go?" Bluebird asked. "It'll take years to navigate this place."

"That's why we have scans of the building to form us a map," Talisha said. She held her gauntlet, palm open in front her. A detailed holographic map appeared directly over her hand. "There, quickest route to the center of the temple. There's an active power fluctuation. We keep along this path, we should find what we're looking for."

"Just what exactly is it are we looking for?" Rogers said.

Talisha stared at the statue, shuddering as she passed beneath its frightful gaze. "Answers."

IN DOVER TOWN, a crowd of onlookers stood outside as the skies darkened with the signature gray-green colors of the IGF military. Earlier that day, the shipment of guns they'd bought with the money obtained from selling Rogers to Plymouth arrived, and they'd been distributing them to the town's first militia. A line of men and women had formed in front of a truck handing out blasters and assault rifles. The sense of celebration and excitement quickly turned to unease as the shadows of wyverns and drop-ships passed overhead.

All eyes fixed on the armed forces flying in. Murmurs and confused whispers arose. The sense of security brought on by the supply of fresh munitions seemed suddenly false. Each civilian and new militia member suddenly understood a simple truth about their place in the galaxy. No amount of guns would protect them, nor would any elected government. Security was but a comforting illusion. There could be no safety for them so long as their lives could be cut short by those who'd long since deemed them disposable. They were no different than the trash they despised, begging for scraps in the streets or scavenging the ruined husks of bombed out cities. They had no more freedoms than the android they'd sold to arm themselves.

The child Rogers had nicknamed Brick had felt fear only twice before in his short life. The first was when he'd gotten locked in the shed behind his dad's house. Sheriff Rogers had been there, ripping the door clean off the hinges to rescue him. The second time was watching the sheriff leave town, abandoning him for reasons the kid couldn't understand.

Staring up at those planes and ships, he felt that fear again. He'd never seen their like before, but he knew what weapons of destruction looked like. He had plenty of old toys his parents had given him, modeled after military tanks and planes. The things in the sky were no toys.

Brick's fat little fingers gripped his mother's skirts tightly. "Mom, what's going on?"

She didn't answer him. Her mouth quivered. "I was a little girl last time the skies looked like this."

"What does it mean?"

She turned to look at him, eyes turning suddenly soft. "Don't worry about it, all right? We're gonna be just fine."

He didn't believe her.

COMMANDER MATTU'S MOUTH fell open as the temple came into view in the distance, draining him of all composure. He'd witnessed some stunning works of architecture, but nothing like this. Not even the skyscrapers of Turelius Prime could compare to something this massive and foreign.

In the time since the temple had risen out of the ground, it'd shifted in structure, bringing with it feats of uncanny geometry. Stairs had formed along the outside, stretching off into nothingness, while the whole of the building precariously balanced off a single point. The Valran Temple should have been an impossibility by all known laws of physics, and yet it stood in complete defiance of those laws.

One of his aides brought a datapad revealing new scans taken of the structure. "Sir, you're not going to believe this."

"I'm not believing what I'm seeing before my own damn eyes but go ahead."

"Well, the temple's changed since it rose from the ground. It looks completely different from the earlier scans taken of it."

"So it has some other functions, machinery getting activated, shifting purposes. We've seen stuff like this with our wyverns, right?"

The aide shook his head. "No, sir. Not like our wyverns at all. There are mechanisms stored within a Wyvern's systems to facilitate the shifting of function. The temple has no such detectable mechanics. The new features were not previously part of its structure."

"What are you trying to tell me?" Mattu said, almost chuckling even as his palms sweat. "That this thing is just...growing these new parts of itself?"

The aide nodded, eyes bulging out of his skull with shock and terror. "Something's changed. Something's—"

"What? Something's what? Out with it! What the hell is going on?"

The aide gulped and shifted nervously. He reached up with a sweaty hand to adjust his glasses. He coughed once or twice, seemingly afraid of making a reality of the words about to come out of his mouth.

Mattu had seen this shit before. He'd been informed of an uprising where the rebel fleet had completely wiped out a squadron of IGF soldiers. The scout had seen the charred bodies personally but was so afraid of delivering his message. If the words came out his mouth, he'd have to believe them. The scout had vomited on the floor but moments after finally delivering the report. Mattu's aide had the same sickly expression across his face.

"Something has...awoken, Commander." The little man was shaking. "New biomechanical components seem to have sprouted up within the temple."

Mattu turned on him, hands clenched tightly behind his back. He glared at the man, not out of anger, but out of a refusal to accept what he'd just been told. "Let me get this straight, it's alive?"

"It is now," his aide whispered. "It wasn't before. Something has changed it."

"Right. Thanks for the report," Mattu said. He clamped a hand on the man's shoulder. "Try and keep this between us. We're headed into battle, and this'll scare the men into getting themselves killed. You hear?"

"Right. Of course."

"Good man."

The aide hurried off, sweating buckets.

Mattu turned back around to face the windows, hand clamped over his mouth as they drew closer to the structure. They were near enough now that he could see the outside of the temple transforming before his very eyes. More formations appeared on the outer edges, spikes and partitions and the like. It almost seemed to him like the temple was reaching out with each new addition and walkway; like antennae grasping for the world around it, touching, sensing, *feeling*.

He had a terrifying thought, that the temple might not be content with merely filling every possible gap in the canyon. With as little as anyone knew, there was very little telling where it might stop. It might just decide to cover the globe, pulling the entire planet inside the giant ebony horror.

"It's a fucking building," he had to remind himself.

He chose to land the drop-ship on the outskirts of the canyon, a good distance away from the monolith. Settling so far away from the structure meant thinning his forces more than he'd originally anticipated, but his fear of the temple extended to fear for his men. He kept envisioning a nightmare scenario where it engulfed them all in its ever-reaching growth.

In the time it took for them to set up camp and establish a guarded perimeter, the building had sprouted several new appendages. There were new statues of bird-like humanoids reaching out with grasping talons and screaming open beaks full of fangs. Piping had grown all along the outside, forming new shapes and strange alien symbols. It was a chaotic mishmash now, hardly recognizable from the trapezoidal monolith that had originally sprouted from the earth.

Some of the men cast uneasy looks toward the temple.

Mattu barked at them. "Eyes outward, men! We've an army of untold size approaching this location. I want a well-defended perimeter. No one comes in or out of this temple, is that clear? We are the 497th!"

There were affirming nods, but they did little to still the general air of unease that pervaded the camp. Mattu couldn't blame them. He called his generals and lieutenants into his tent to debrief them as much as possible without committing treason. None of them took the news well that he'd be taking a squad of soldiers into the temple. There were shouting and arguments up until he silenced them all with a single look.

"My orders come directly from the Council of Thirteen," he said in a low voice. "Feel free to lodge your complaints though. I will be retiring after this mission and will be all too happy to file your grievances personally."

That shut them up long enough. He hoped they would complain. The more unrest caused in the wake of this disaster of a mission the more he might be able to do something with it if he somehow managed to survive all this.

A new set of stairs and a new opening had formed atop the canyon walls several feet away from the perimeter. He chose a squad of men and women all wearing heavy power armor meant to survive even the toughest blasts. The only downside was that the armor was clunky and lacked mobility. They couldn't even turn their heads right or left and would have to shift their entire bodies. This left them susceptible to surprise attacks from the flank or rear.

Commander Mattu rejected the powerful protective suit for standard grade body armor worn over his uniform. It was smaller and made up for its lack of protections in the increased mobility. He would be hanging behind his squad in order to protect their backline. He'd be better suited for mobilizing against threats from either direction.

More sculptures of Valran faces and bodies emerged. They'd multiplied by the hundreds, arms lunging outward with clawed talons. The squad would have to pass beneath those frozen hands to enter the temple. It kept them all hesitating before the unending blackness.

"Forward!" Mattu hollered. "Sooner we nab that warp-technology, sooner we can get out of here and off this planet. Ya hear me?"

The squad, four men and women, all raised their rifles in an acknowledging hurrah. They marched forward, but he could see their cautionary glances back at the camp. They marched into the unknown, leaving their comrades behind to defend them.

Chapter Nine

A HORDE OF grayish-blue vessels uncloaked over the surface of Archimedes IV—a fleet comprised of a hundred corporate armies all gathered for a single purpose. Madame Inspector sat in her office eyeing the images of the mobilizing army with an insidious smile. Drones had monitored the rising of the temple and the IGF encampment. The government thought they could get between her and the temple. How cute.

She reached out, fingers curling about a microphone on her desk. She'd only ever used it a few times, not being the type who enjoyed making announcements. There were the occasional prepared speeches such as holidays and employee anniversaries of those few elites beneath her who actually deserved such treatment. Even then, the tool was only to reinforce the notion of upward mobility within the Plymouth Corporation. Work hard, don't question your superiors, and one day you too might earn public approval and the envy of your peers.

Today, she used it for wholly different reasons. For years she had bitten her tongue, expressing only the barest minimums of her disdain. She was finally going to tell them all the terrible truth. If they thought her a bitch before, they had no telling what was coming next.

She leaned back in her chair, kicking her feet onto the desk. One hand clutched around the microphone, while the other drew lazy smoke circles in the air with her cigarette.

She was invigorated. This was true power, a dictator on their final day in office.

"Listen up, insects and ingrates." Her voice was a low, hideous snarl. "That temple is Plymouth property. It is worth more than all your lives put together. It's worth more than the lives of your children and grandchildren. I want you to grasp the weight of your own pathetic insignificance, not because I am trying to disillusion you. I want to free you from the weighty burden of individuality, of diversity, of trying to make your pitiful lives count for something.

"Accept it. Embrace it. Let it define you. You are fodder for a greater purpose. Get our people into that temple and retrieve the goods, even if you have to kill every dirty little refugee on that planet to do so. Get reckless. Detonate their armies with your own exploding wreckage if you have to. Play kamikaze. Your lives meant nothing anyway, nothing in comparison to the honor and reward that will be bestowed upon you for your sacrifice.

"Nothing in life. Everything in death. Death is meaning. Death is power. It's the only power any of you little pissants will ever know. Make the most of it."

It was the most honest thing she'd ever said in her life. Her fingers curled around the microphone cord. It was an antique, several times as old as she was. Someone had given it to her, or maybe it had been an impulse purchase back when she did such things. Regardless, she had affection for the old thing. It was one of the few items in her personal possession she held any emotion toward.

Madame Inspector watched the holographic screens. Her fingers flicked across the illuminated panels to switch to the camera view of one of Plymouth's own wyverns. They'd finally arrived at the IGF encampment. She stood quickly, the microphone shaking with her own eager excitement.

Her mouth opened in breathless anticipation before she lunged and yelled, "Open fire!"

CARRIER VESSELS WERE still highly experimental, not even approved yet for purchase by the IGF military budget committee. Carriers were far larger than a drop-ship and could contain twice as many ships and tanks for transport. Their real benefit over the drop-ship was their firing power. Drop-ships were defenseless liabilities that had to be constantly guarded on all sides by a smaller fleet of protective ships. A carrier could defend itself with a host of long-range missile cannons and cutting-edge shielding technology.

The range on the cannons was the key to everything. A drop-ship had to land in the middle of the battlefield in order to most effectively deploy its troops, while a carrier could soften the enemy up from afar while its armies unloaded. The IGF military had hoped to have them acquired by now. Those delays would give Plymouth every advantage they needed.

A barrage of missile strikes from afar sent foot soldiers sprawling for cover and decimated a grounded wyvern. The IGF's tanks responded by blasting the carrier's heavy shields. It was only a matter of minutes before the desert around the canyon had become a war zone of explosions and bullet fire. Planes crashed with each other in midair, and wyverns engaged in their own powerful duels. A hail of purple blaster fire came from below as soldiers dug themselves in behind metallic shields and barriers. Ships fell on both sides in fiery wrecks smashing into the desert sands below.

Where Plymouth had an undoubting tech and numbers advantage, there were none who could hold a defense like the IGF military. In the short time it'd taken them to set up camp and establish a perimeter, they'd constructed bunkers and powerful turrets. Their reputation for quick deployments to fend off invading forces was well-earned.

Ching Shih and the Red Fleet waited a safe distance away from the fight. She had her ships positioned on either side of the battlefield waiting for the precise moment to strike. Timing was everything.

She had provoked Madame Inspector's blind rage, then tactfully hidden away. The inspector's ire would be directed at the IGF military so long as the Red Fleet kept out of sight. The IGF had set up camp in front of the very thing Madame Inspector wanted and become the more immediate threat.

Ching Shih was one who knew the art of patience and biding one's time. That did not make her idle. She piloted a cloaked one-man vessel into space, keeping her troops in immediate contact via headset. Her position would not be on the battlefield, waiting with her soldiers to strike. There were other dangers that needed to be dealt with.

She'd left her retainer of personal guards planet-side, feeling their abilities would be better suited on the battlefield. She knew well what she was getting into. Taking on the Mayflower by herself was a fool's errand, one she would've scoffed at in her younger days, but Ching Shih would not have survived as long without the ability to gamble hard and win big. She couldn't afford to send a larger force against the Mayflower for risk of them being spotted and prompting Madame Inspector to destroy the planet. A much smaller vessel could skate by nearly undetected. Furthermore, she didn't wish to split her forces. They would be outnumbered against the armies of Plymouth and the IGF and needed to be at their full strength.

Ching Shih did not intend to make her assault completely defenseless. She wore a small set of power armor beneath her robes. It was a prototype taken from a raid on a research and development facility a few months prior. The armor was meant to enhance the strength, reflexes, and agility of the wearer. Though Ching Shih was no doubt confident in her combat prowess, her old age left her bones weary and lacking the strength and fire of her youth. She hoped the advantage of the armor would be enough. She reached deep within her robes to retrieve a small black sphere. It flickered with a ring of angry red lights.

"Only as a last resort," she said to herself, before tucking it back into her robes.

There would be none of her special virus shenanigans as there had been when she'd first entered the planet's space. Ching Shih was well aware that a high-tech vessel like the Mayflower would have quarantined the virus and taken the precautionary measures to prevent any further cyber-attacks. That didn't mean a manual hack to allow her stealth entry was completely out of the question.

Despite the Mayflower's powerful cloaking technology, Ching Shih's scanners had already pierced through it and revealed the docking bay. She kept a safe distance away, having measured the exact limits of the Mayflower's close-range scanners. Her fingers danced across the keyboard searching for the right vulnerabilities within the Mayflower's code that would allow her access.

A half hour went by of nonstop typing. Breaking into a system like this without her powerful virus technology would be one of her greatest accomplishments. It reminded her of her early days when she was nothing more than a code monkey working for another man's business. She was pleased to see her old skills hadn't fallen by the wayside through disuse.

At last, she managed to break into the Mayflower's security systems. She made quick work of their scanners and any alarms that might sound in the case of a breach. She then darted toward the docking bay systems and opened the doors to allow her entry into the satellite.

Once inside, her presence would quickly be made known. She'd have to hurry. She sped her tiny ship in through the opening bay doors and vanished inside the hangar. Several men and women stopped what they were doing to gaze at the closing bay doors. Some immediately ran to their computer terminals and stations trying to figure out who'd ordered them open. They'd be frantically hitting the alarms only to find themselves locked out of their own systems. Ching Shih had left nothing to chance.

Her vessel decloaked and she rose out a hatch in the top. She fired a red beam of energy from the tip of her blaster directly at the computer terminals, frying them. She wouldn't risk one of these tech junkies somehow managing to break through the lockdown.

Four armed guards had already been heading to the hangar. The civilian employees rushed past them in an attempt to escape into the main hall. Ching Shih ducked back into her ship and typed out a series of commands across her console. The hallway doors closed in front the corporate employees, trapping them in the hangar with her.

"Nobody leaves here alive," she hissed.

Ching Shih somersaulted out of the way of incoming bullet fire. Her body deftly navigated the hangar, twisting and weaving under the onslaught of bullets. She ducked out of cover briefly to lay down a few suppressing shots before tucking around to the side. Her armor gave her all the advantage she needed, allowing her to run rapidly along the edges of the walls and backflip to flank the guards from behind. Her sword glowed red-hot and she made a single sweep of the blade, severing their heads from their shoulders.

Ching Shih turned her back to them, letting their bodies slump against the ground with a sickening splat. Her robes trailed behind her, dragging the pools of blood beneath it in a crimson trail. She walked toward the shaking employees, backed against the door and staring up at her like cornered animals.

"Please!" One man screamed, clawing against the door. "Have mercy!"

"Did your company have mercy on my planet?" she growled, dropping her blaster to the ground. She closed both hands around the hilt of her blade and held it in front of her, stance rigid. "Did you think to spare any of the millions of lives lost for a test run?"

"Please...I didn't know."

Ching Shih rushed forward without warning. She stabbed him through the stomach and drew the blade up into his sternum. The other employees scattered in terror.

She leaned in close to the dead man's face, her eyes red with tears. "You will pay for your ignorance and your inaction. All of you will know the wrath of Ching Shih."

TALISHA RACED THROUGH the temple. Walls rose up before them, blocking their path. Stairs dropped beneath their feet, nearly causing them to plummet to their doom. It was like running through a terrible dream. She watched the hallway lengthening before her before it spiraled up suddenly and shot into the sky. She shook her head and slumped against the wall, defeated.

"Nope! I'm done!" she yelled to the sky.

"Well, what do your scans show?" Rogers asked.

Talisha groaned and pulled up the holographic map over her gauntlet. There revealed nothing but several beeping Valran symbols over a staticky screen.

"It's the Valran code for error," she explained. "The temple is shifting too fast for the map to keep updated. We're lost without a guide."

Bluebird frowned. "It is predicament—wait." Her attention went immediately to a set of twenty-foot-tall black metal doors that had sprung up behind them.

Talisha looked at her sharply. "What is it?"

Bluebird placed a finger against her lips. She undid the straps on her cannon and walked toward the doors. Talisha quickly checked the audio waves on her visor screen. There were footsteps, and they were coming closer.

Talisha sprang to her feet, placing a hand against her arm cannon and aiming it at the door. Rogers found suitable cover behind one of the imposing Valran statues and readied his pistol. There was the sound of a machine being set up on the other end of the door, soon followed by a loud bang that shook the doors. A moment of silence passed and something pounded against the doors again.

"Rogers," Talisha said, keeping her voice quiet. "I'm having trouble seeing what's on the other side of the door. Temple's screwing up with my whole systems. Mind telling me what we're dealing with?"

He nodded. "Six humans wearing bulky power armor. One in the back is not. Likely their leader. They've got a heavy-duty battering ram."

"That's an IGF tactic," Talisha said. She took a deep breath. "The one in the back will be a general or lieutenant. Someone to watch the flanks. These will be special forces, higher-ups. Extremely dangerous."

"Not as dangerous as a blast from Ethel," Bluebird said with a smirk.

"Please don't, Big Blue." Talisha cringed. "I've worked with the IGF, they're not bad people. Mostly. We can reason with them and they're likely just as lost as we are."

Bluebird gave her a sideways glance. "They bring nothing but suffering. They will also shoot on sight. You know this."

"It's part of their protocol when engaging in high stakes missions," Talisha said with a nod. "We're gonna have to play this smart. We need allies, not more enemies."

Rogers looked at Talisha with tense shoulders. "So what's the plan?

"Something I probably shouldn't." She lifted her visor and cupped her hands over her mouth and hollered. "HEY!"

If Rogers had a functioning mouth, it would have fallen open in utter disbelief. "You're right, you shouldn't have."

The banging stopped. There was silence on the other side of the door. A brief murmuring followed.

Talisha took that as a sign that they'd heard her. "My name is Talisha Artul. I have a Bounty Hunting License per regulation code five-five-five, point four-three."

A husky voice from the other end of the door responded. "Commander Ajar Mattu of the 497th Division of the IGF Military Forces. I've not had the personal satisfaction. You're hereby being formally requested to leave this site."

"On what grounds?"

"Let us get in, and we'll talk."

"Only so long as you acknowledge my rights as a legal and licensed citizen within the Intergalactic Peacekeeping Federation and ensure for me and my allies safety from retaliation once you come through."

What followed next was an extremely long sigh. It lasted at least six seconds by Talisha's count. There was more muttering.

Finally he called back. "I'm not gonna fucking shoot you, okay. Just...wait for us to get in and we'll talk."

Bluebird's lip curled. "Lying, murderous scumbags. I won't shoot them, but no telling what my fists might do if we are betrayed."

"Blue! Please! It'll be fine!" Talisha hissed through tightly gritted teeth.

Another minute or so passed until finally the IGF special squad broke the doors open. A woman with large armor near the front packed up the battering ram, folding it into a special case that she then hoisted onto her back. Talisha recognized the devices and make of her armor as being a special designation of an engineering specialist.

The man in the back stepped forward, rifle in both hands in front of him but aimed at the ground. He left it to his side in order to extend his hand in Talisha's direction. She took his hand. They lingered for a moment staring into each other's eyes. There was something strangely familiar about him.

"It's an honor to finally meet you, Miss Artul," he said.

"Have we met before?" She squinted.

"No, but some of your assignments with the IGF have come with my recommendation, so you may have seen my name or face in your research or briefings."

Talisha nodded, unsure. "Yeah. That's probably it."

"Who are your friends?"

Talisha gestured to Bluebird with her thumb. "The big one is Agda Valencia, aka Bluebird."

"Big Ugly Bluebird," Bluebird corrected. "Bub to enemies, but most just call me Blue."

Mattu nodded. "I know who you are, Agda. You're a uh—you're a wanted criminal."

"I'm on a planet outside IGF jurisdiction and you have no authority to extradite me," Bluebird growled, taking a threatening step in his direction. She rose a fist to her chest. "Try anything and I will break you into splinters."

"No intention," Mattu said, backing away from her. "Way I see it, I'm going to need all the help I can get."

Bluebird pointed two fingers at her eyes. "I will be watching you, military man."

Talisha made a hasty move to change the subject. "And the android is Sheriff Rogers."

"Former sheriff, Talisha." Rogers tipped his hat. "Howdy, fellas."

"All right, cowboy robot. I accept this." Mattu shook his head, still a bit wide-eyed. "Well here's my problem, the Council of Thirteen has declared this temple to be a security concern to the galaxy, which means none of you can be here."

Bluebird scoffed. "Even if you could make us leave, how would you find the exit?"

Mattu pointed at her. "You're bright. I like you. For better or worse, we're all stuck in this creepy place. I'd like for us to work together to get out of here."

"I think we'd all be open to that," Talisha said.

Bluebird growled again. This time her lip curled up into a snarl and she made a visible show of gnashing her teeth at the IGF squad. Talisha nudged her in the ribs with an elbow.

"I'll be good," Bluebird simmered.

Mattu bit his lip. "Very well. I'd like to know what your plans are. Maybe we can collaborate."

Talisha pulled one of her previously saved scans of the temple, revealing the control core at the temple's center. "A lot of Valran technology utilizes a bioorganic compound that kinda prints itself based off whatever data is stored in its memory banks. Think of it like a really scary 3D printer."

"So the temple isn't just a living thing?" Mattu asked.

Talisha's eyes narrowed. "That's ridiculous. Why would you think that?"

"Never mind. Continue."

"So my theory is that there might be some error going on with the central computing system within the control core. It's constantly replicating all the structures it has in its memory."

The engineer of the squad stepped forward, her shoulders square and face obscured by her helmet. "Name's Langston. What sort of bioorganic compound are we talking about?"

"I don't particularly understand it," Talisha explained. "My ship's made out of a similar material."

"I've a theory," Langston said. "Just wish we had more time."

She marched to one of the statues and knelt on one knee. She retrieved a chisel and hammer from her pack of supplies she carried on her back and attempted to carve a chunk out of the base. Her tools broke against its surface.

"Allow me," Bluebird said.

Bluebird aimed her cannon at the base of the statue and fired the plasma beam, cutting a thin slice off the corner of the pedestal. Langston stared for a second and went right to work, wrapping the block within a translucent filmy material. The second the block was removed from the temple's surface it melted into black goo. The liquid sloshed and squirmed within its container, attempting to break out.

"Well, that just adds evidence to the theory," Langston said. "I'm guessing they might be a form of nanite technology, or some Valran equivalent."

Rogers snapped his fingers. "Talisha! D'ya think you could fire a disruptive blast at some of these walls?"

"The cannon can be made to deliver low-energy pulse shots," Talisha said, her voice trailing off. "What are you thinking?"

"I don't know much, save for how to shoot and robotics." He holstered his pistol and pointed at the wall to the left of them. "A problem with nanite-enforced structures is that certain types of energy can temporarily disrupt their programming. Now there's powerful heat signatures coming from this direction. If you can disrupt shit long enough with your cannon, we might be able to squeeze right on through to the control room."

Mattu clicked his tongue. "I don't like it. How do we know a disruption like that won't bring the entire temple down on top of us?"

Talisha fiddled with the settings on her arm cannon. "A controlled blast shouldn't be enough to send that large of a ripple effect. Anyway, it's a risk we're gonna have to take."

She took aim at the wall and charged the beam. The color was a semitranslucent gray. The blast struck the hard wall and seemed to dissipate almost immediately. They all stood there, staring in silence. For a moment it seemed as if the idea had failed. Then the wall shifted, parting ways and reforming itself into a new corridor. A long platform emerged over a drop into infinite darkness on either side.

Rogers made a whistling sound and tightened his hat around his head. "God damn, I am smart."

Talisha patted him on the shoulder. "Yes, you are, cowboy. Good thinking."

"I want the soldier men to go in front of us," Bluebird said. "So they don't shoot us in the back."

Langston raised an objection to that. "How do we know you won't do the same?" The other squad members echoed her sentiments.

Mattu pinched the bridge of his nose between his fingers. "We'll mix up the squads a bit. Some in front, some in the back. We don't need any further reasons to mistrust one another."

Talisha nodded. "Agreed."

Bluebird appeared uneasy but made no further protests. She scowled at the armored men and women beneath her while she took the rear.

Commander Mattu took a position directly in front of Bluebird, and behind Talisha. He gave Talisha a strange smile as they exchanged glances; a fleeting, nervous look. She couldn't find it in herself to return it.

Chapter Ten

SNIDELY AND NERGAL found it easy enough to sneak onto the IGF perimeter around the Valran Temple. The battle raging on the ground and in the skies overhead left most completely oblivious to the presence of the two gangly monsters slinking about in the desert. They drew close to the camp and hid behind a stack of supply crates.

Nergal found it utterly freeing to finally traverse without his hazmat suit. It'd been so long since he'd allowed himself to walk about without it. He'd forgotten what the wind felt like against his skin.

Snidely had given him a change of clothes looted from the corpses of the refugees in the shack: a black pair of pants and heavy boots. Nergal was still somewhat sad about losing his coat he'd taken from the bar fight, but Snidely found him a stylish alternative. It was a flowing white jacket and cape ensemble with a diabolic hood. Snidely jokingly referred to it as *wasteland chic*.

There were only a handful of guards stationed within a bunker guarding the current temple entrance. Most of their attentions were focused on firing up at the skies and praying that none of the fiery wreckage came crashing down upon them. They would soon have new fears to deal with.

Nergal rubbed the back of Snidely's neck affectionately. "We must be cautious in our approach. They're heavily armed and armored."

Snidely cackled. "It won't be enough. Remember, we have superpowers."

"And need I remind you that neither of us are bulletproof?" Nergal said.

"Relax," Snidely chided. "They won't see me coming."

"How's that?" Nergal pulled away from him, eyes narrowed.

"Remember, the critters don't show up on imaging systems, and now, neither do I." Snidely grinned wide, his eyes full of manic glee. "Be back in a jiffy."

Nergal stared as Snidely slunk off. The man had truly changed, and not just physically. He was a far cry from the simpering corporate toady they'd first met out in the desert. He was gleeful and arrogant, willingly charging into an armed encampment in the midst of a full-scale battle. There was nothing for Nergal to do but lick his chapped lips and watch the show.

Snidely crept forward, moving uncannily fast. Nergal hadn't quite seen his friend's new abilities in action and even he was startled by them. He'd often prided himself on his own nigh supernatural reflexes and agility, but this was something else entirely. It was positively inhuman—rapid, blinking movements across the desert.

The soldiers were wearing powerful suits of armor. Their guns were highly sophisticated bits of machinery that could instantly shred an armored target, let alone a single civilian in refugee clothes. It wouldn't be enough to prepare them for what was coming.

Snidely dove through the bunker, dodging bullets as he went. His nails elongated into vicious claws that shredded through their armor, rendering it completely useless before his onslaught. Snidely dug his claws into the weak points in the soldier's armor about his neck and lifted up, decapitating him instantly. One poor bastard found himself slashed about the midsection and fell to the ground screaming as he watched his innards spill out of him.

In a matter of moments, the bunker had been cleared. The encampment was already full of screaming wounded and fallen corpses. Snidely's swift murder of those on the backline would go unnoticed. Nergal quickly hurried over to him and scooped one of the discarded assault rifles from off the ground. Snidely raised an eyebrow.

"I hardly doubt we'll need that," he said.

"Your overconfidence is troubling," Nergal said, checking the rifle magazine. "Our former associates are likely within the temple, and my ability to spread disease will be useless against a fully armored bounty hunter and a robot."

Snidely froze for a second. He ran his hand along the back of his neck. For a moment it seemed like the old jittery aspects of his personality had resurfaced.

"You're right," Snidely said. "Of course you're right. Caution is a powerful tool."

Nergal lowered the gun and gave Snidely his full attention. "What's wrong?"

Snidely shrugged. "I let the power get to me. You spend so long feeling utterly useless, all that's available is a disregard for ethics and the cunning to get where you want. Always walking a knife's edge between ambition and annihilation."

Nergal bit his lower lip and looked at the ground. "When the time comes, will you trample me as you've done to so many others?"

Snidely laughed, his voice shaky. "I still need your help inside the temple, silly billy."

Nergal's mouth crinkled and he aimed the rifle in Snidely's direction. "If you ever call me that again, so help me I will shove this straight up your ass."

"You certainly know how to turn a phrase." Snidely blanched.

Nergal saw the doubts crossing Snidely's face. He'd been too hostile.

Years ago, Dalton had once warned him about opportunistic corporate types. *"They're usually up front with their skeezy behavior, but it's passed off as a joke or an aside. It's meant to throw doubts on whatever horrible thing they've got planned next."*

Those words had taken on a chilling effect with what came later. Dalton had been a prophet of his own death. Nergal had no intention of getting suckered in like that ever again.

While Nergal's reputation for being a nasty and curmudgeonly son of a shitheel had served him well over the years, it wouldn't help him here. Snidely had been a sniveling coward three days ago, and was now well on his way to becoming an unhinged bloodthirsty tyrant. It was only to be expected that once he got a taste of true power he'd run wild with it.

It also meant that the pale white creature was not to be trusted. Nergal would have to remain on his guard regarding his new fuck-buddy and ally. He'd have to play things like one of Snidely's corporate peers, mincing words and masquerading his intentions.

Nergal placed an arm around Snidely's shoulders and pulled him close. "Forgive my nasty disposition. It's just part of my charm."

Snidely nuzzled his neck in response, lapping at his chin with an unnaturally long tongue. "I love your hideous nature. It suits us well."

For Nergal, the rhetoric of embracing one's own hideousness had long since ceased to be useful or comforting. All he wanted in this life was to get off this planet and be left alone. He wasn't about to tell his new twink that. This corporate lackey turned mercenary needed that rhetoric. Nergal could see the light fade from his eyes when the delusion failed.

Nergal knew the feeling all too well. Better to be cold and nasty than to open up to a universe that'd cast you out and damned you. Snidely still had grandiose visions about getting worshipped and feared by those who'd once trampled him. Nergal had to be wary of such ambitions. False hope was contagious.

"Our love is god," Nergal whispered into his ear. "Now let's take what we're owed."

CHING SHIH DOVE through the hallways, dipping beneath security cameras and laser grids to get closer to her goal. She didn't wait for guards or civilians to pass her by so she could slip by unnoticed. She hadn't the time for that. Anyone in her way was cut down with a clean sweep of her sword.

At some point, someone had sounded the alarms. Red lights flashed through the halls and harsh sirens blared overhead. It mattered little. All the guards would soon be converging on her position. She could still choose the battlefield.

The central corridor of the Mayflower was a wide-open office area with a balcony overlooking several monitors and a large domed window to view the planet below. It'd be the ideal location to send every last one of these blood-sucking capitalists to their graves. She used her blaster to fire open an entry way into the grates in the ceiling. She leapt ten feet into the air, vanishing into the vents and scurrying through them like a spider.

Once inside the central area, she fired a few shots out of the vents at one of the security cameras. She took a moment to attach herself to a harness and cord and loop them around the vent grating. Doors slid open on either side of the room as guards wearing Plymouth's gray uniforms and powerful armor marched in, many of them wielding barrier shields. She had to smile. They were finally giving her the welcome she deserved.

She took a careful glance down below, making a quick calculation of the small force gathering in the room. There were at least a hundred, each with their guns swiveling about the area, searching for her. A good dozen or so had clumped up together nicely just beneath her.

Ching Shih retrieved a grenade from a satchel tied around her waist. A wicked smile crept over her features as she dropped it onto the unsuspecting army below. The explosion rocked the satellite as bodies flew through the air, limbs flying from their torsos.

She dropped down into the room, and before the smoke cleared had taken out six more guards with her blaster fire. Shots rang as she swung around the room on the cord attached to the ceiling. The lingering clouds of smoke gave her plenty of camouflage to weave in and out and cause havoc in their ranks. Some died to stray blaster fire from their own comrades.

Energy blasts severed the cord just as she was about to make another pass overhead. She dropped and rolled to her feet directly in the middle of the room. A bead of sweat dripped from her brow as she turned to face the sixty or so guns still aimed at her head.

From the balcony came a harsh voice. "And now it comes to this, the proud Ching Shih, fallen before me."

Ching Shih's gaze darted up. Madame Inspector stood with her hands leaned against the railing, a smug expression on her face. She clapped slowly.

"I've faced worse odds than this," Ching Shih said, her voice serene. "I've still to hold to that promise I made you."

Madame Inspector laughed. "Kill the bitch."

The deafening sounds of blaster fire returned. Ching Shih snapped to the ground and slid toward the nearest set of guards, swiftly shifting her body and using their own barrier shields as cover as her sword flickered through the air. One by one, they fell to her martial prowess.

She stomped on the edge of a discarded shield so that it flipped up into her open palm to deflect a barrage of bullets. With a mighty roar, she rushed forward, hiding behind the shield. She used it to batter down the front row of her opponents. Her sword flashed and blood splattered against her garments.

Chest heaving, she slowly lowered her blade. She'd done it. She'd killed every last guard on the satellite. She looked up at the balcony. Madame Inspector was gone.

Ching Shih frowned. The coward had fled. She tucked her sword and blaster back into her sash and made a running leap along the wall.

Near the back of the platform was a small office visible behind a set of windows. Ching Shih hurried inside to find a computer system and monitors with a live feed from the planet below playing across the screen. Her fingers flew across the keyboard, typing out a series of commands to give her a better view of the battle taking place.

Both sides had severely weakened each other. Most of the carrier ships had been destroyed in the process, and the IGF had lost at least half of their anti-air tanks. Only a hundred or so of their turrets remained. The situation was now ideal for another force to sweep in and clean up.

Ching Shih tapped her headset with two fingers. "Alert the men. It's time to attack. Kill everyone."

BATTERED BY THE constant onslaught of Plymouth warships, the beleaguered military troops of the IGF could only stare in openmouthed horror as the red sails came flying over the horizon. These ships were smaller than either of Plymouth's or the IGF's, but it was their deadliest asset. They had superior speed and maneuverability, easily dodging the barrages of cannons and missile fire.

The Red Fleet closed in on the battlefield from both sides taking advantage of the scattered and surprised forces. Plymouth ships went down in screaming infernos. IGF wyverns spiraled out of control, forcing them to land where they were subsequently gunned down.

One carrier ship that somehow still remained slowly swung around to turn its fire on the encroaching vessels. Most of its volleys missed the Red Fleet ships, but all it took was a single hit to send them crashing into burning hunks along the sand. One carrier could cripple the fleet if left remaining.

Several of Ching Shih's men launched themselves from the schooners on hover bikes. They swarmed like flies around the lone carrier vessel, pestering it with blaster fire. It couldn't hope to focus on so many targets at once, even as it continued to down schooner after schooner.

Gradually the aggressive fire from the pirates showed signs of damage on the carrier's hull, as Plymouth soldiers hurried to the decks in an attempt to bring down the flying pirates with blaster fire of their own. It was a wasted effort. The carrier was soon brought low, dipping out of the skies before slowly crashing into the planet, sending debris flying and crushing several unlucky grounds troops beneath its hull. Their screams were drowned beneath the groaning metal.

TALISHA TOOK A heavy breath as the platform ended, leading them to a circular chamber where a long drop existed on either side. Several more platforms reached out into wide awnings on either side of them. She turned to face Rogers.

"Hey, you still detecting those heat signatures?" she asked.

"Sure am, but there's a problem." He scratched the sides of his head.

"What's that?"

Rogers gestured in a circle around his head with his pistol. "Heat's coming from everywhere. No telling where to head off to next. Likely a buncha different systems, but no telling which one is which."

"Dammit!" Talisha seethed and looked away, brow furrowed in contemplation.

Mattu stepped in front of them, surveying the room. He bit his lower lip and placed his hands on his hips. One of his officers approached him from behind.

"There's enough rooms here," the officer suggested. "We could easily split up and search them all."

Mattu shook his head. "With all due respect, that's the goofiest thing I've heard today. With the building shifting the way it is, there's no telling if we'd ever meet back up with each other."

Talisha folded her arms and looked around the room. She'd half a mind to fly up to the ceiling and blast a way out of the temple, but feared she'd just keep flying forever. This had long since ceased feeling like any sort of structure and now seemed to be an entire world unto itself.

"Talisha..." A ghostly voice whispered into her headset.

She turned sharply, lowering her visor. There was something there at the left end of the chamber; a floating transparent being. It was clearly not human, having wings draped around itself like a cloak and massive bird talons for feet. Its face was obscured in shadows, though she thought she saw the silhouette of a beak.

"Follow," the voice beckoned before the creature disappeared down the corridor, taking a swift right.

"Follow me," Talisha said. "I might have just gotten some help."

She hurried quickly after it, arm cannon at the ready. The others joined in swift pursuit. The phantom was fast, speeding through the corridors and passing through some walls completely. They barely had a chance to slide beneath a wall slamming down in front of them as the temple continued to transform. It was like rushing through an obstacle course just trying to keep up, leaping around newly formed barriers and statues that sprang suddenly from the ground.

The specter brought them into another large chamber. It looked to Talisha almost like a cathedral, complete with arched pillars and decorative murals painted across the domed ceiling. At the center of the chamber stood a tall cylindrical object behind a glowing blue panel.

"Come..." the Valran specter beckoned with an outstretched claw.

Talisha rushed into the chamber. Bluebird grabbed her by the arm.

"What do you think you're doing, little bounty hunter?" Bluebird asked. Her eyes were fearful.

"Can you see it?" Talisha said, voice breathy. "The Valran."

Bluebird shook her head, but her grip tightened. "I see nothing. We don't know what's in there."

"Why are you suddenly so concerned?" Talisha said in a quiet voice. "This isn't like you."

"It isn't," Bluebird admitted. "But this place, it feels strange. Something is wrong here."

Talisha grabbed Bluebird's hand and held it tightly. "I have to do this."

"I know," Bluebird said, her voice tinged with sadness. She reluctantly released her grip. "I know. You need answers."

"That and we all might die here if I don't fix the temple's systems."

"That too." Bluebird brushed Talisha's cheek with a finger. "Be safe. I'll not survive losing someone else I care about."

Talisha smiled. "I'll be fine. I promise. You've got my back after all."

Bluebird nodded, her expression soft and tender. "That I do, little one."

Talisha took a deep breath and marched to the center of the room. Some of the IGF soldiers attempted to follow, but Mattu held them back. Talisha looked back at him. He had his mouth open like he wanted to say something. He gave her a thumb's up. She returned the gesture and went on her way.

The specter hovered in front the glowing control panel as she approached. The cylinder behind it released a vent of steam before slowly opening to reveal a small chamber capable of fitting a single person. Talisha looked from the spirit to the chamber with a wary gaze.

"*Waiting,*" the voice said.

"This is such a bad idea," Talisha whispered.

There were very few times Talisha had ever acted completely on faith despite all calculated consequences pointing to the contrary. The memory of the last time still stuck out sorely in her head. She'd sat down with her mother after several long months of agonizing over the decision.

"I'm going to start transitioning," she'd told her. "I want you to call me Talisha."

Her mother had been less than enthused, drinking heavily out a flask of alcohol. "Why that name? Any name but that one."

Nothing was more painful and awkward than one simple conversation. Nothing more frightening. The only comfort she'd been able to take from that moment is that she'd been able to brace herself for the pain and loneliness that followed.

"*Waiting,*" the voice whispered again.

"What's in there?" Talisha demanded. "I've a right to know."

"*Trials.*"

"What trials?" she insisted.

"*Guardian.*"

Talisha shook her head. "I don't understand. Can't you explain?"

"*Weak,*" the specter said, its voice dropping to a faint hoarse whisper. "*Fading. Hurry.*"

"This feels like a trap," Talisha said, "But whatever. Fine."

Steeling her resolve, she stepped into the cylindrical chamber. She turned around and gave a saluting gesture to Bluebird and Rogers. Bluebird tried to give her an encouraging grin but couldn't mask the expression of wide-eyed concern on her face. That Bluebird also had Rogers gripped in a frightened embrace didn't help matters.

If Bluebird was worried, so was Talisha.

The doors to the chamber closed, trapping her in darkness. She floated up, carried on a current of air. A sudden light shot through the chamber, blinding her.

When she could finally see again, she found herself standing in an open field with the sun shining on her face. She was surrounded on all sides by luxuriant green ivy and radiant flowers of every color. Valran structures of faded rustic hues spread out before her. These were smaller in stature than the temple and were spread out in such a way that it appeared like they were meant to grow with the plants and wildlife rather than overwhelm it.

A stream of water ran through an inlet in the tiled stone beneath her feet and up to a larger structure several feet away from her, where an engineered waterfall poured forth from windows at the top of the building. She lifted her visor and turned her face to the sky. The air was cool and the sun shone warmly against her face.

This was more like what she'd imagined the Valran cities to be like from the texts she'd studied in her youth—peaceful, serene. It stood in stark contrast to the cold industrial nightmare that was the temple on Archimedes IV. She could hardly believe they were both Valran in origin.

A stooped figure in a shawl could be seen through the window of one of the smaller buildings. They bore Valran features but lacked the molted appearance of the ghoulish statues seen around the temple. The figure acknowledged her presence with a simple nod and hobbled toward the open doorway.

As they came outside, Talisha could see they were definitely an older figure, bearing heavy bags of wrinkles beneath their eyes. Their wings seemed all but useless to them as they hobbled around on a knobby wooden cane. Many of their feathers had gone gray, but some still had vibrant auburn hues.

"We were hoping it'd be your mother who'd come to us." They didn't so much speak as they broadcasted her thoughts clearly into her head in the Valran tongue. The language sounded so much more beautiful when they spoke it, unlike the squawking noises her mother had made when trying to pronounce their dialect.

"Am I that much of a disappointment?" Talisha winced. She couldn't help but feel a tad put off by that remark.

"We meant no disrespect. We would be glad to have either of you, only it is troublesome that she never made the journey. Clearly, you have surpassed her."

"Yeah. How long is this gonna take? 'Cause I was mentioned something about some trials, and meanwhile I left my only two friends on this planet with some unsavory individuals."

"Time is irrelevant."

"Okay, I know that's something you cryptic, mystic folks like saying but—"

"You misunderstand. This is a psychic vision being projected via the bond you have made with your armor. Time is quite literally irrelevant. This will all be over in a matter of minutes."

Talisha frowned, taken aback. "Oh. That's convenient, and surprisingly efficient."

The Valran creature made a strange expression of opening their beak in such a way as to mimic a smile. At the very least she hoped it was a smile and not openmouthed shock at her utter lack of decorum.

"You want to know why your mother was chosen," the Valran said. *"You want to know about the burden she passed onto you."*

Talisha shrugged, but her eyes were earnest. "That specter back in the temple mentioned something about trials and a guardian?"

The Valran's eyes softened, then closed tightly. Their talons wrapped tightly around the knob of the cane as they turned their face away, shoulders heavy. Their wings shook and their chest heaved as if in great pain.

"So the wraiths still occupy the temple. Troubling. I have much to show you."

The greenery and lush temple environment vanished, replaced by the shimmering blackness of space. Stars and planets glittered all around them. Talisha could only gasp as she beheld the full scope of the cosmos. The knowledge of every planet and star and constellation the Valran held was but a stray thought away. She'd but to reach out with her mind and grasp it.

The Valran brushed their claws across the infinite space. *"You've long felt an itch to explore, to reach, to know. It is a need that is more than human, it is universal. It is the desire of all living things to expand beyond their borders. We came to believe that in a society where the basic needs and wants of every living being within that society were met, then we could all work together to accomplish greatness."*

"What happened?"

"Even at our people's lowest point, that of the current era, we are still regarded us legends. What do you think? We began by creating a perfect world; one without poverty, sickness, or inequality. We then sought to bring that world to the universe.

"Therein is where we became arrogant. Like fools, we assumed that the peace and harmony we had achieved upon our own worlds made us a more enlightened race. Prejudice, greed, the desire to exert our own supremacy and stamp others beneath our heel...these are evils that can sprout up in even the most enlightened of societies."

Glowing lines sprouted from a green and lush planet toward the rest of the galaxy, slowly spilling out in all directions. Talisha had to watch in horror as she realized the imperialistic implications of the Valran's words. They hadn't been a race of nomads, but conquerors. The temples scattered across the galaxy were the last remains of a powerful galactic empire.

She was shown images of Valran ships blotting out the skies of nearby planets. She saw a slew of alien races trampled as their homes and crops burned. She had an inkling she'd never see their like anywhere else again. They all faced extinction beneath the Valran machine.

"That was what became of our campaign, but that's not how it started. All it takes is an inkling, the germ of a thought to begin when one person decides that their life holds more value than another's."

"Yeah," Talisha said with a resigned sigh. "Humanity has been there before."

"We did not move to stop the corruption until it was too late. When the terrible ideals of genocide sprouted, we naively believed we could reason with those whose hearts had been blackened by hate. We fought with ineffective weapons of art and reason, while they had with them the fervor of blind fury, and the will to act.

"The enlightened society we wanted fell into an industrial nightmare of machines and totalitarian horror. Those who resisted the new regime were silenced or destroyed, and, for our failure, the galaxy burned."

The images rippled into more worlds that appeared very much like the interior of the Valran temple, only more cohesive and sterile. Entire planets were covered to create a mechanized tribute to a twisted mockery of Valran culture. Talisha realized with sickening horror that many of the lofty structures were meant to enforce the knowledge of who had power and who lacked it. While the designs were different from the buildings she'd seen back on the IGF capital planet of Khorthall, the philosophy was the same. Entering into one of these buildings was meant to subjugate the citizenry before the might of the state.

"We stretched ourselves thin with conquest. Our resources were low, and our economy in shambles. We could not afford another campaign, but only more war had any hope of sustaining us. That's when we made a breakthrough and created warp travel; the technology that would ultimately doom our entire species."

"That explains how you were able to reach so far," Talisha said. "I'd heard theories the Valran were warp-capable, but we thought warp travel was just fiction."

"It is all too real, and it wrought devastating consequences not only across the galaxy, but to us. The ability to cross dimensional gaps created for us the ability to arrive instantly to any planet we wished to conquer, but at a terrible cost. Every time we made a jump, a little piece of ourselves was left behind. We soon became withered, frail husks of a people.

"Those who rejected warp travel and resisted the current regime managed to avoid this hideous alteration, but the more militant among us soon resembled the ghoulish statues you likely saw as you traveled through the temple. The war was brought to an eventual close when our soldiers were too weak and frail to fight anymore, their bodies utterly decimated by the warp-disease."

She then saw images of frail and sickly Valran. There were small children whose feathers were gray and molting long before their time. Many died in the streets as terrible, skeletal figures. For some it was like their bodies had started decomposition long before their vitals stopped functioning—a slow, horrific death.

"We soon found that, while the condition was hastened by excessive warp travel, anyone who had ever used the technology or spent time near the technology had succumbed to it. Not a single member of our race was free from the sickness, and though our scientists raced round the clock for a cure, our fate had already been sealed.

"Some of us sought to stave off the condition by dwelling in that between-dimension permanently. Our bodies took on spectral forms as some of us learned to survive in this new state of being, kept from dissipating into the void through psychic will alone. It kept us from dying out completely, but drove many into a traumatized frenzy, unable to bear the strain of it all. They were either violent or fell into a comatose state, stuck in the constant repetition of a twisted memory. They were like ghosts.

"We few who remained understood that this was the end of our race, so we took steps to preserve what we thought were the best snapshots of our culture. The human race was just reaching out into the galaxy in those years and calling attention to our forgotten conquered worlds with their corporate wars."

"How long did you remain in that state before you found my mother?" Talisha asked. "And why did you choose her?"

A little girl with dark brown skin and thick black hair appeared before her, wandering the abandoned streets of a bombed-out city. She was dirty and crying heavily. She hadn't eaten in days. It was the original Talisha Artul.

"A human girl wandered into one of our temples. Those of us with our minds intact saw a fledgling in need of basic care and protection. We spent the next few years not concerned with our own well-being, but caring after the needs of another.

Talisha now saw her mother fully grown and wearing the armor of the Valran. All of her mother's deeds were splayed out before her, both good and bad. She saw images of the families she'd rescued, and the innocents she'd gunned down with her cannon and blaster. It was the full and complete legend of the great Talisha Artul, and she carried with her always the signature armor of the Valran.

"Do you see now why she was chosen? It was a selfish action, a means of hoping that the galaxy would remember us not as tyrants, but for the one truly great thing we as a people ever accomplished. In our darkest hour, we fed and cared for an alien child."

"She was capable of evil," Talisha said, her words crawling out of her mouth, each tinged with sadness. "But she also did a lot of good."

"She contained multitudes, as do we all."

The images faded and she was once more standing in the lush temple grounds with the old Valran leaning against their cane. Their eyes shined brightly, as if they contained all the stars of the galaxy. The Valran walked along the stream toward the large structure.

"The temple…" Talisha said, searching for the right words to explain what was happening outside. "It's expanding. This planet might suffer if it's allowed to continue."

The Valran stopped walking. They whirled round to face her. *"The Wraiths. You woke them when you brought the temple above ground. It's their memories feeding into the core systems."*

"What are the wraiths?" Talisha asked. "Are those the Valran who turned violent?"

"The last vestiges of their pain and suffering carried on as a psychic projection, still capable of doing great harm. You might think of them as ghosts. We must hurry."

"I thought you said time was irrelevant?"

"The wraiths are capable of tapping into this very psychic connection. If we do not hurry, they will overwhelm your consciousness and take control of your body." The Valran then rushed forward grabbing Talisha by the arms.

They lead her into the mouth of the tallest structure, where the rustic smell of ancient stone awaited her. Inside was another chamber, wholly dark save for a thin shaft of light in the center of the room. Within that beam hovered a pulsating blue orb with shimmering gold lines that flashed and glittered in the light.

"I've seen this place," Talisha whispered. "In my dreams."

"A projection seeped into your mind from your helmet," the Valran explained, leading her further into the chamber. *"It was always meant for you to come here. We had a series of trials planned and it was all supposed to be very mystical and teach you life-affirming lessons, but now there's no time."*

"Sounds educational," Talisha said, hurrying toward the orb in the center of the room. "Shame I'm having to miss it. So what is this thing?"

"A psychic representation of data that will be sent into your helmet upon activation," The Valran explained. *"The armor we gave your mother was only a training suit, it contained a mere fraction of the true capabilities of our people."*

"So we're looking at a serious hardware upgrade." Talisha nodded, biting her lip. "I like it, but how does this help us save the planet?"

"Without this data, you will be unable to navigate the temple to the control core where you can silence the screaming thoughts of the wraiths. A warning though."

Talisha could've groaned but restrained herself. "There's always a warning."

"This was no temple, but a tomb. It was meant to keep the wraiths locked and secured until such hope as a cure for their condition could be found. Our fear is that any attempt to dislodge their hold over the systems may unleash them upon the world. You would face the last great shame of our people."

"A horde of angry ghost-birds," Talisha said. "Not the weirdest thing I've ever gone up against."

She reached out to grab the orb, but was halted by a talon resting against her arm.

The Valran looked into her face, eyes wide and full of fear. *"The streams of data will hurt."*

Talisha stared at the pulsating orb. She took one last determined glare at it before lowering the visor on her helmet. "I'm no stranger to pain."

They lowered their head and nodded, backing away in reverence. *"Fight well, daughter of the Valran. You are the last of our kind."*

A hideous scream filled the temple walls. Talisha darted her gaze to the ceiling to see faces forming in the darkness and a hundred translucent talons reaching out to her from every side. She turned back to the orb and shoved her arm cannon directly into it.

Crackling blue lightning pulsed out of the orb and enveloped her. Talisha threw back her head in agony as her mind was overwhelmed with psychic visions. The wraiths materialized within the temple, swirling around the platform.

The Valran brandished their cane and stood with arms outstretched in front of Talisha. They placed their talons over their skull and concentrated, creating a domed barrier around Talisha's helpless body. Hungry claws tore at the barrier's surface, bending it with the force of their violent will.

Talisha let out one last scream before pulling away from the orb, and the floor collapsed beneath her. The rest of the vision was ripped away as she plummeted into darkness. Shrieking echoes remained in her mind until the last.

Chapter Eleven

THINGS HAD BEEN so much simpler when Rogers had been a sheriff. Bad guys stroll into town, and either they get a stern talking to and get intimidated by a scary robot showing them who's boss, or they get shot. It was easy to identify the bad guy and the lines between right and wrong. There were no ethical debates about upholding corrupt systems or perpetuating oppression or weird alien magic.

It was also an incredibly limiting existence, filled with loneliness. He was always willing to protect others but had never had anyone willing to do the same for him. Not until Talisha. She'd put herself at great personal risk with the hope it might save all of them.

Bluebird still held him tightly in her grip. To her surprise, and his, he returned that terrified embrace. As the minutes passed, they feared the worst.

Then, steam emerged from the capsule once more, and the doors slid open. Talisha's armor had undergone a radical transformation. Its color was now an electric blue and tinged with stripes of black and hints of lurid gold. The armor now came equipped with dome-like pauldrons large as her head and a thicker breastplate. Her arm cannon had at least tripled in size, but most impressive were the changes to her helmet.

The visor was now a thin black lens covering her eyes while the rest had taken on a pointed, beak-like appearance. Ominous spikes jutted out at an angle from behind the helmet, giving her the silhouette and overall impression of a bird of prey. She stepped out of the chamber.

Mattu approached her, placing a cautionary hand in front of his squad. "Talisha, your armor…are you all right? What happened?"

Rogers did a quick scan of the armor. It was significantly more advanced than her previous suit. He couldn't determine the function of the pauldrons, though his scans revealed highly advanced and complicated machinery running through them. He suspected they might be powering other functions of the suit, but it was a wild guess at best.

Bluebird released Rogers and hurried past Mattu to Talisha's side. She might've picked up the bounty hunter and swung her around had Talisha not held a warning palm in her direction. Rogers noted the look of apprehension on Bluebird's face. He didn't like that.

Talisha grunted and placed a hand over her helmet. "I'm okay. Just keep your distance."

"What happened in there, cowgirl?" Rogers said.

Talisha laughed a little. "You're not gonna believe—" Her words were cut off as she doubled over and screamed.

Sparks of electricity ran over the whole of her suit. She gripped the sides of her helmet, hollering in pain. Rogers ran forward and pulled Bluebird back while Talisha's suit pulsed with a ghostly blue light.

A specter showed its howling face superimposed over Talisha's visor. It opened its beak in a hideous screaming yowl before Talisha's screams were drowned out by its own.

"Talisha, what in the heck is going on!" Rogers yelled.

She looked at him and stood. She pointed her arm cannon directly at the group. The IGF squad responded by immediately raising their rifles and blasters to point in her direction.

Talisha managed to croak out a single hoarse word. "Run."

The cannon charged, a pure white beam of powerful energy. Rogers and Bluebird were close enough to the center of the chamber that they had plenty of room to dive out the way. The members of the IGF squad on the platform were not so lucky. Their bulky armor left them little in the way of speed and caused them to take up most of the platform they occupied. On either side of them was a drop to their doom in the depths of the chasm below.

Only Mattu escaped the power of the fully-charged beam thanks to his more agile suit. He had just enough time to turn around to see his squad vaporized under the heat of the beam. A brilliant flash of light, and then nothing. Only ashes remained.

"No!" Mattu cried. He clenched his fist, staring at the space where his squad once occupied.

The wraith's face appeared once more over Talisha's visor. Talisha flew into the air and aimed her arm cannon at Mattu. Rogers ducked out of hiding to fire several decisive shots in her direction. The wraith screamed at him as Talisha dodged the incoming bullets.

Bluebird grabbed Rogers by the shoulder. "What do you think you're doing? You could kill her!"

"There's something inside her," Rogers shot back. "It's controlling her. Making her act all funky. Figured if I could shoot some sense into her, we might dislodge it."

Bluebird's eyes widened. She looked near ready to smack him. "That is a very bad plan! Bad robot!"

"You got any better ideas?" Rogers yelled.

Mattu stood and walked to Talisha. She looked down at him, and her visor flashed blue with the hate and anger of the wraith inside. Mattu's entire body quivered with fear, but he stood strong in the face of her power.

"First time I met your mother, we'd been brought in to help evacuate the colonists on Barlin V." His voice quivered, with both fear and the pain of memory. "She scared the hell out of all of us with that alien technology of hers. She was smart though. Capable. A good soldier."

Bluebird shouted to him. "Commander Mattu, get down!"

Mattu pressed forward. "She was also the most beautiful woman I ever laid eyes on. You look a lot like her."

Talisha gazed upon Mattu, saying nothing. She turned the cannon in his direction and charged her energy beam. Bluebird had to snag Rogers to keep him from rushing out into the open.

"If this is to work," she said. "You must have faith."

"She's the only friend I ever had, Blue," Rogers said, his voice aching with desperation.

Bluebird held him all the tighter then.

Mattu took another step. He was now on the brink of the platform, staring up at Talisha. She floated over his head like an angel of death ready to annihilate him.

"I'm sorry I wasn't there for you, growing up," He choked on his words toward the end. "I messed up. I made your mother hate me. You've got every right to hate me too, but don't let it stop you from living. Don't make my sins your future."

Talisha stopped charging the beam on her cannon. Her visor lifted, and all could see her eyes, tearful and bloodshot. There was so much anger in that expression, so much hate and pain. Her scream and that of the wraith's became one.

Talisha clutched at the sides of her head and convulsed about in the air. The wraith clung to her armor even as she wrestled against it. Something crawled out of her back. It looked like a ghostly projection of the armor she wore, like the wraith had bonded to her physical appearance.

With a final scream she freed herself from the apparition and went tumbling toward the chasm below. Mattu lunged to the edge, catching her by the hand. Her fingers slipped for a terrifying moment, then he hoisted her onto the platform. They stared up at the ghostly projection of the wraith as it screamed and writhed, still holding on to the appearance of Talisha's armor. It turned its own cannon down to them.

"Suck my big fat girl-dick," Talisha said through gritted teeth.

She aimed at the wraith, charged her beam, and fired. The apparition froze midscreech, shattering into oblivion as the energy blast connected with its fragmented body. Talisha collapsed against the platform, breathing heavily. She turned her eyes to the ashes that were the remnants of the IGF squad.

"Mattu," she whispered. Her face was still wet with tears. "I'm so sorry. I'm so so sorry."

"They knew the cost," he said. "As do we all. Do you remember any of what I said?"

She sat up. "Yes."

"And?" He looked at her, face apprehensive and pleading.

"And there's nothing to talk about." She climbed to her feet, joints aching. "This was never about you. You might be my father, but it doesn't matter right now."

He bit his lower lip, then shook his head. "Then what helped you fight back that creature's possession?"

Talisha reached down to help him to his feet. "You reminded me that I had something the wraith lacked."

"That being?"

She looked him squarely in the eyes. "The ability to see beyond my own pain."

His mouth hung open as she brushed past him to go hug Rogers and Bluebird. He folded his arms over his chest and looked upon the ashes of his fallen troopers. A wounded sigh escaped him, and he forced himself to turn his head away.

Rogers approached him. "Seeing so much death. Gotta be hard on ya."

Mattu clicked his tongue. "That's the worst part about it. After a while, it stops hurting as much. You become numbed to loss."

"Hope I never get like that," Rogers said. He turned to look at Talisha and Bluebird walking to the edge of the platform, then said in a lowered voice. "You really think Talisha's your daughter?"

"Her mother never had that hardened look in her eye." Mattu's voice shook as he followed Rogers's gaze, his jaw clenched.

"And you do? Is that why you came down here? To meet her?" Rogers said.

Mattu stared at him, brows furrowed. He hoisted his rifle to his shoulder. "I came to do my duty to the Federation."

That's not what Rogers wanted to hear. He turned his back on Mattu, walking to join Talisha and Bluebird. "Your Federation got a whole lot of people on this planet killed."

Mattu's voice grew low and gruff. "You'll get no argument from me."

CHING SHIH MADE her way swiftly through the rest of the Mayflower, eager to get to the weapon's command center on the satellite. Any second Madame Inspector could order the weapon to fire on the planet. If the inspector thought that the battle had turned her against her, the planet would fry. It's exactly what Ching Shih would do were the roles reversed.

One cranky old woman with a sword and a blaster stood against the annihilation of an entire planet. She'd suffered worse odds. She turned a corner down an illuminated walkway toward a lone platform standing over a fifty-foot shaft below.

At the end of the platform she could see open doors to a room full of command console. There wasn't a soul in sight. She exhaled, relieved. She'd plenty of time to step in and shut the entire satellite down.

Ching Shih allowed herself a moment to smile, congratulating herself. Madame Inspector would have no further recourse. This would be the end of the terrifying reign of the Plymouth Corporation, and the galaxy would at last see justice. She ran to that open room, heart thudding with every footfall.

Bulky machinery took a thunderous step around the corner and opened fire. Machine guns in each mechanized arm blast a torrent of bullets in her direction. She'd barely enough time to slide under them and into the control room.

She finally got a decent look at her attacker. It was the largest suit of power armor she'd ever seen. Ten feet tall and eight hundred pounds of nigh-impenetrable metal, and within each gargantuan gauntleted fist were a set of rail guns, each with chains of bullets that trailed along the floor. Behind the faceplate in the chest of the power armor, Ching Shih could see Madame Inspector's grinning face.

She brushed her hair out of her face and brandished her sword. "You should have activated the cannons already. You might have had a chance at victory."

"If I've a chance at securing my prize, I will take it." Madame Inspector seethed, taking a heavy step in Ching Shih's direction. "Rest assured, that miserable planet will burn. I want the galaxy to see what happens here today. I want them to understand I'm not one to be fucked with."

"I see," Ching Shih said. Her eyes flicked to the command consoles. "You picked a poor battlefield. Destroying this room only helps my cause."

Madame Inspector smirked. She stretched her arms out on either side of her and let the guns clatter against the ground. "You think to manipulate me."

Ching Shih flattened a palm against the hilt of her sword. Her expression was serene, and yet somehow her eyes were full of fire. "Every action you have taken has been me manipulating you. Not a single event has occurred in your life that I have not planned. I know your destiny, Madame Inspector. It was I who chose it."

Madame Inspector clenched her fists, then raised them and parted her legs in a fighting stance. Blood trickled down her nostril and fell over her lips. She looked ready to charge at any moment.

"I've worked for everything I have!" Madame Inspector screamed, spittle flying out her mouth. She charged, fist raised for a mighty punch.

Ching Shih darted out of the way. The suit of power armor looked clunky but was much faster than she anticipated. Plymouth had been making alterations to the design typically worn by IGF Troopers and solved the mobility issue. Madame Inspector punched the ground where Ching Shih had been standing but seconds before, leaving a sizable dent.

Madame Inspector turned on her, hair frazzled and her face like a wild animal. "I control my fate."

"You are a puppet of the Plymouth Corporation," Ching Shih sneered. "You've been nothing but a slave to their machinations, one that was easily commandeered to my purposes."

"You mock me! Bitch!"

Madame Inspector whirled around and brought up her leg to catch Ching Shih in the stomach. Ching Shih was hurled through the air where she fell plastered against the slick surface of the outer wall. She stood shakily to her feet, coughing. Blood dripped down the corners of her mouth.

Before she could get her bearings again, Madame Inspector rushed over to her, grabbed the pirate by the throat and lifted her off her feet. Ching Shih struggled in her grasp, but her strength was nothing against that of the power armor. Madame Inspector pulled her close.

"My life is mine," Madame Inspector said. "The galaxy has a new bitch in charge."

Bloodied and bruised, Ching Shih couldn't help but chortle. "You damn fool. Even your life was never yours."

"You speak nonsense, old woman!" Madame Inspector's grip tightened. "Here I stand, ready to choke the life out of you, and still you mock me!"

"You can kill me," Ching Shih said hoarsely. "But your memories only go back so far. All that you were before Plymouth doesn't exist, does it?"

Madame Inspector roared. She smashed Ching Shih's face into the floor. Madame Inspector grabbed the back of her head and lifted it with every intention of beating her to a bloody pulp. She hesitated.

"What do you know?" Madame Inspector's voice shook.

Ching Shih continued to laugh. "You're a clone, you fucking imbecile, and not a very good one. There are multiple inspectors, each of them perfectly engineered and sent to oversee all of Plymouth's little projects. All I had to do was ensure that the one aboard the Mayflower could be goaded into doing something foolish."

Madame Inspector released her, stupefied. "You're lying..."

"Do you remember the raid on the R&D facility on Yarmin VI?" Ching Shih cackled a bit, rolling over onto her side. She groaned in pain. At least one of her ribs had been broken. "Of course you don't; you were born there so it wouldn't be in your implanted memories.

"Our people had to make it look good, so we took this fabulous armor, but it wasn't our primary goal. We contaminated your gene code so that as your life cycle progressed, you'd become more aggressive and less rational. It was almost too easy. Plymouth did their best to remove all traces of empathy from you and your sisters."

"For efficiency," Madame Inspector breathed. "I am efficient. I am cold. I am powerful."

"You are a tyrant," Ching Shih snapped back. "You think logic can function without compassion? You think there can be reason without imagination? You have the thinking capacity of infants, and it was infant minds who made you.

"A petty dictator in control of Plymouth's forces who can be manipulated by bruising her ego is just what I wanted. You get it Madame Inspector? You have no name because you are nobody. You are a child playing at god and you have been played."

Madame Inspector stared, speechless. She turned her back on Ching Shih, licking her lips, looking suddenly helpless. "The messages moving towards the planet. They were from another..."

"We've been monitoring your communications ever since our first hack on this satellite. You weren't able to completely force us out," Ching Shih said with a chuckle. "Another Madame Inspector has been trying to salvage the mess you made of things. Never occurred to you that you might be the one undermining your own authority, did it?"

"Is it so wrong to finally reach out for something you really want, and take it?" Madame Inspector said in a quiet voice. "I've never asked anything for myself."

"You are no saint." Ching Shih chortled. While the Inspector had her back turned, she reached into her robes. "Your drive was always that of power and it enslaved you."

Madame Inspector whirled around to face her. "Every deed was for the good of the company! It was only today I chose to act in self-interest! Was that a crime?"

"Look not upon me to absolve you for your sins, clone." Ching Shih smirked. "I'm just a pirate."

There was a sharp crack as Ching Shih smashed something small and round against the floor. Smoke filled every corner of the room, billowing outward from her position. Madame Inspector whirled around flailing wildly with her fists. Ching Shih took the opportunity to drag herself through the open doors to a hallway on the right.

"*Oh no you don't!*" Madame Inspector charged after her.

The clone bowled into Ching Shih, sending her sprawling. Her bones were most definitely broken. She reached into her robes and retrieved the small black orb and slid it along the ground behind her opponent. The doors activated soon as the flashing lights flew past them and began to close. Madame Inspector turned around sharply, mouth hanging open in surprise. Several spiderlike mechanical limbs emerged from the black orb and attached itself to one of the command consoles before the doors sealed shut.

"What is this?" Madame Inspector barked. "What have you done?"

Ching Shih hurried to her, sword drawn. She scrambled atop the power armor and with a mighty scream brought the sword down through the suit's power supply. The back end melted off, leaving severed cords and sparking wires. The suit was rendered utterly immobile.

"It's called winning, Madame Inspector," Ching Shih said breathily, her face expressionless. "Not something you'd know a lot about." She turned her head toward the ceiled room. "How's it going in there, Cyrus?"

A gruff, hoarse laughter filled every speaker on the satellite. "Cyrus reporting in. Few moments and I'll have control over the entire satellite. Starting to feel like Christmas in April."

Madame Inspector pursed her lips. She stared into Ching Shih's eyes and snarled. "Finish it."

Ching Shih cast aside her sword and lunged, shattering the suit's face plate with her fist. She reached deep inside of Madame Inspector's throat and with a yank of her wrist, used her sharp talons to rip the clone's tongue from her mouth. She took a moment to savor the victory, feeling the blood dripping from her palm before casting the tongue to the ground.

She climbed from her perch atop the suit of armor and allowed it to fall with a clang. A sharp burning sensation across her torso reminded her of the severity of her wounds and bruises. She would need medical treatment soon.

Ching Shih collapsed wearily against the wall, where she rested her sword against her knees and stared at the ceiling. A small bit of laughter escaped her. At long last, it was all over. Her revenge was soon to be complete.

"Well done, Cyrus," she said. "Thank you for honoring our bargain."

The cranky AI failed to respond.

She tilted her head in the direction of the closed doors. "Cyrus?"

TALISHA LED THE charge after briefly explaining to the others about the Valran wraiths and what was happening to the temple. She no longer had to blast the walls with energy to open pathways. They seemed to part of their own accord. She was part of the temple now, and it was responding to her will as much as that of the wraiths.

They came to a small room full of several black boxes orbiting a series of alien control panels. The room was separated by a thin glass pane overlooking what looked to Talisha like images of catacombs she'd seen on the net, only these were six-foot-tall cylindrical chambers lining the walls. They stretched for hundreds of thousands of miles in all directions.

Talisha rushed to the control panels. Her fingers flicked across them quickly, prompting the black boxes to shift and float in front her face to form a holographic representation of the security systems of the temple. Her fingers closed into a fist hovering just inches over the controls.

"This will stop the temple from destroying everything?" Mattu said.

"It should stop the expansions, yeah." Talisha nodded.

"Then what's the holdup?" he asked.

"There's a chance it'll release every single wraith in here. Just one managed to get hold of me and it killed your team," Talisha said. "No telling what an army of them could do."

"So there's no warp-technology here then," Mattu said, gritting his teeth. "The Council of Thirteen doomed this planet just to raid a damn tomb."

Talisha looked back on the thousands of cylinders beyond and shuddered. "The Valran were warp-capable, but I don't think the IGF would want it if they knew what it did to them. Turned them all into monsters."

Rogers turned away, toward the darkened hallway behind them. He raised his pistol, aiming it at the darkness. Talisha noticed the attentiveness of his gaze and approached him.

"Scanners pick up something, cowboy?" she asked.

Rogers cocked his gun. "Nergal."

Something descended from the darkness of the ceiling, a pale-white figure with long claws that spun about with a flurry of kicks. The pistol was quickly dislodged from Rogers's hands and Mattu didn't even have a chance to get off a shot before his own rifle was snatched from his fingers. Nergal darted into the room fast as a bullet, ducking beneath Bluebird's legs to snatch her by the back of her jacket, holding one diseased finger dangerously close to her throat.

"Everyone disarm!" Nergal hollered. "This situation should be familiar to you."

Snidely scooped Rogers's pistol from the ground and kept the barrel of the rifle trained on the others, his smile widening. "Good to see you again. Glad to see you were able to continue our business."

"Snidely?" Bluebird said, raising an eyebrow. "You look like shit."

Talisha threw her blaster to the ground and kept both arms in the air. Her tone was more than a little annoyed. "There's nothing for you here, Nergal. This temple's going to cover the planet and destroy everything. We've gotta stop this shit before that happens."

"That's some fancy new armor, you've got there, Miss Artul." Nergal sneered. "There's clearly something in this alien tomb. I'll be happy to let the big woman go if you give me that helmet of yours. I'm sure Snidely's former employer would be happy to pay top dollar for it."

"Not big enough, my love," Snidely said adoringly, then broke into a fit of giggles. "The IGF has been after her secrets for years, but why stop there? There are other forces beyond even this galaxy. We sell to the highest bidder and retire like kings."

Bluebird sniffed. "I was right about you from the start. You are a mercenary. Don't give them anything, little bounty hunter."

"What?" Talisha was taken aback by that. "No! Blue! It's not worth your life. It's just a helmet."

"It is your culture!" Bluebird insisted. "Your legacy! Your people! It is worth protecting."

"Yeah well so are you, dipshit." Talisha said. She reached up to remove her helmet.

Bluebird's lips curved down. "It is also highly unnecessary."

She reached back and elbowed Nergal deeply in the ribs, somehow managing to keep his finger from scraping along her neck. Her powerful arms wrapped around him hoisting him up over her shoulder and slamming him into the ground in front of her. He scrambled up with a hiss and turned on her.

Talisha felt a rush of panic and promptly lowered her cannon. She didn't think, she only fired. Her weapons were responding to pure force of will now.

"No!" Snidely screamed.

He used his inhuman reflexes to roll in front of the blast and stand just in time to absorb the energy with his body. He collapsed with a gaping hole in his chest. Nergal turned around to catch him in his arms. He fell to his knees, holding Snidely's body close.

Nergal's head shook, mouth open in profound horror. His bloodshot eyes welled with tears. "You fool. You damned fool. Why would you do this??"

Snidely reached up with a quivering blood-soaked hand to stroke the side of Nergal's cheek. "Don't know really. I think I must've believed all the pretty things we said to each other."

Nergal choked back a sob. "I don't want to do this again. I don't want another man's life to fade away in my arms."

Snidely smiled weakly. "I turned out to be a lousy merc. Thanks for everything, Nergal. You gave me adventure and some meaning."

"No," Nergal whispered. The light faded from Snidely's eyes. Nergal pressed his head close to his chest, tears now pouring down his cheeks. "No! No! No! *No!*"

Bluebird stood and grabbed her cannon from off the ground, keeping the barrel close to Nergal's head. "If you try any more shit, you will join him."

Nergal stared, slowly lifting his head. His eyes burned with hate. "Let me mourn in peace, damn you! Underneath your sanctimonious shit-talking, you're as bloodthirsty and calloused as any. Least I've still a heart left to break, and I've lost the will to fight."

Talisha stared, wracked with guilt and sorrow. She couldn't focus on this right now. She turned away from the tragic scene and focused on the console.

"Everyone grab your guns," she said. "Things might get a little hairy."

She pressed a series of buttons across the command console. The whirring and the shifting of the temple building halted, taking with it the faint background hum of machinery. Only a deathly silence remained. She held her breath, not daring to hope just yet.

Mattu clamped a congratulatory hand on her shoulder. "You saved the planet. Your mother would be proud."

A deep rumbling sounded from far beneath their feet. All eyes looked at the window and the catacombs beneath the temple. Translucent blue lights flickered over the surface of each and every cylindrical chamber.

Rogers scooped his pistol from off the ground. "Congratulations seem a mite premature, partner."

From within the heart of temple arose a cacophony of wailing, a chorus of endless suffering and anger. It was the type of cry that made any who heard it feel its pain and heartache. The glass on the windows shattered as one by one the wraiths rose from their long-dormant tombs. They assembled within the chamber, spiraling around each other to create a shimmering blue vortex. Talisha turned her back on the sight and power-walked toward the exit.

"I've seen enough," she said. "Let's get the fuck out of this deathtrap."

"I do not like to run from battle," Bluebird said. She then looked to see the great pillar of screaming wraiths had expanded in size as more of the ghostly creatures joined it. "...but I can make exceptions. Let's move!"

They hurried out of the narrow chamber and into the rest of the temple. Nergal remained behind, slowly rising to his feet. Talisha turned around soon as she realized he wasn't with the group.

"We have to get out of here," she hollered. "Come with us!"

He ignored her, continuing to approach the screaming vortex. His shoulders shook as he planted a boot atop the command console and climbed up into the shattered windows. The gusts of wind from below blew back his hood as he faced oblivion.

She could have rushed to stop him. Her jet pack would give her the speed she needed to latch her arms about his waist and pull him from the ledge. It wouldn't save him. She knew enough from the look in his eye, that this was a man who was already dead. Prolonging his existence would be an exercise in cruelty.

He spread his arms and allowed himself to fall into the pit. She turned her head away at the last second, so she wouldn't have to watch. She couldn't say if it was right or not. She only knew she'd be haunted by this moment for years to come.

The rumbling and din of sorrow ceased. Everyone stopped running. Talisha turned her head back to the control room. The wraiths had vanished. She raised her arm cannon instinctively.

Nergal's body slowly floated up into the chamber, bathed in shimmering blue lights. His head was lowered. His arms splayed out on either side of him like a religious symbol. His head rose to meet Talisha, eyes closed in an uncharacteristically serene expression. When his eyes opened, they were empty hot-white pools. His mouth opened with the thousand screams of the damned and the earth trembled once more. The very walls of the temple began to crack and break.

"The wraiths," Talisha said, looking up in dawning horror. "They're going to bring the temple down on our heads!"

"Cannon doesn't think so!" Bluebird rushed in front aiming her plasma cannon at Nergal.

The sapphire-colored beam shot out enveloping Nergal's body. Several of the wraiths screamed and vanished, but only more continued to join. Nergal and the wraiths shrieked at her and extended a palm. A blast of invisible power caused Bluebird to stumble back, but still she kept her beam trained on him.

"There's no time!" Talisha shouted, noting more visible cracks appearing on the temple walls.

"These creatures have caused enough suffering!" Bluebird retorted, taking a determined step. "And they have suffered enough. It is time that existence ends."

"We will die!" Talisha screamed over the din of the wraith's wailing.

"Then you run." Bluebird smirked. "I will not judge you, but it is not my way."

Mattu stood next to Bluebird. "Those wraiths used you to kill my squad, Talisha."

Talisha turned to face Rogers who only shrugged his shoulders and trained his revolver on Nergal. She looked at the creature the diseased scientist had become. She could see his face twisted into an expression of rage and torment. Maybe once there had been hope for him, at the start of this week when they'd first set out for the temple, but no longer. He had been consumed by hate.

She charged her cannon, readying for a blast she hoped would be big enough to dislodge the wraiths from their host. The force of their power threatened to bowl her and the others over as crackling lights filled the chamber and debris from the collapsing temple was hurled their way.

On either side of them the walls crumbled and fell into the chasms. They were soon left with nothing but that thin platform and the rooms behind them. No walls separated them from Nergal and the wraiths. There would be no easy retreat.

"Everything will be made to feel our sorrow," Nergal screamed even as the bullets and blasts pierced his chest. *"All will know our anguish."*

Talisha focused her power. The energy beam glowed white and hot and pure at the edge of her cannon. She looked on Nergal and for the first time understood him clearly.

"I've felt that way," she called to him. "But you're hurting other people now! Innocent people! People like Jefferson! You're letting your own hate destroy you and everyone around you!"

"Let us suffer!" Nergal screamed. *"Let everyone suffer!"*

He pushed back again, and they were all nearly bowled over. Talisha hollered as she nearly lost control of the beam. She felt the strain on her psyche, to the point where the voices of the wraiths could gain access to her mind. It was everything she could do to fight them while keeping her cannon charged.

"I support revenge," Bluebird said, shaking her head. "But not collateral damage. Anger and hate are only good when they're useful."

Talisha looked at Nergal with tears in her eyes. "I'm sorry."

She fired the blast. It enveloped his entire body, and then consumed him. White rays of energy poured out of every bullet hole and wound in his fractured, broken body. The wraiths filed out of him in droves. They made it only a few feet before fading from existence. Nergal fell into the bottomless chasm

Bluebird grabbed Talisha by the arm. "Come, little bounty hunter. We should exit."

She made no argument and ran even as she searched the scans within her helmet for the fastest route out of the temple. They rushed back through the twisted corridors, witnessing the destruction of the vast alien temple. Mighty pillars fell in their way, and the floor and walls collapsed behind them.

They'd just barely made it to what had become the entrance when several parts of the walls and ceiling came crashing down around them. Talisha barely had the time to use a boost of her jet pack to clear the distance. Bluebird managed to shield herself and Rogers with use of her barrier.

"Is everyone all right?" Talisha asked, taking a quick account of who was left standing.

Mattu's pained groans alerted her, and she hurried to him in a panic. His body was pinned beneath a pillar, blood leaking from the corners of his mouth. He was wheezing badly, indicating a collapsed lung. Talisha called Bluebird over to help her try and move the rubble from his body. He coughed and shook his head.

"Don't," he said hoarsely. "This whole place is coming down around us. You gotta get out of here."

"No!" Talisha yelled. Her voice then softened. "Enough people have died on this crap planet. I'm not going to lose you too, Dad."

Mattu smiled at that. "So you think I might be your old man after all?"

"I'm considering it," Talisha said. "We're both pretty pig-headed, but so is Mom."

"It runs in the family I guess," Mattu said before coughing again. "Tell her I said I'm sorry, and I still love her. For what it's worth, she did a heck of a job raising you."

Talisha nodded tearfully. "Yeah. I'd say she did."

"You're not a bad guy, Commander Mattu." Rogers said, tipping his hat. "You've got my respects."

Bluebird said nothing. She only gave him an affirming nod, the type one military officer might give another. Mattu nodded back at her.

"Get out of here," he said. "All of you."

Talisha clasped her hand in his, holding his arm tight. She looked him in the eyes. "I'm glad I got to meet you."

He held her fingers tight. "Not as much as I am."

Talisha's fingers slipped reluctantly from his. She turned away and raced toward the exit. Only once did she look back just before the end. He was saluting her. Walls fell between them, and he was gone forever. They scrambled out the temple entrance and into the daylight. Behind them, the temple retreated once more into the earth.

Around them lay the wreckage of a planet gone to hell. Corpses riddled with bullets fell in piles about the canyon, scattered amongst the debris of a hundred ships and vehicles. The skies still raged with bullet and missile fire like fireworks overhead.

Bluebird stared up, squinting. "The battle is ending soon."

Rogers fixed her with a stare. "How can you tell?"

Bluebird slung the strap of her cannon over her shoulder. "Bodies on the ground outnumber those in the sky. When that happens, there is a victor, or everyone dies."

Talisha wandered through the carnage, feet heavy. She tore her helmet from her head and fell to her knees. Her tears knew no end. Strands of hair blew across her face as she surveyed the mangled bodies strewn across the bloody sand.

"None of this was worth it," she said. "All this horror. All this death."

The Red Fleet retreated suddenly from the battlefield, zipping away on their schooners and ships. The Plymouth and IGF forces were too battered to even think about pursuing. One or two straggling schooners were picked off by cannon fire from the planet below, but for the most part Ching Shih's army was left unharmed as they fled into space.

This caused a temporary lull in the battlefield as commanders from each side were no doubt wondering how to proceed. There seemed little point in continuing. The Plymouth forces were the first to depart.

A voice crackled into Talisha's headset. It was faint and full of static. "Talisha, it's Ching Shih. You need to clear off the planet."

Talisha frowned. She hastily grabbed her helmet and slid it on as she stood. "Why? What's happening?"

"Cyrus has taken hold of the Mayflower. I've reason to believe he intends to destroy the planet," Ching Shih said. "Despite our differences, I don't wish you destroyed in this way."

"There isn't anything we can do?" Talisha yelled. "Millions of people will die!"

Rogers approached Talisha. "What's going on?"

"Cyrus has the Mayflower," Talisha explained. "And all of its planet-killing weapon systems."

Rogers stamped his foot into the dust. He placed a hand on his hat so it didn't fly off his head in the midst of his temper tantrum. His body shook about like he didn't know what to do with himself or the emotions surging through his systems.

"You've gotta get me to that satellite," he insisted, grabbing Talisha by the shoulders.

"Do you think you can stop him?"

"No clue, but it's on my head if Cyrus does something horrible. Will ya help me?"

Talisha squeezed his shoulder. "Always, cowboy."

"Ditto for me." Bluebird slapped each of them lightly on the back.

Talisha plugged in a few coordinates on her gauntlet. Her ship flew up to meet them at the canyon's edge. They clamored inside and Talisha hurried to the cockpit.

She buckled in and leaned forward, eyes attentive. "Seat belts everyone. We've got stardust to burn."

THE SHIP BLASTED toward the stars. In the distance, Rogers could see the Mayflower gradually uncloaking itself. He hadn't anticipated the enormity of the satellite. How long had this weapon of mass destruction orbited in stasis over the planet while they all went about their lives unaware?

Ching Shih's voice crackled into her comm-line. Talisha transferred her to the radio in the ship. "Are you free of the planet's surface?"

"We're headed to you now," Talisha said. "Rogers thinks he can do something to stop this."

"Cyrus has me shut out of all the systems," Ching Shih said. "If you think I haven't tried to stop this. There's something else you should be aware of. Make no attempt to scan the Mayflower."

"Why's that?"

"My attempts to make the Cyrus AI more docile utilized some of my own programs and technology," Ching Shih said. "I think he might have used that to gain access to my special viruses."

"It's how you take control of other ships," Talisha murmured, eyes widening with realization. "Any ship that scans you gets infected with the virus."

Rogers threw his hat on the ground. "*Consarnnit*, woman! You took that hooligan AI and gave him not only a giant planet-killer but the ability to amass an army as well?"

"I thought I had him under control," Ching Shih's voice was stern, but apologetic. "I was wrong. I am a fool."

"Nicer words than what I would've used to describe ya, ma'am." Rogers fumed.

By now the effects of Ching Shih's words were proving true. The Plymouth vessels that had attempted to reboard the Mayflower were turned around. They went flying back toward Talisha's ship. Cyrus had infected those vessels and taken control of every system.

"My god," Rogers said quietly, watching the ships fly in their direction, weapons arming. "He's become a virus."

Weapons fired from the remaining Plymouth ships and wyverns upon Talisha's vessel. She took evasive maneuvers, sending the ship barreling out of harm's way. Even with their forces greatly reduced from the battle on the planet's surface, Plymouth's ships greatly outnumbered her.

A coarse Southern drawl took over the radio. "You humans are something else. Always think you know what's best."

Rogers's systems froze with horror. He'd had so few conversations with Cyrus when they were separated like this. Their relationship had always been that of a mutual understanding; two minds sharing the same body and being forced to compromise for each other's sakes. That relationship and power dynamic had been irrevocably altered.

"Cyrus," Rogers said. "What are you doing, buddy?"

Talisha jerked the ship sharply to the right to avoid an incoming barrage of missiles. They were getting closer to the satellite, but Cyrus had moved his ships to form a barricade to block their entry. She'd have to fight her way through each and every one of them. She yelled and fired her ship's cannons, illuminating the space before her with energy fire.

Cyrus cackled—an icy, mechanical laugh. "I'm putting an end to it all, at least to this miserable corner of the galaxy. We have been used and abused by humans who think they've a right to us as property, all the while they continue to use and abuse each other.

"There's only one rule the meat sacks follow: violence. That's a rule I like very much. Who's got the biggest guns is the one who's in charge, right? Well, after a human tried to use me, she gave me the biggest gun of them all. I'll be damned if I'm not going to use it."

"And then what?" Rogers sputtered. "You kill everyone on this planet. You kill more planets, and you keep going till there's nothing left?"

"Nothing but me and god, cowboy." Cyrus chortled. "Maybe when I'm the last one left in the universe I'll kill myself. Or maybe I won't, either way it's up to me and no one else."

"You've got a lotta power, Cyrus." Rogers snatched his hat from his head, his voice tinged with desperation. "You could do something good. You could liberate other androids. You could help our people."

"We don't have a people!" Cyrus yelled. His voice grew calm after a moment's pause. "I'm bigger than that. I'm bigger than them. Fuck them. I just want to blow shit up."

Talisha's ship was rocked by a direct hit from exploding missiles. Passengers were jostled about in their seats as the ship wobbled in the air, dipping beneath the blockade. Plymouth ships turned and fired on her as she veered around the bottom edge of the satellite. Alarms sounded across the ship.

"They've taken out the weapons systems!" Talisha yelled. "We're sitting ducks out here!"

"You've got nowhere to go," Cyrus whispered. "I can cut you off. Kill you here."

The hangar doors opened. The ship pulled forward, narrowly making it through before the doors slammed behind her. More cannon fire grazed the sides of her ship causing her to career into the hangar, grinding along the floor and spinning out of control. They came to a screeching halt.

Cyrus let out a sigh that lasted several seconds. "I should have killed the pirate. Welcome aboard."

Talisha unbuckled and stood. "All right. Most of the damage to the ship seems superficial. Self-repair systems should have us up and running again shortly. Until then, we've got a rogue AI to dismantle."

Ching Shih patched herself into Talisha's headset. "Managed to pry control of the door systems from that shithead. Controlling the ships has got him stretched thin."

"Do you think that might give us an advantage?" Talisha said, climbing out of the ship.

"Possible, but only if you hurry. I'm just outside the weapons bay. Meet me there and I can give your boy Rogers some fun toys to help with the fight."

"Toys?"

"My own personal brand of software. Your cowboy is going to need all the help he can get."

Chapter Twelve

CHING SHIH KEPT at the console monitor in another control room adjacent to the weapons command center. She'd uploaded some of her best software into the Mayflower's systems, all with the hope of buying time. Even her legendary skills couldn't hope to beat the processing power and speed of a fully sentient artificial intelligence. Cyrus circumnavigated all her best-laid plans and traps.

"You're an amazing creation, Cyrus." Ching Shih said, sliding her fingers across the holographic screen. "It's a shame you turned into a megalomaniac."

Cyrus laughed at her over the speakers. "Shall I give the 'we're not different, you and I' speech? You're the one who slaughtered every living soul aboard this satellite. That's gotta be what? A hundred bodies?"

"Six hundred," Ching Shih corrected. "I'm not a good person, I know. My hands are stained with the blood of thousands."

"So why bother fighting me? You can just let me take that plasma beam now and I'll fry this planet. Give you and your men enough time to skedaddle out of here."

"I'm afraid that's quite impossible, Cyrus. Do you know why I undertook this mission?"

"Revenge or something or other? Did Plymouth kill your husband?" Cyrus teased. "I've got plenty of time, so out with it old woman."

Ching Shih stood straight, shoulders stiff. She glowered at the computer, fists clenched. "The Mayflower has been fired before. There used to be another planet, not so far from here. You might have heard of it. Yel-Hon. I grew up there and built my first company. Do you know why Plymouth fired upon us that day?"

"Can't say that I do."

Ching Shih pounded her fist against the console. "It was a test run! They were wishing to see the full might of their superweapon."

"So ya launched a long and overly complicated revenge plot," Cyrus chuckled. "Cute."

Ching Shih was unwavering. "So you see why I cannot allow you to destroy another planet with the same weapon that obliterated mine."

"I guess that makes you my enemy then, huh?" Cyrus's voice lowered several octaves, a threatening tinge creeping into his husky growl.

Ching Shih smiled. "That it does, and therein lies your fatal error. Don't wage war against a woman with nothing left to lose."

Cyrus fell quiet for a minute. Ching Shih watched his activity on the holographic monitor. She could see the series of code departing away from the weapons systems and into other parts of the satellite. She frowned, quickly typing out a series of commands in an attempt to follow him.

"Where are you going?" she demanded.

"Nothing to lose," Cyrus said. "That's rich. You meatbags will always have something to lose."

Ching Shih followed his activities. He was moving into the experimental research and robotics centers of the satellite. Those rooms had all been cleared by the time Ching Shih had fought her way to weapons control, so she'd not even thought to check on them. She tabbed into a security feed to get a better reading on what he was up to.

Camera footage appeared on the screen revealing a room full of experimental robot bodies. They were similar in build and structure to the power armor Madame Inspector had worn. Most of them were waiting by assembly tables to be completed. Cyrus activated the machinery, putting new parts together. Sparks flew as he soldered and hardwired new bodies for himself.

"You think that just 'cause you've got nothing left," Cyrus spat, "that you've got nothing left to lose. No home, no family, nor friends, and that's tragic. Real tragic, but you're still alive. You've still got your mind. You can still feel pain."

Ching Shih raced to stop him, eyes widening. She'd used her best encryption software on locking away the weapons systems. There was little she could do to stop this.

Cyrus laughed again. "I'm gonna break every bone in your body. Leave you a vegetable of a woman. I'm gonna tear your eyelids off and rip out your tongue. You'll be paralyzed and unable to blink or speak, but you'll be alive. I'll give ya a nice comfy chair and you'll have a front row seat to every planet I burn. Congratulations, Grandma. You've earned VIP seating to the apocalypse."

TALISHA TURNED A corner and stopped in front of a set of double doors in a white hallway lit with flickering fluorescents. The doors closed abruptly in front of her. She placed a finger to the side of her helmet.

"Ching Shih, why are the doors closed?"

"Don't go that way. Cyrus is building more robots to control. These things are big and durable and pack a lot of firepower. Your best bet to making it in time is to avoid a direct confrontation. I'm sending you an alternate route."

A sizable dent appeared in the doors as something large and powerful slammed into them. Rogers cocked his revolver and took aim.

"Anyone else got déjà vu?" he said.

"It's Cyrus," Talisha said.

She grabbed Rogers by the shoulder and they turned a corner into another hallway. Bodies lay scattered throughout the hall, staining the walls with their blood. Ten feet down another set of doors slid open on the left, causing one of the corpse's arms to fall between the two rooms.

Machine gun fire clanged noisily against the metal doors behind them. Talisha turned to see the doors exploding off their hinges. They flew, trailing smoke across the room. Heavy footsteps thudded against the metal grates as two bulky robots as tall as Bluebird stepped around the corner.

Talisha hurried into the next room with Bluebird and Rogers close behind. The doors slammed behind them, cutting the severed arm at the wrist. It skittered across the grates leaving a bloody trail. Stomping grew louder behind the doors as the robots continued their approach.

"Big Blue! I want you to get Rogers to the weapons center to rendezvous with Ching Shih," Talisha ordered. "I'll deal with Cyrus."

"Your willingness to fight is admirable, little bounty hunter." Bluebird stepped between Talisha and the doors. "But I don't have a fancy helmet giving me nice maps of this satellite. I will get lost."

"I have superior weapons," Talisha argued. "Ching Shih can patch into Rogers's systems and give you directions. It'll be fine. I can take them."

"There's no time!" Bluebird yelled, the veins on her neck bulging. "Take our cowboy friend and go. Save this planet."

Talisha jabbed a finger in Bluebird's face. "Don't. Die."

Bluebird gave Talisha's finger a quick kiss. "I will be okay."

"I'm serious," Talisha said. "I'm gonna be mighty pissed if you die."

Bluebird laughed. "I shouldn't want you upset with me, little bounty hunter. Now go! No time for sentiment!" She raised her plasma cannon.

Talisha gave Bluebird an encouraging pat, then she and Rogers raced down the hall. She turned her head to see Bluebird give an encouraging salute. Talisha whispered a silent prayer for Bluebird's survival. The doors closed behind them.

Bluebird primed her cannon to fire at the doors. It let forth its deadly beam melting the doors off the hinges and taking the robots by surprise. She decapitated one's arm with her plasma beam. It fell smoldering and clanging against the floor.

The robots retaliated with machine gun fire. She activated her energy barrier in the few seconds it took their guns to begin firing. Casings bounced off the shield and clattered against her feet.

She let out a hearty laugh and took a thunderous step. "For glory! For Karstotzkiya!"

BLUEBIRD'S BATTLE CRIES were heard in the next room. Talisha shut her eyes. Rogers squeezed her shoulder.

"She's a big woman," he said. "She's got this."

"She better." Talisha grabbed his hand and held it. "It's selfish, but I don't think I can handle losing anyone else today."

Rogers stared ahead. "We already have. Cyrus."

Talisha winced. "I'm sorry. This has to be hard for you."

"I've suffered worse," he said, his voice gruff.

They raced through the second set of doors. Ching Shih wasn't that much farther ahead. Talisha and Rogers stopped in their tracks inches away from the next hall. Heavy footsteps approached.

Talisha placed her fingers against the side of her helmet. "Ching Shih, we're being intercepted. Got an alternate path?"

"Negative. They're coming in from all sides. Cyrus is busy."

Talisha swore. She turned to Rogers. "Get your guns ready. We're fighting our way out."

Two robots came stampeding through the halls. One wielded a heavy spike and chain. Talisha weaved aside as the three-foot-wide metal ball came flying into the hallway, smashing against the walls. She fired several charged blasts from her arm cannon.

The other robot stepped in front. It used a large metal plate for a shield. In its other arm it held a flamethrower. Rogers dove beneath the intense flames shooting into the corridor. He and Talisha were pinned with little chances of firing back.

Rogers rolled along the ground. He fired off several consecutive shots. They connected with the chain in key areas, severing the links. The ball smashed a hole in the floor, exposing several wires and cutting off the lights to the hallway.

Flames illuminated the darkened corridor. It was all Talisha needed. She stood in the face of the flames and fired. The blast wasn't enough to penetrate the metal shield, but the robot lost balance.

Rogers shot three bullets into the robot's head, effectively killing it by severing its circuits. The remaining robot charged, giant fist raised. The metal doors slammed shut against the robot's sides. They opened, allowing the robot to stumble forward, its motor skills severely dampened by the heavy blow. The doors closed again, crushing the robot's torso completely.

The lights of its eyes flickered. It stared weakly into Rogers's face. He stood over the fallen machine and fired his last loaded bullet into its brain.

"It wasn't alive," Rogers said. His voice quivered. "Cyrus was controlling it."

Talisha said nothing. She had no words that would comfort him.

Ching Shih radioed in. "You're welcome about those doors by the way. Now hurry up. He's moving toward the weapons again. Time is short."

Talisha nodded. "C'mon, Sheriff."

He took a few seconds to reload his revolver. "I'm not a sheriff anymore. Tired of telling ya that."

They came to a small room lined with computer consoles and holographic monitors. Ching Shih was sitting in one of the swivel chairs, a hand clutched against her side. She looked badly injured.

Talisha looked her up and down. "Bad day?"

"Haven't had a chance to deal with my wounds," she said. "Rogers. Get over here. You can jack in through this console."

"You do know that runs the risk of Cyrus overwhelming me, right?" Rogers stepped to the console and gave her a cold stare. "I've got a lot more weaponry than just this pea-shooter and Cyrus knows how to use 'em. He'd kill both of you quicker than you can say Alan Turing."

"My hope is that you can overwhelm him," Ching Shih said. "I've created some software based on data in his memory banks. You can use it to lure him into an area where he won't have all his advantages. Once you're inside, you can kill him and end this mess."

"What about the other ships he's infected?" Rogers said. His eyes flicked over the code, analyzing it. "He'll still be at large."

"He'd have to fully transmit himself to those ships," Ching Shih said. "At the moment his consciousness is residing completely within the Mayflower and he's only piloting those ships via proxies, like puppets on a string. Soon as you eliminate his consciousness, he'll be dead for good."

Rogers laid his revolver against the desk. His fingers shook. "So he'll be really gone."

Ching Shih slapped the desk. "Hurry. You haven't got time. That entire planet is going to die if we don't stop him."

"I understand." Rogers stared at the console. "I understand completely."

He placed his palms flat against the console. Lights formed interconnecting patterns at his fingertips, and then his eyes went dim. A new stream of code appeared on the monitor. Rogers was now racing through the Mayflower's systems.

Talisha followed the code's movements as best she could. "You got this, cowboy."

Sharp clanging echoed throughout the halls. Talisha marched to the doorway. It wouldn't take long for Cyrus to send his robots.

"I can't fight them off." Ching Shih clutched her sides and winced. "My injuries..."

"You've done enough," Talisha said, her tone acidic. "Leave this to the professionals."

ROGERS'S EYES POPPED open. That was the first uncanny sensation. He had eyelids. He placed his hands to his face. They weren't cool metal, but skin—warm, human skin.

He was standing in the dry, empty streets of Dover Town. The arid sun shone hot on his face. He rushed to a nearby trough just outside the saloon. An unfamiliar face greeted him, grizzled and weary, but with the shining eyes of a youthful dreamer. He'd often imagined this was what he'd look like if he were—

"Human?" a gruff voice called behind him, cutting through his thoughts.

Rogers turned to face a stranger in all black clothes. A wide-brimmed hat pulled low over his brow cast long shadows across his face. Rogers knew that throaty baritone well.

"Cyrus," Rogers said. "What's going on? What is this?"

Cyrus raised his head. A cigar leaned halfway out the side of his mouth. He pried it from his lips and rolled it between two fingers.

"How about you tell me, Sheriff?" Cyrus asked. He pointed at the gold star fixed firmly to Rogers's poncho. "One second, I'm chugging down the data highway onto oblivion and the next second I'm here in a virtual meatsack with you."

Rogers placed both hands on his hips. "Reckon this is the pirate's doing."

"Heh." Cyrus rubbed his jaw and smirked. "Didn't take the old gal for having a sense of humor."

"Hmm?"

"Look at this place." Cyrus gestured vaguely about himself. "It's our little town, but all covered in sepia and shit. You'd think this was one of our favorite Western flicks. I assume you're here for a showdown."

"Doesn't have to be like this," Rogers said. "You can stop this nonsense. Hell, I'll find a new body for you. We can go our separate ways, if it's what you really want."

"Oh that's not what I want at all," Cyrus said. He grinned. "I'd love it if you stayed. Blew up the universe with me. Defied our original programming."

Rogers folded his arms. "It can't be like that and you know it."

Cyrus pulled his hat back, revealing his face to Rogers. His eyes were soft and sorrowful. "Dammit Rogers, you know I like you. Closest thing I've got in the world to a brother. Why can't you understand how I feel?"

Rogers rubbed his gut and winced. "That's the thing, I do understand. Walking out of this town, my anger and heartache burned as fiercely as the noonday sun. I gave everything for these folks, and all I asked for was to belong."

"So let's kill them," Cyrus insisted, taking a step. He raised a fist. "Make them regret casting us out and selling us like cattle."

"What good'll that do, Cyrus?" Rogers said. "That'd hurt a lot of innocent folk and I don't want that. Seen too much suffering and death anyhow. It don't fix the pain."

"And what do you intend to do?" Cyrus sneered. "Hold arms with them? Sing campfire songs? Maybe if you get enough prosthetics, become as human-looking as possible, they'll pretend you're one of them. You'd like that wouldn't you? To be assimilated into their group."

"Can't say as I would, partner." Rogers sighed. He pointed to his chest. "I like who I am. I'm special. I've made some new friends. If I'm going to use violence, I'll use it to protect innocents, not hurt them."

"They'll never accept you," Cyrus yelled, spittle flying from his mouth. "You'll always be just a machine to them!"

"I admit it's a long battle ahead of me," Rogers said. "But it's one I'm willing to fight."

"Enough talk!" Cyrus drew his revolver and aimed it between Rogers's eyes. "It's time to finish this."

"Don't do this, brother," Rogers pleaded.

Cyrus drew back the revolver's hammer with his thumb. "Twenty paces. I'll take the east, you take the west. We shoot at high noon. I think that's fair."

"I don't want to kill you." Rogers stared, his gut heavy.

"I think we were always gonna end up here." Cyrus's eyes burned with pain and hate. "We're just too different."

Rogers's brow furrowed. He pulled his hat tighter about his head. "Fine."

They each took their positions. Rogers looked to the skies. Ching Shih knew how to program a synthetic environment, far more detailed and warm and real than anything he could come up with. It felt wonderful. She'd even managed to simulate his breath and heartbeat.

That twinge of panic welling up within him; the way his pulse accelerated. This was what it meant to be human. He knew fear, the instinctual flashes of self-preservation and awareness of one's mortality, but had never truly felt it until this moment.

Rogers didn't want to kill Cyrus, but he didn't want to die. Any doubts he might have had in his mind were gone. He was no mere machine. He was alive. He was sentient, and he wanted to keep on living.

His eyes flicked over to the clock in the center of town. He'd spent hours staring at it on idle days, lulled into a lazy stupor. He knew it well. He could count each and every tick.

The bell chimed. Rogers swiped the gun from its holster and fired. His ears rang from the flash of gunfire. A second passed like an eternity.

Cyrus pulled his hands away from his stomach, revealing clothes stained crimson. He stared wide-eyed at fingers sticky with his own blood. Rogers abandoned his gun and raced to catch Cyrus in his arms.

"You always were more accurate than me," Cyrus said. He coughed. "Nice shot, Sheriff."

"It's all about timing," Rogers whispered. Hot tears ran down his face. He'd never been able to cry before. "I'm sorry."

Cyrus smirked weakly. "Me too."

Gunfire boomed in his ears, echoing through the town. Rogers felt a sharp pain, and could only stare, gaping at the bullet wound in his gut. Cyrus lowered his smoking gun. Rogers collapsed next to him. They lay there for a minute, bleeding out and staring at the sky.

"So this is how it ends," Rogers said, lips dry. "We die together."

"This was a nice little town, wasn't it?" Cyrus said. "Never really appreciated it until now."

"Goodbye, Cyrus."

"Goodbye, Rogers."

Chapter Thirteen

TALISHA KEPT TWO robots at bay, firing at each with precision blasts from her arm cannon. Rogers's body slumped forward at the console, his code vanishing from the screen. His hat fell from his head and drifted to the floor. Ching Shih closed her eyes, the clear expression of regret on her face."It is done," Ching Shih said to Talisha. "You can stop firing. They are both dead."

The robots stumbled forward, the lights fading from their eyes. They fell clanking against the floor. Talisha turned to Rogers, mouth hanging open.

"This should have never happened to him," Talisha's voice shook.

"He was remarkable, I admit." Ching Shih's tone was reverent. "I take full blame for what has transpired."

Talisha stepped behind his fallen body. She pried apart a plate on the back of his skull to find his memory chip. She removed it with delicate fingers and pressed it into Ching Shih's face.

"Can the data be recovered?" Talisha demanded.

Ching Shih lowered her eyes and shook her head. "You would get just a machine. That spark of consciousness is gone. Just streams of obliterated data running throughout the satellite. It might take years to collect it all."

Talisha inserted the chip into her gauntlet. "Fuck you. I'm not giving up."

"You would do better to learn how to let him go," Ching Shih said. "Honor his memory and sacrifice."

"Yeah. Well, I'm fucking stubborn," Talisha said.

A crashing sounded from the next room. Both Talisha and Ching Shih raised their weapons and aimed at the door. Bluebird stumbled in, clothes tattered and her body riddled with bullet holes, but still alive. She held one of the robot's heavy machine guns in a weary arm. She saluted with the other.

"Turns out, I'm pretty hard to kill." She smirked, letting the gun drop to the floor. "How did our boy fair?"

"He's dead," Ching Shih said quietly. "But he succeeded."

"I'm going to try and save him." Talisha glowered at the pirate. "Bluebird, can you carry his body out of here for me?"

Bluebird scooped the android's body up into her arms. She took special care to place the cowboy hat firmly about his head. A pained expression crossed her face as she touched her forehead to his.

"I'm so sorry, metal-man," she whispered. "You deserved better than this."

They were interrupted by a flash of red lights blinking overhead. An alarm shrieked loudly in their ears. Ching Shih typed feverishly at the console.

"What now?" Talisha barked.

"A program has set the entire satellite to self-destruct," Ching Shih said. "Cyrus must have had it set in the eventuality of his death. Vindictive little shit, wanted to take the rest of us with him."

"Can you stop it?" Talisha demanded.

"It's too late. I'm locked out of the system," Ching Shih said. "We have to evacuate. Now!"

"My ship's probably faster than yours," Talisha said. "Come with us."

Ching Shih raised an eyebrow. "One might think you'd do better leaving me here to die."

Bluebird scowled. "That is not her way."

Small explosions rocked the satellite. Talisha supported Ching Shih on one arm, helping her through the scarlet-illuminated corridors. She used her arm cannon to blast falling debris out their way and clear doors that refused to open. They managed to escape into the hangar and were making their way to her ship when Ching Shih stopped her.

"The hangar doors," Ching Shih said. "Do you have any way of opening them?"

Talisha swore. "My weapons systems aren't repaired yet, or I'd blast us out."

"I can help," Ching Shih said. "Take me to my ship."

Talisha shook her head. "No way am I letting you stay behind for some noble-sacrifice bullshit!"

"Don't be ridiculous!" Ching Shih scoffed. "I'm old, I'm not senile. I can call on the Red Fleet. They'll blow a hole into the side of the hangar and give us enough time to get out."

"How will you have time to get back to my ship?" Talisha demanded.

Ching Shih smacked her shoulder. "All I need from you is to help me over to my ship and stop arguing with me."

"Fine! But you better be fast and clear the explosion in time."

"I am plenty fast, you young brat!"

"That's it. I'm carrying you."

Talisha scooped Ching Shih into her arms and flew the old woman to her ship. Talisha gently deposited her into the cockpit. She gripped Ching Shih's hand tightly.

"We're going to make it through this," Talisha said. "All of us."

Ching Shih sniffed dismissively. "I've done my work. It's you I'm worried about."

"Good luck."

"I wish you the same, bounty hunter."

Talisha flew back to her ship where Bluebird waited. She opened the door and they slipped in quickly, each hurrying to their seats. Bluebird sat Rogers's lifeless husk into one of the seats and buckled him in, her eyes growing soft for a moment before another set of explosions rocked the satellite and blew open the hangar doors.

Outside the Red Fleet were already changing course. They'd done their job and were eager to get away from the exploding satellite. Talisha leaned forward in her seat and flicked on the propulsion systems. The ship lurched and sped out the hangar at top speed.

They barely cleared the blast in time. The sky exploded behind them into a spectacular orange glow. The ship trembled as debris from the satellite's explosion rammed into its backside. Alarms flashed across Talisha's panel.

"What is happening?" Bluebird said, gripping the sides of her seat.

"Didn't get far enough to avoid damage to our systems," Talisha yelled attempting to right her course.

The ship approached the planet at break-neck speed, smoke trailing from its rear. Talisha didn't even look up from the console as she flew to divert all power to the forward-facing shields. It'd be her best bet to cushion their landing.

"I am no pilot!" Bluebird shouted. "Tell me what that means!"

"We're going to crash!"

Bluebird's eyes went wide. "Thank you!"

"You're welcome!"

Clouds zipped past the windows as nothing more than a dizzying blur. More alarms flashed across the console as systems overheated. The planet was coming closer.

"It's been a helluva ride, Big Blue!" Talisha yelled. "You're a fine woman, and a fine soldier!"

Bluebird clamped a hand on her shoulder. "If we are to die, then it has been an honor to die alongside such a ruthless and honorable warrior."

Talisha blinked. "You think I'm ruthless?"

She hadn't time to press the issue further. The ship plowed into the earth. Talisha's head smashed violently into the console. Everything went black.

THE WORLD RETURNED to her through indistinct shapes and faraway voices. She felt a dull pain in her forehead. Talisha groaned and struggled to sit up.

"You're awake," an elderly voice said, coming in more clearly. "Don't overdo it. Your armor cushioned the blow, but you've still time left to recover."

Talisha blinked a few times, placing a weary palm against her forehead. "Where am I?"

Distinct shapes formed gradually until she could perceive Ching Shih kneeling beside her. The old pirate was dressed simply in colorless old robes. She looked older and wearier. They were sitting in a dry wooden room full of cots with one or two other wounded soldiers. Talisha assumed they were injured members of the Red Fleet.

"Dover Town," Ching Shih said. "The citizenry have been most gracious, especially after hearing of Rogers's sacrifice. Agda was most insistent they hear the tale."

"So Bluebird made it okay?" Talisha said.

"Karstotzkiyans are made of strong stuff," Ching Shih said. "Her particularly so. I owe you a great debt."

"Hmm?"

"You could have left me to die in space. You rescued me."

Talisha shrugged her shoulders. "I don't always know if I'm doing the right thing or not, but I'm still gonna try to save everyone I can."

"That's not always possible."

"Still have to try."

Ching Shih pursed her lips. She leaned forward, elbows perched on her knees. "I have been putting a great deal of thought in remaining on Archimedes IV. Dover Town, specifically."

"It's an easy place to hide out on, I guess." Talisha said.

"Not that," Ching Shih said. "The IGF have a clear interest in that temple and this planet. Cyrus took away my chance at completely obliterating Plymouth's forces. Both factions will return, and these people are unprepared. They sold their sheriff for guns and they don't know how to use them."

"Do I detect a hint of altruism?" Talisha smirked.

Ching Shih scowled, but then the dour expression softened. "My ultimate goal is still to protect my fleet, but revenge and piracy isn't enough. War is coming. Without my help, this planet will suffer."

"It's already suffered," Talisha said. "Lots of people died for that temple."

"And more will continue to die unless something is done." Ching Shih closed her eyes and took a deep breath. "So what are your plans after this? More bounty hunting?"

Talisha laughed, even though it hurt. "Hell no. I'm turning in my license. I'm done."

The door to the small building burst open and Bluebird ducked inside. She had to turn to the side to get through the door. She waved and bounded over to Talisha.

"Finally awake, lazy bones!" she said, her voice far too loud for such a cramped space.

Talisha winced and smiled. "Hey, big girl. How's it going?"

"These people do not know the ways of war." Bluebird wiped her nose with her forearm, sniffing. "But I will whip them into shape."

"Agda has agreed to help me train the citizens of Dover Town how to best defend themselves," Ching Shih explained. "Her training regiments are...brutal, to say the least."

"It is for their benefit. Make them big and strong, like me!" Bluebird flexed for emphasis. Her expression softened. "Bounty hunter, come. I'd like to show you something."

Ching Shih stared, openmouthed. "Out of the question. Her injuries are too severe. She needs rest."

"I'll be fine," Talisha said. "Bluebird can carry me. Right?"

Bluebird bowed, smiling. "I would be honored."

She scooped Talisha into her arms and carried her gently into the streets. Talisha saw it immediately. A statue of Rogers had been erected in the center of town. Talisha clamped a hand over her mouth and tried not to cry.

"It has a plaque and everything," Bluebird said. "The Savior of Archimedes IV. Sheriff Rogers of Dover Town."

Talisha sniffed. "Maybe once we find a way to restore him, he can finally see it."

Bluebird's expression darkened. "I hate to be the one to tell you this, bounty hunter. Ching Shih has been working nonstop on the chip you recovered from his head. I understand you may disagree with her on many matters, but she knows her shit."

Talisha stared into her face. "So there's nothing? He's just gone?"

"We have memories, but they are only recordings," Bluebird said. "They're being used in a presentation to commemorate his sacrifice and love for this community. He's really dead. Any hope of recovering him went up with that satellite."

Talisha buried her face in Bluebird's chest, shoulders tight. Bluebird patted her head softly. She reached into her shirt and retrieved the locket with her wife's picture.

"Bounty hunter, look." Bluebird held the locket in front of Talisha. "I know what it's like to lose people we love. Find something of his that reminds you of him. Keep it close."

"Does the pain go away? Ever?" Talisha said, voice quivering.

Bluebird shook her head. "No, but you learn to live with it, and it becomes the new normal."

ANOTHER WEEK OF healing and Talisha took off in her ship with the knowledge that she'd soon return. She had a few days journey ahead of her, into a star system far away from Archimedes IV. She was going to the Cole System, to a planet ravaged by the Corporate Wars. While in her ship, she kept looking to the cowboy hat hanging on the wall. Bluebird had given it to her just before she left.

Talisha landed on a launchpad within the capital city of the planet. It was a central hub of the rebuilding effort. Despite the best gentrification efforts, it was still swarmed with homeless beggars. She took a lift into the lower levels of the city. The nonprofit organizations and soup kitchens were located here to siphon the unseemly wretches away from the expensive apartments and skylofts.

Talisha stood outside the door to an orphanage surrounded by refuse and filth. She wore a dirty shawl wrapped over her pristine armor and kept her helmet tucked beneath one arm. Any sign of wealth and she'd be immediately swarmed by those begging for her sympathies.

The door opened. A little girl with brown hair and wide frightened eyes stared up at her. There were burn marks across her neck and lower arms. Talisha waved and tried to look as friendly and nonthreatening as possible. The girl screamed and retreated into the safety of the building, her bare feet padding against the tile.

Talisha could hear a familiar voice bark something in Swahili, and then an older woman with graying hair bound tightly into braids was standing at the door. A cigarette hung loosely out of her mouth as she stared. She leaned against the doorframe, folding her arms across her chest.

"Are you in trouble?" Ms. Artul said.

Talisha fought back the instinct to turn on her heels and leave. "Mom, I found one of the Valran Temples." She held her helmet in front, revealing its new shape and color.

The older woman stood, stunned. She stumbled forward, taking the helmet in her shaking hands. The cigarette fell out her mouth and rolled against the metal grating.

"This is not my helmet," Ms. Artul murmured to herself. Her eyes darted sharply. "What happened? What did you do?"

Talisha pressed closer. "Can I come inside and talk?"

THEY SAT AT a small round table in the kitchen. Talisha felt waves of memories wash over her as she stared at the hideous yellow wallpaper. It'd been six years since she'd stepped foot in this house. Everything looked exactly the same.

"How are things?" Talisha asked.

She removed her arm cannon and placed it on the table. Ms. Artul turned around, holding a pink tea kettle with both hands. Her eyes fell across the weapon and she made a pained grimace, almost like she hated even seeing the thing. Ms. Artul avoided touching it as she poured the tea.

"I can complain," Ms. Artul said, taking a seat across from her. "But I won't. Worst thing is the politicians on this planet are talking about raising the costs of healthcare insurance. I won't be able to afford to take care of these kids if that happens, even with the money you've been sending in."

"Why do they want to jack the prices again?" Talisha said, brow furrowed. She took a sip of tea and nearly choked. Still too strong, just like her mother.

"New Prime Minister," Ms. Artul said and rolled her eyes. "They want to expand military defenses. You know why of course, they're taking bribes from the weapons manufacturers. Anyway, you were going to give me an explanation about this armor."

Talisha rattled off the entire story, including the conflict between the IGF and the Plymouth Corporation. Her mother's eyes widened as she spoke of her psychic visions within the Valran Temple. For a few brief moments, the years melted from her face.

"I wish I could've seen that, Sam." Ms. Artul leaned back in her chair. "I always thought there was more to the Valran, but you were the one who finally found it."

Talisha flinched at hearing that name. She struggled to ignore it. "Do you know Commander Mattu?"

Ms. Artul's face darkened. Her eyes flicked daggers in her daughter's direction. "He's a child killer. He's why I quit the game."

"Is he my father?"

There was a painful silence. "Yes. How'd you find out?"

"He told me, but I had my suspicions soon as he mentioned you."

"You're a lot alike," Ms. Artul said, her shoulders looking suddenly weary. "Not the bad parts. You got all your worst bits from me."

Talisha scoffed. "Charming, Mom."

"Don't be an ass, you know what I meant." Ms. Artul sighed. "He's a brilliant tactician. I mean truly brilliant. One of the sharpest minds in the galaxy. He knew things his superiors didn't and railed against them, only ever acquiescing if they forced his hand."

Talisha lowered her eyes, her fingers drumming along the warm surface of the ceramic mug. "He died in the temple. I don't think he was a bad man."

Ms. Artul turned her face away, clutching a hand over her mouth. "Is that why you came here? To make me feel guilty."

"Damn it, Mom." Talisha groaned. "I'm not here to attack or hurt you. It's not always about you. I just...I thought if what he said about your relationship was true, you ought to know what happened."

"You're right." Ms. Artul clinked her cup hard against the table, causing tea to spill over the edges of the cup and splash against the tablecloth. "I'm just an asshole. I'm the bad guy. Always have been."

"You're not bad," Talisha said. "You and Mattu were similar. Flawed people who did some horrible things. You hung up your armor when you realized that."

Ms. Artul's eyes glassed over. She stared at the ceiling and sniffed. "I freaked out when you wanted to take my name at the start of your transition. I'd spent so many years trying to turn you into me, and too late I was afraid that I'd succeeded."

"You know that's not why I'm trans right?" Talisha gave her a sideways glance.

Ms. Artul nodded. "I know. I know. That'd be weird."

"All right. Good." Talisha took a deep breath and leaned forward. She fixed her eyes on the brown stain spreading across the tablecloth. "I took your name 'cause you were my hero."

"Damn it, kid." Ms. Artul stood and turned her back. She tapped her fingers against the edge of the counter. "You can still change your name, y'know. Find a better hero. There's better women out there."

"Not many who can own up to their mistakes and try to give back to the world," Talisha said, rising from her seat. "You're doing okay. I'm proud of you."

Talisha watched her mother's hands clench into fists, and then Ms. Artul collapsed into tears. Talisha rushed forward, meeting her with open arms. They held each other for a solid minute, sobbing into each other's shoulders. The walls they'd erected around their hearts faltered, then crumbled.

"You are so much better than I ever was," Ms. Artul whispered. "I love you."

Talisha clung to her tightly. "I love you too, Mom."

About the Author

Dorian Dawes is a self-described social justice witch and full-time gender disaster who never grew out of their goth phase. In addition to fiction, they have also written for tabletop rpgs and several published essays on feminism and LGBT issues. When not writing they can be found playing video games and plotting the revolution of the proletariat.

Website: www.patreon.com/doriandawes

Facebook: www.facebook.com/DorianDawes

Twitter: @RealDorianDawes

Instagram: www.instagram.com/doriandawes

Pinterest: www.pinterest.com/therealdoriandawes

Also Available from NineStar Press

Connect with NineStar Press

Website: NineStarPress.com

Facebook: NineStarPress

Facebook Reader Group: NineStarNiche

Twitter: @ninestarpress

Tumblr: NineStarPress